Whitney shook out the material again and waved a pair of paint-smeared black silk breeches under his nose. "Have you missed these, my lord?"

His lost breeches. He reached for them, but Whitney was quicker. She packed them away in her little box. "You cannot have them back now. They've come in quite handy."

"You shrew," he whispered in horror.

"If I was a shrew, I'd have already told your intended what you were doing the night before you met her," she warned.

He looked away, feeling guilty and ashamed. The one night he'd been incautious of his honor in society was the one time he'd truly felt free. Having the woman turn out to be Whitney Crewe, cousin of an earl, an acquaintance of his intended bride, was a source of embarrassment to him. If he'd known her name, connections, he'd never have touched her. "Why haven't you?"

PRAISE FOR THE TROUBLE WITH LOVE

The Trouble With Love blends fanciful with emotional and begets exceptional. If nothing else, Whitney and Acton prove that life has a sense of humor and sometimes the heart is the last to know, what the head has already discovered.
~ Isha Coleman, I LOVE ROMANCE

Ms. Boyd has created two characters that cause the rest of their world to fade with their vibrancy and willingness to be passionate about life.
~ Dianne, TOME TENDER

…it's the slow building type of romance with a sexual chemistry just waiting to boil over. The Trouble with Love is a great addition to this series and sees one more distinguished rogue find his own HEA.
~ JG Baldos, DELUGUED WITH BOOKS CAFÉ

HEATHER BOYD

BESTSELLING AUTHOR

The TROUBLE with LOVE

Distinguished Rogues

8

The characters and events portrayed in this book are fictitious. Any similarity to real persons, living or dead, is purely coincidental and not intended by the author.

THE TROUBLE WITH LOVE
Copyright © 2017 by Heather Boyd
Edited by Kelli Collins

All rights reserved. No part of this book may be reproduced in any form by any electronic or mechanical means—except in the case of brief quotations embodied in critical articles or reviews—without written permission of the author.

Dedication

This is for my dear friends Michelle, Donna, Crystal, Anne, and Kelli. Thanks for holding my hand (virtually) when I needed support the most, and for laughing along with me when it was almost too hard. Love you.

Prologue

London
March, 1814

Making merry didn't come easily for Everett Dean. The Earl of Acton did his duty, even if the weight of responsibility threatened to choke him at times. He sipped champagne slowly, casting an admiring glance over the lovely ladies who glided past his spot in the avenue of tall birch trees as if he'd not a care in the world.

Those who'd come to enjoy the Fairmont Bachelors Ball on the grounds of the expansive Fairmont estate were having a marvelous time without his participation. He could probably ask any one of the ladies to dance with him, but he did not want to give rise to unreasonable expectations beyond this one night.

Tomorrow it would be whispered that he was finally surveying the marriage mart and that could not be avoided. Those rumors would be true, if a little late. Everett had already chosen his bride, so he was uncertain why he'd felt a keen need to come to this unholy revel alone.

When he'd left his home, he'd originally had no intention of directing his driver to this spectacle but here he was, watching other people enjoy themselves. His hosts were not considered good *ton*. Lord and Lady Fairmont were more than a little eccentric in their habits, and in the company they kept. Within the manor behind him had been gathered mystics and fortune-tellers, determined to predict his future in exchange for coin. He'd pressed through their number without partaking or being taken for a fool. Acton did not need a fortune-teller to determine what his future path would bring. His future was already determined.

He would take a bride within the next month and that was that.

Miss Alice Quartermane was a fine choice for him. She was not in attendance tonight; she was not out in society yet, and her parents would certainly have shielded her gentle soul from boisterous depravity such as this. He had negotiated the marriage contract with her father last year while riding to hounds at a friend's estate, and he was looking forward to meeting Alice tomorrow in quieter surroundings at last.

Everett accepted another glass of champagne from a passing waiter and looked along the avenue of trees. He would not dance tonight out of respect for Alice, and would dissuade any damsel who might encourage him. Pretty women were in general a distraction from the serious business of being the head of a well-known and respected family. That was why he'd chosen the innocent Miss Alice Quartermane to be his wife. Her father knew his interests. They both agreed that Alice would be the perfect woman to become mistress of Warstone Manor, and his countess. It was the best possible arrangement for all concerned.

A flash of long bright red hair weaving through the trees ahead caught his eye. There were others following her, men and women making the most of the moonlit evening to dance gaily.

Everett was drawn toward them too, and smiling widely.

He'd lost his innocence to a redhead in Leeds at fifteen, been caught rutting with a russet-haired maid at eighteen, and after one final indignity—falling head over heels for a married countess—he wisely chose to keep his amours confined to fair-headed damsels ever since.

Miss Alice Quartermane was reputed to be blessed with very fair hair.

The redheaded woman was garbed as a gypsy—a prosperous lady, judging by the silk caressing her curves and the gold glittering on every finger under the torchlights as she weaved between the tree trunks. Her thumbs sparkled with gold bands too but her face was veiled, so all he could see were a pair of laughing, merry eyes.

But he felt her exuberant laughter as if she was stroking her jeweled fingers over his skin. She broke from the trees onto the clipped lawn and Everett followed. She lifted her skirts a little as she danced with careless abandon, revealing slender ankles and bare feet gliding upon the neatly trimmed lawns.

He drew closer, intrigued by the way she moved with unhindered sensuality. It was as if the darkness was her natural element, and she a flame in the midst of the chaos around her. She did not seem to care, or notice, that she was making a spectacle of herself.

He wasn't the only person who admired this woman. She continued to draw a crowd of admirers, even among the fairer sex. People stared, smiled at her transparent energy, and made a game of trying to copy her movements with varying degrees of success.

Everett was utterly entranced, and found a spot to watch as the redhead suddenly grabbed a lady, swinging her into her wild dance. They laughed in giddy joy, and soon the entire crowd was swaying to a beat that Everett had never seen before at a ton event.

The energy was compelling, the sounds and movements drawing him ever closer to the mass of humanity. He found himself surrounded, touched by strangers as they spun about on their merry way.

The redhead paused in her mad flight right in front of him and looked him directly in the eye as she had no one else so far. He acknowledged her with a dip of his head, unsure of what else he should do. He had not meant to curb her dancing. He'd been enjoying watching her sensual movements too much to desire that, but he was glad she had stopped.

He did not recognize her in the half dark but wanted to know her.

She held out her hand to him, fingers wriggling in invitation. The gems winked and he stepped forward.

Redheads were his weakness, but he suddenly didn't care one whit for caution or restraint or propriety. He took her bare fingers in his firmly. Her skin was soft and warm within his grasp and he didn't want to let go.

She tugged, and he followed her away from the crowds and into the house where it was quieter.

Their fingers still entwined, the lady led him toward a drinks table without a word, hips gently swaying ahead of him. She requested punch from a footman as she lowered her gauze veil.

"Dancing is thirsty work," she apologized in a husky tone between sips of her drink. "Why did you not join in and dance with us?"

He requested another beverage for the lady when she finished the first, trying to better see her face in the candlelight. She looked young, and very, very pretty to his eye. "How do you know I didn't dance?"

Her pretty green eyes glowed with delight. "Because I was watching you watching everyone else at play since you arrived in the garden. You are too serious, sir. Did you not read your invitation? Guests were supposed to leave their cares at the door."

"Life cannot be all fun and games."

"I don't see why not," she insisted. "As long as you hold reasonable expectations, it does not have to be full of misery. A little fun never hurt anyone."

"Is that so?"

The lady, having quenched her thirst, reset her veil over her face. "Indeed. Come with me."

She caught his hand again and pulled him along in her wake and into a deserted long gallery. Holding his hand firmly, she studied the paintings of their hosts' ancestors. "Look at this. You can tell just by looking at them that living life to the fullest extent was their goal. Don't you want a similar happiness for your own life?"

Everett gave the paintings a second longer glance, noting the couple closest to him were surrounded by hens and other farmyard fowl. "It is widely acknowledged that the Fairmont family possess a great number of eccentrics."

"I like eccentrics," she told him. "In fact, I have become one already. I will never do what is expected of me by society no matter how many long noses, and disapproving looks, bear down upon me."

His lips twitched in amusement. The woman had no idea of the trouble that attitude would cause her one day. "Already a rebel to propriety at your tender age."

"I am older than I appear to you, sir," she said, twirling a strand of red hair around one slender, bejeweled finger. "In my family, our looks change very slowly."

"Lucky you," he murmured. There was already streaks of gray in his hair at the temples and the odd strand at his crown. He felt time rushing past him—particularly so when he collected rents and saw how many men of his age had children old enough to work their farmland. But this woman had her whole life ahead of her. "Your hair has very distinct coloring."

"I'm wearing a wig," she confessed with a soft laugh.

It shocked him that she might really not be as she appeared tonight. He stretched out his hand and gathered a lock of her hair between his fingers. She felt real enough to him. "It's a very convincing wig."

Her brows were penciled, darkened with kohl, but he thought he detected a little bit of ginger underneath.

He lost his grip on her hair as the lady brushed her hair back over her shoulder. "Has anyone every told you that you are a very pretty fellow?"

Everett coughed in shock at the bold question. "Not to my face," he said, feeling his cheeks heat with embarrassment.

"But you are," she insisted. Her lips curved into a broad smile and she brushed her fingers across his cheek. She turned his face this way and that, studying him. "You have a face deserving serious consideration."

Her fingers were so firm and warm against his skin that he was astonished to feel himself become aroused just by her touch. "I would like to see more of your face, too."

The woman ignored his words as she traced each of his eyebrows, the shape of his nose, and again caressed his jawline, rasping her fingers against the grain of his new beard growth.

Her attention dropped to his lips, and he discovered he'd captured one between his teeth.

"Can I have you?" she asked.

He was flattered. A dalliance with the redhead wasn't wise, given his plans for tomorrow, but with her fingers still caressing his skin, his reasons for resistance began to erode. What could it hurt, this one last night to taste temptation before he became a properly devoted husband? "For tonight, but no more than that."

Her fingers slipped around his face to trace the edge of his ear. "But I could spend many days and nights studying this face." Her lips parted slightly.

She could not have more than this one night to know him, so he grabbed her hips firmly and tugged her close. "Only tonight."

She stood inches under his height of six feet three, slender but utterly feminine in silk. Her body was so soft and warm as she pressed against him. She burrowed her nose against his neck and inhaled as her arms slipped under his coat. Her hungry moan shocked him because it matched the way he was feeling.

Everett had some idea of the layout of the Fairmont estate, so he propelled the woman into a nearby chamber before anyone came along to interrupt them and closed the door.

"What is your name?"

"My friends call me Trouble," she whispered. "Undress for me."

It bothered him only a moment that she did not ask for his name before he removed his coat and kicked off his shoes. "Not completely."

She drew back, her eyes narrowing on his lower half. "Then please remove the clothing that is in the way of what I want to see."

It was hard to miss her meaning when her attention dropped to the region of his hips and the erection he should be hiding. He wasn't usually so easily aroused, but he put his hands to the waistband of his breeches and slipped the buttons free. He pushed his shirt up and lowered his smallclothes to reveal his cock. "Is this what you want?"

She purred, coming closer before she wrapped her fingers around him. Everett hissed at the sensation of her hand on him. He couldn't help but thrust his hips forward as she proved her experience without a doubt or hint of shyness.

"Remove your veil," he whispered.

"Why is it that you are alone?" she whispered back without complying.

He covered her hand and slowed down her strokes, trying to see past the veil to learn more of her identity. "I'm not alone now."

Everett lifted the veil a little and leaned forward to deliver a kiss to her cheek, but the woman jerked back, her fingers catching on his clothing momentarily.

The woman clucked her tongue and resettled the rings on her fingers. "Kissing is for romantics."

"Most women enjoy kisses."

"I'm not most women," she promised him.

"I see that." Cautious of scaring her off again, he brought her hand back to his cock and closed her fingers around him. "So you are not romantic *at all?*"

"I am the furthest thing from it as a woman my age can be." She resumed stroking him firmly. "I am practical. I give and take my pleasures where I can, without any hesitation or regret, sir. I have no need for a husband or protector, but I do desire being with pretty men from time to time. You interest me tonight, and I want you."

"I'm flattered."

She clenched the top of his cock and held still. "Stolen moments of pleasure bring meaning to my life. A quick dalliance can satisfy far better than a drawn-out love affair can, and with far less trouble. Do you agree to my terms?"

She squeezed him a little harder, and he groaned when her hand slid down his length again and clenched him at the base. "Yes."

He let the veiled woman have her way, quite frankly because he was utterly under her spell. He'd never known a woman to speak so boldly of pleasure on first making his acquaintance. He'd never inspired such passion before, and her focus on him went to his head.

She stroked him almost to the brink of completion then stopped. "Take off your breaches and the rest of your clothes. They are in the way of what I want now."

Feeling a little desperate for her to continue, Everett stepped back, stripped off his waistcoat and shirt, and everything else he was wearing until he stood nude in the room. He let everything fall to the parquetry floor but heard a button or such bounce away. He couldn't care where it landed right now. He wasn't one for unguarded romps, but this woman, Trouble, had him twisted around her dainty bejeweled fingers. "Satisfied, madam?"

"That's better. Now I can determine that all of you deserves to be worshiped. The real you is exquisite, rather than the carefully constructed society gentleman keeping himself apart from happiness." She took a pace toward him, her glance admiring and decidedly hungry. She unwound the fringed shawl she'd tied about her waist and dropped it onto his clothing. "This moment is when lovers are the most raw, most vulnerable. I must have you."

"Honestly, I think I must be had," he said with a strangled laugh as she returned and took him in hand again, torturing him with lazy strokes. He caught her hips, kneading her curves and considered having her against the wall if she was agreeable. "By you, and all night," he agreed.

The woman cupped his ballocks, kneading him carefully with

one hand, but he still moaned. She traced the muscles of his back with her other hand and then cupped the back of his neck. "Lovely," she whispered. "I'm so glad we met tonight. This is an auspicious beginning."

He was glad he'd come tonight too, but... "I'm to be married soon," he cautioned her.

The woman released him so suddenly he cursed out loud.

"Married? When?" she demanded.

"Just as soon as I meet the woman." He said it with a laugh but his companion did not join in.

"You... You are engaged to be married without ever meeting her first?"

He nodded, puzzled by her outrage. "Yes, that's the way it's always been done in my family—for generations."

"Sir, this is a bachelors ball. Hen-pecked husbands and panicking engaged men were not invited." She bent to snatch up her shawl from the parquetry floor and hugged it to her chest. "I thought you knew the rules for this evening's revel."

"We were hardly doing anything out of the ordinary, and I am not engaged yet."

"Merely intending to be so from tomorrow?" Her gaze hardened, but then she rolled her eyes. "And people wonder why I'm opposed to marriage. An arranged match? I suppose she comes from a wealthy family too and has only just come out?"

"She's not out yet," he confessed, feeling just a touch defensive on the subject. "The money from her dowry wasn't why I chose her, but it is vital for the future of my estate and our children."

"Fortune hunter!" She nearly shouted. "No wonder you look so sad, but I will not pity you. I pity the poor child, married before she's even had a chance to enjoy her first season and a little attention."

"Now just a minute," he protested. "I'm not going to marry the chit tomorrow."

The woman advanced on him, stabbing him in the chest with her finger. "You, sir, should really consider if this arranged marriage is what you want before it is too late to remove the scowl you wear when you speak of it. Goodbye."

"Wait!"

"For you?" She looked him up and down coldly and then shook her head. "I'd rather drink paint."

Chapter One

———◆———

Worcestershire
August, 1814

Whitney Crewe stepped from the dark carriage into torchlight, casting a wary eye up at Lord and Lady Taverham's country home. She shook out her rumpled travel clothes once more, considering the subtle intimidation of the large building looming above her.

So this was Twilit Hill.

The property name had implied she'd discover an elegant, almost delicate structure but Whitney wasn't prepared for the enormity of the reality. Dear God, this place was a cold monstrosity, and she was expected to paint those who lived here into some semblance of a happy family. No wonder the lady of the house had run away.

For the first time, she wasn't sure she was up to the challenge.

"Miss Crewe, you've come at last!" Lady Taverham cried out as she hurried down the manor's steep front steps to meet her on the drive.

Surprised by her hostess' sudden arrival, Whitney smiled broadly and rushed to meet her. The Marchioness of Taverham was a dear friend of her cousin's, and by association, now hers, too. Whitney thought Miranda the most remarkable woman she'd ever met, but not one given to enthusiastic greetings likes this. "Miranda!"

The woman caught her by the shoulders, puffing slightly. "My dear, what kept you? I've been fretting for hours that something had happened to you after we parted."

"Forgive me." Whitney kissed Miranda's warm cheeks, noting that although out of breath from her dash down the stairs, Miranda's eyes seemed to glow with happiness. "I met the most charming newly married couple after you had been driven off, and when they learned of my accomplishments, they commissioned a sketch to be done to mark the occasion. Since it will be weeks before I pass that way again, I decided not to lose a moment and had them sit for me there and then."

Miranda's smile slipped. "I was beginning to suspect you'd tricked us all and changed your mind about coming to visit."

Whitney smiled and hid the truth. She *had* thought about it several times since leaving London. She still doubted the wisdom of taking this trip even now. "I just stole a few hours for myself."

And in that time apart, she had put her plan into motion. The inn where Lady Taverham had last seen her had been the perfect spot to dispense with the fussy companion her cousin, Lord Louth, had foisted upon her at the last moment. Finding the woman already waiting for her in the Taverham's carriage upon leaving London had soured her good feelings toward her cousin considerably.

"Well, no harm done, I see." Miranda squeezed her hand. "With all that has happened this season, I can understand you might feel overwhelmed and need the peace. It must be difficult to venture so far from your cousin and his growing family."

"I have no qualms about leaving my cousin in Iris' capable hands." Her cousin had recently married Miss Iris Hedley, a love match she wholeheartedly approved of, and discovered himself a father to an illegitimate child. Neither situation required her supervision or involvement.

Especially not when Martin was always too protective of everyone.

Whitney collected her case containing her paintbrushes and such from an overeager footman and tucked it under her arm. She was very ready to be on her own at last. To make her way in the world with no one to answer to. She had money enough, and she had no responsibilities. She was free to live how she chose. "Besides, I promised Christopher art lessons, didn't I?"

The woman smiled broadly. "So you did. Christopher tried so hard to remain awake long enough to greet you, but Kit had to carry him up to bed over an hour ago."

"He must have loved that," she said with a laugh. Miranda and Kit's son might be too old to be carried but Kit was very new at being a father to him. "Well, tell Christopher that I always wake early so we can meet first thing in the morning, if his tutor will release him to be with me that is."

Miranda nodded and looked beyond Whitney's shoulder. "Where is your companion, Mrs. Fry?"

Whitney shrugged. "She, ah, remembered friends she simply had to visit immediately and went on her merry way."

Miranda sighed heavily. "Martin warned me you'd try something underhanded, but I told him he was worrying for naught. Oh, he's going to be so angry with us." Miranda closed her eyes briefly.

"Only with me," Whitney promised Miranda. "I'm sorry, but I told you—and Martin—many times that I do not need or want a companion following me about anymore."

"It is expected, Whitney. You're not married yet. You must think of your reputation."

"I'm five and twenty, Miranda."

"And look as young as anyone fresh on the marriage mart." Miranda sighed deeply. "But it is done now, and I trust you compensated the poor woman for the trouble of being dismissed after a mere two full days' employment."

"I did indeed. She has a glowing reference and fifty pounds, and that should ensure Mrs. Fry never has to work for an obstinate, headstrong spinster like me for a while," she said soothingly, experiencing a twinge of guilt that she made the marchioness worry over her. Miranda wasn't always in good health, so Whitney led the marchioness up the long flight of stairs by taking her elbow. It was Miranda's heart, of course, the organ most likely to give a lady trouble. Tonight, the marchioness did seem to lean on her arm, so Whitney held her up a little more firmly. "How are things with you?"

"Very well. The dowager moved out to the dower house as if the devil chased her upon my arrival. She expects our son to visit her daily but other than that, we are quite civil. Of course, she dotes on Christopher, so she tolerates me for his sake."

Whitney winced. Miranda and her husband hadn't had the best start to married life, and the dowager, the most fearsome woman she'd ever encountered, was said to have favored another woman for many years. It had been a messy situation all round. Love did that. "Perhaps I'll ask Christopher to escort me to the dower house when I go to pay my respects tomorrow morning." Only for the sake of peace for Miranda, of course. "I suppose everyone else has gone off to bed by now."

"Heavens no. The dowager is here, and the entire household remains awake and waiting on your arrival. Lord Acton and his guests have joined us, too."

"What is Acton doing here?" Whitney groaned. "Last I heard, he was in London."

Not that Whitney was keeping track of the scoundrel.

"He is our nearest neighbor and my husband's good friend," Miranda reminded her. "He called earlier in the afternoon with the Quartermanes and a friend, Mr. Thompson, so Kit invited them all to stay for dinner. When I heard them arrive, I at first thought, hoped, it was your carriage."

Whitney had no acquaintance with a Mr. Thompson, but Miss Quartermane was a young lady she'd met early in the season. She was nice if a little forward and competitive for attention. Her mother gave Whitney a megrim though. Mrs. Quartermane had stated very plainly that she disapproved of Whitney's avoidance of matrimony, which had made for some awkward encounters during the last few weeks.

As for Lord Acton, she couldn't imagine why he'd choose to linger in wait for her, unless he wanted the breeches of his she'd accidentally taken returned before he wed the innocent Miss Quartermane.

Miranda squeezed her hand. "Miss Quartermane is quite lovely, and I'm sure we will become great neighbors and friends one day. But promise me you'll behave around Acton? He really has been on his best behavior since the reconciliation, especially so since his sister went to live in Bath."

Whitney smiled, but inside she was seething. Lady Brighthurst, Lord Acton's sister, had attempted to take Miranda's place as marchioness through devious and despicable acts that could have ended Miranda's son's life, by all accounts. Whitney knew enough of the facts to know not to trust Lady Brighthurst or her brother, even if he protested his innocence. "I'll not say one word to upset the starch in Lord Acton's smile."

"Oh, Whitney. If I can forgive him for the unsuspecting part he played, surely you can." Miranda sighed. "He is trying to make amends, but I caution that you must not say a word about his sister before the Quartermanes. I don't believe he has revealed the true state of affairs to his betrothed yet."

Whitney came to a complete halt beneath the wide front portico. "Alice is on pins and needles to meet Lady Brighthurst and win her approval. She told me so the last time we spoke together in London."

"I agree it is badly done of him to keep such a secret, but as far as I'm concerned, it is his business to manage." Miranda smiled. "All I ask is to never see the woman again."

"Yes, but surely the right moment to tell Alice that Lady Brighthurst isn't a good person was long ago. Acton announced their engagement in the first weeks of the season. Is he afraid to tell Alice?"

"I wondered about the delay myself," Miranda whispered as a servant approached. "Hush now. The less said, the better."

An aged man wearing livery approached from the shadows of the hall and bowed. "I am Anders, Lord Taverham's butler. May I take your coat, Miss Crewe?"

"Indeed you may, sir." Whitney moved to a mirror set above a marble-topped hall table and put her treasured paint box down. She shrugged out of her coat, removed her bonnet, and shook out the skirts of her favorite pink gown. She fluffed out the cap sleeves and then peered at her face in the mirror, noting that her bright red hair looked far from elegant again. It did gleam nicely in the candlelight of the Taverhams' front hall though, so Whitney did her best to tame it. Largely unsuccessful, she teased a few strands into ringlets beside her ears and hoped that would do. Still, she looked like she'd recently tumbled out of bed, or off the top of the carriage she'd been grudgingly allowed to drive a few miles on the way here. What an exhilarating experience that had been!

"Barely presentable," she apologized.

"You always look lovely," Miranda promised.

The old butler nodded too and then hurried away with her coat and bonnet. Whitney tucked her paint box under her left arm again and smiled. "Ready."

To be nice. To be civil. To bite her tongue rather than say what she really thought of Lord Acton's impending marriage to Miss Quartermane.

Married by arrangement?

She shivered. Whitney did not approve of that sort of thing.

The butler returned to open a tall set of doors to the left of the marchioness, and Whitney stepped into an elegant drawing room beside her.

She was barely in the room before her eyes found Acton's.

As always, the man turned his beautiful body toward her without a sliver of shame or awkwardness in his bearing. It was as if they'd never almost climbed into bed together one decadent night.

What a mistake she'd made, thinking she'd met a kindred soul at the Fairmont Bachelors Ball.

Chapter Two

Despite her distaste for Lord Acton's past behavior, Whitney couldn't stop herself from admiring his appearance. As usual, Acton dressed with restrained elegance, appropriate to his location. His blond hair was always just a tad too long, brushing the collar of his coat and making her itch to run her fingers through it again. His maroon tailcoat barely contained his wide shoulders and long arms. His chest was wrapped in a brown, striped silk waistcoat, and his long, powerful legs encased in another pair of black silk breeches, above pristine stockings and shoes.

Quite simply, he was a very well put together earl, and as someone who knew what lie beneath his clothes, she was nearly breathless after her brief scrutiny.

Tongue-tied yet again, she only nodded to him before hurrying toward his future bride—a woman Acton had coldly chosen for her obscenely large dowry without ever knowing one thing about the young woman he would wed.

Miss Quartermane appeared a delicate creature. Soft curves and a nervous giggle. Blonde hair, almost silver in a certain light. Her full cheeks were tinged with a delicate blush from pinching them too often. Beside Alice, Whitney felt too tall and far too red. "My dear Miss Quartermane, what a delightful surprise," Whitney murmured.

"Forgive me for the surprise of being where I wasn't expected,"

Alice said as they shook hands. "But when Lady Taverham mentioned your coming for a visit, I convinced Mama and Papa that we must accept Lord Acton's invitation to visit, too. So here we are, all in the wilds of Worcestershire, together again."

"How marvelous." Whitney had tried to avoid Alice when she was with her future husband many times in the past month, without much success unfortunately. She exchanged a cordial greeting with Mr. and Mrs. Quartermane, and then curtsied deeply to the Dowager Marchioness of Taverham. The older woman's eyes were keen with bright intelligence—like a hawk focused on its next luncheon of raw meat. "My lady."

"Miss Crewe," the woman replied stiffly.

Whitney faced the Marquess of Taverham next.

She knew the marquess well now. He had been a good friend of her cousin's for many years. Whitney especially enjoyed teasing him lately—mostly because he seemed so unsure of how to react. At least at first.

Of course, she liked him better now that he was living with his wife again and had cut Lady Brighthurst completely from his life.

He looked well, and happy, too. The resumption of his marriage appeared to have done him no harm. Whitney stifled a laugh. *Must be all the lovely sex he and Miranda are engaging in now.*

"Hello Kit," she said with a wide grin. "Thank you for inviting me to visit."

His eyes narrowed but then he smiled. "Welcome to Twilit Hill, Trouble."

They embraced briefly, a rare thing in polite circles.

The dowager frowned. "Trouble?"

"Yes, all my cousin's friends end up calling me that, I'm afraid," Whitney apologized as she glanced at the other gentleman present. His face, quite handsome too, wasn't familiar, but since Miranda had said Thompson was Lord Acton's friend, Whitney was immediately unsure about him.

"Mr. Thompson, I presume," she asked, intent on introducing herself when no one spoke up.

"Yes, indeed." He came closer, hand outstretched. "Mr. Alexander Thompson, at your service."

Mr. Thompson had wide, clear blue eyes, dark hair cropped

close to his skull, but the cut of his clothing wasn't quite in the same league with Lord Acton's. Whitney had always paid close attention to people, and always noticed when what they wore was at odds with what they said of their situation. Mr. Thompson had not mentioned his connections or where he lived, which made Whitney like him all the more. At a guess, Mr. Thompson might be a younger son of someone important, especially so if he could claim a place in Lord Acton's tight circle of friends.

She let him take her hand and was not unduly surprised when he lifted it to his lips. Many men did, thinking the action would warm her heart to them. Being known to have funds had definite drawbacks, especially when a woman was not married or did not want to be.

Thompson's lips grazed the back of her hand, and she felt…absolutely nothing for him. His eyes might reveal interest in her person, but Whitney was too wise. There was always a chance new acquaintances, men particularly, had more interest in the size of her bank account than in herself.

"A pleasure to make your acquaintance, sir."

"The pleasure is all mine, I promise you." His smile grew warmer as he held her hand a touch too long.

Oh, Thompson was interested, but Whitney was decidedly not.

She pulled her hand back and glanced around the large room, avoiding Alice's questioning gaze, and cast her eye over the portraits hanging on the walls. She loved to study the work of better-known painters. And these were very good.

She dragged her attention back to the people who'd waited to greet her. "Forgive me for missing dinner, but I had the most eventful journey after being left behind."

"Nothing serious, I trust," Acton asked, finally finding his voice. It was so rare that he spoke to her, and that was by her choice. She worked very hard to forget such a man existed.

They had only danced together once after their proper introduction where names had been exchanged and connections revealed. They had danced a short and extremely awkward set the night his engagement to Alice had been announced. She had only accepted him because her new cousin Iris had dared her to, and offered a reward of new canvas for her art.

She believed she made Lord Acton very uncomfortable, too. Their first anonymous encounter had been an incredible memory…tarnished, of course, the moment she'd learned he was to marry, then ruined utterly once she'd discovered his identity.

She let everyone—her cousin and his wife, Miranda and Kit too—believe her dislike of him had begun when she'd learned of Lady Brighthurst's scheming. That was terrible of course, but not the whole reason.

She arched her brow. "A chance encounter on the road brought about a very pleasurable interlude with a rather handsome gentleman," she told him, smiling as his cheeks grew red with discomfort.

She did not finish her tale on purpose, a subtle dig only he would understand, and had no doubt he'd leapt to conclusions about the nature of that meeting, believing the worst of her.

After all, she *had* almost seduced Lord Acton at the Bachelors Ball, another stranger. Whenever he met her now, he frowned. Especially when she was enjoying herself. Whitney did not discriminate between duke or footman, but he clearly did. Everyone was interesting to Whitney. Even Lord Acton sometimes still. The wary way Acton watched her made her wonder if he considered her an immoral creature of insatiable appetites about to launch herself upon him again. The man grew so tense when they met, she kept waiting for him to split apart.

Miranda nudged her. "Tell them the nature of the encounter before they believe you were imposed upon by an unwanted admirer."

Whitney laughed softly, breaking eye contact with Acton. "A commission for a marriage portrait in charcoal. The couple was so gloriously in love that I could not possibly refuse the fellow's beautifully worded request that I capture the image of his blushing bride for posterity. The money was most happily spent by them, and most graciously received by me in the exchange."

"Well, I never," Mr. Quartermane began, glancing at his wife in obvious disapproval.

Silence fell, awkward and absolute. A lady engaged in trade, even the production of harmless little portraits, wasn't considered very highly among members of the *ton*. But in the art world, simply giving away her work placed her at a distinct disadvantage.

It was Whitney's opinion that the prestige of having a portrait done by a lady painter must always be equal to that of a man. Money was merely a means of deciding popularity.

Whitney wanted to be popular for the only thing she could always control in her life—her art.

She cared little for approval outside of the art world. What she enjoyed was recording the people she met and places she went to. When coins were exchanged for the final piece, those funds always went toward Whitney's next project.

"You are a most generous lady," Miranda murmured, and to her surprise, the dowager nodded, too.

"You would have given the family a treasure for generations to come," the older woman added.

"I do hope so," Whitney said before meeting Miranda's startled expression. The older woman and Miranda actually agreed on something. "They seemed such a lovely couple, and now I am looking forward to the projects you wish completed too, my lady."

Miranda had requested a family portrait be completed during Whitney's stay. She was looking forward to the challenge very much, far more than socializing with Miranda's nearest neighbor.

"The space you requested has been cleared out as we discussed," Taverham told her before he motioned for everyone to sit. "It is in that direction, at the end of the house. Ask Anders to show you the way in the morning. Just don't keep our son up at all hours, if you don't mind."

Whitney sat opposite Lord Acton and his betrothed, set her paint box at her feet and grinned at her hosts. "I promise to chase Christopher back upstairs if he's neglecting his other studies."

"I wouldn't advise running in the house," Kit said, grinning in return. "My boy is disturbingly against recklessness of any kind."

"I am not surprised at his caution," she murmured, casting an accusing glance at Lord Acton. "Christopher will come to understand soon enough that when I chase him, it is purely for the purpose of play, and holds no danger."

Acton regarded her steadily, giving nothing of his feelings away. Did he feel some responsibility or guilt over what his sister had done in terrifying that poor boy? Christopher, calling himself Simon at the time, had run away to an orphanage, lost to his mother because the earl's sister had discovered his existence and made an attempt on his life. Luckily, fate intervened and brought the family back together earlier this year.

Acton cleared his throat and crossed one leg over the other. "Will you teach him to paint field mice on this visit?"

Whitney smiled at Acton but without any warmth. Painting a mouse had been her own special project, a test of her skill at rendering in paint an object small and highly fidgety. She was annoyed anyone knew about that, and couldn't account for how he *could* have known, unless her cousin had opened his mouth. Perhaps it wasn't too late to strangle her cousin.

"Perhaps you'd like to offer up yourself as an alternative subject, my lord. I could paint you instead," she said with a teasing laugh that brought an immediate scowl to his unfairly handsome face.

It was a harmless suggestion. Acton wouldn't agree.

"Oh, yes," Miss Quartermane cried out. "I should like to have a portrait done of dear Acton before we wed."

The man's cheeks grew flushed with color while Whitney struggled not to laugh at his misplaced modesty. The only men Whitney painted or sketched lately were nude, and since she had viewed all of Lord Acton before, she could probably paint him from memory if the unlikely mood every struck.

"If there is time," she murmured without committing herself to fulfilling Alice's request. Whitney would make sure she never found time to paint any portrait of Lord Acton. She would make sure her work for Miranda, lessons for Christopher, and her own work stretched out until the very last day of her visit, if need be. "Lady Taverham's commission and young Christopher's curiosity are the reasons I've come to Twilit Hill. As soon as the work is complete, I will be on my merry way."

"Oh, I hope that is not too soon," Alice fretted, glancing at her betrothed. "I so hoped you would be willing to extend your visit a while."

Acton stilled, clearly discomforted by the suggestion.

Whitney tore her gaze away from him as Alice's words sank in. "Have you finally set a date for the marriage to take place?" she asked, resisting the urge to look at Acton again for confirmation.

"We're to be wed in the village chapel on a Sunday in three weeks' time," Alice gushed with a blushing smile for her betrothed, as if they were truly in love. "Acton has been very patient to let me enjoy the season before we marry."

"How kind of him," Whitney murmured as she hid a scowl. However, she was pleased the delay to marry was deliberate. Alice had to see and experience something of society before she gave up her freedom to such a scoundrel. "But I am afraid I will have to disappoint you."

Whitney was glad to know when the wedding would be. She might have to push herself, stay up till all hours of the night to get her work done, but she would be gone before the wedding took place. As much as she might hate to disappoint someone she liked, her attendance at this ceremony was highly inappropriate, given how she felt about arranged marriages in general, and Lord Acton in particular.

"But why?"

"My engagements are such that I cannot remain in the countryside above ten days," she advised. "I will be on my way at the end of this month."

Acton sighed his relief quite loudly.

"The young are always flittering about. To where are you bound next?" The dowager asked, her eyes burning with disapproval.

"To the continent," she said with considerable excitement. Whitney's dream to study abroad was about to come true.

"What? Your cousin couldn't possibly approve of this," Miranda admonished, even as the marquess sputtered out a protest, too.

Whitney waved away their concerns. Martin would know when he received her next letter. She'd already drafted one to him and explained her decision was final. "My cousin has other matters on his mind at present."

Such as doting on his new wife, and pacing the halls with his offspring. Whitney had long ago accepted that Martin would never make good on his promises to join her on this adventure— her own grand tour, of sorts. She understood he couldn't and wouldn't drag his wife from the comforts of home as soon as he'd proven himself deeply in love.

She couldn't wait for her cousin's life to settle down enough that he might escort her.

That was the trouble with love—it made dreams die a slow death. It was worse for women, of course. Women were expected to marry young, bear children quickly, and turn the cheek while their husbands did as they pleased.

Alice and Acton were about to begin a life together that was everything Whitney had never wanted.

"Why on earth are you leaving the country?" Acton asked in a voice full of shock and outrage. "It's not safe."

"I am assured it is." She glanced at him and shrugged. "I am independent. I have sufficient funds at my disposal to make the trip on my own terms."

He shook his head. "Yes, but why leave so suddenly?"

"It is not sudden," she promised him. "I have wished for this all my life. I am going to Florence, and I cannot wait to begin."

"I say, do you need someone to carry your bags?" Mr. Thompson enquired with a short laugh that sounded awfully like derision. "I could do that quite easily."

Whitney stared at him. "That position is filled."

"By whom?" Acton demanded.

She faced him slowly. "Why do you ask? Did you wish to come with me, my lord?"

The Marquess of Taverham roared with laughter. "Be careful, Acton, or she will convince you and your bride to spend your honeymoon traveling with her."

"Oh, yes!" Alice exclaimed. "What fun a grand tour could be for all of us!"

Everyone else twittered, but Acton remained silent as he stared at her.

It wouldn't be enjoyable at all for Whitney to have them come along. "Forgive me, Alice, but this adventure is not for newlyweds."

Chapter Three

———◆———

Everett took one last look at Whitney Crewe standing on the steps of the Twilit estate, and then entered the carriage with a shake of his head. He was glad to be going. Glad she was going away, too. Eccentric wasn't a good enough description for the woman he'd almost made love to one mad evening.

He sat beside Mr. Thompson in the carriage as the women began to chatter amongst themselves.

"Did you ever hear of such nonsense," Mrs. Quartermane burst out as soon as Lord Taverham's home fell behind. "Traveling abroad at her age and jesting that she'd engaged a man to carry her bags when she should be engaged to marry instead. Mark my words, Miss Crewe will come to a bad end."

"I'm sure Lord Louth will have taken steps to keep her out of trouble. Despite what she suggested tonight, he'll insist on a proper chaperone or put a stop to it entirely. I've no doubt about that," Everett promised, with the hope the discussion was over.

"It's high time she married," Mrs. Quartermane continued, receiving a nod of agreement from her rather quiet husband. "Good lord she's almost thirty."

"Five and twenty, mama," Alice chided.

"Well that is even better," Mrs. Quartermane claimed. "There must be some man we know who can bring her to heel."

Her eyes fell on Thompson and lingered there, assessing him.

Everett shifted on the bench. Thompson did not deserve a

woman like Whitney Crewe. It wasn't that Thompson wasn't good enough to marry her, but that Thompson surely didn't need the aggravation. Whitney was *trouble*, and Thompson had more than enough of that in his life already. Disowned by his father, at odds with his siblings, too. Thompson was a good man who'd run afoul of propriety too many times for his family to ever forgive him.

Since making Whitney Crewe's *proper* acquaintance, Everett had been in a constant state of shock at the way she carried on in society. She had no intention of marrying anyone, or so her cousin had once complained within his hearing, and no consideration for moderation or decorum, either.

"Despite her age and disinclination to be courted, she's never lacked for admirers in London," Alice murmured. "She's friends with everyone, even the Duke of Exeter asks her to dance."

"Whitney charms every man she meets," he said grimly, growing hot under the collar. He'd seen her laughing with the duke, a man twice her age but perhaps not quite twice as wealthy.

Learning he'd almost been seduced by an heiress had been another shock. Where had her cousin been the night of the Fairmont Ball? A chaperone? Whitney Crewe's fortune was said to rival his betrothed's dowry, and more besides. Whitney could easily become a target of unscrupulous fortune hunters if she was not wary—the very thing he'd been accused of being.

"Indeed, she does charm without trying," Thompson murmured with a humorous smile his way. "I found her lack of affectation utterly delightful and her age is unimportant."

"I'm very glad I met my Acton before Whitney had a chance to turn his head," Alice exclaimed, laughing.

Everett nearly choked. His head had been turned, upside down and back to front and all in one wild night, and it was before he'd met Alice, too. It was only Whitney's high principles that had prevented them from becoming lovers, for which he was now profoundly grateful. At the time, he'd been furious to be so teased and discarded. "Why do you imagine she could?"

"My daughter is merely teasing you," Mrs. Quartermane said, but cast a warning look at her daughter before she spoke again. "We know your heart is pure, and Alice adores you for your gallantry in allowing her to enjoy the season. Besides, you're much too distinguished to ever fall prey to an eccentric."

Clearly his bride's family didn't know him that well. His gallantry was because of Whitney's parting words the night of the Fairmont Ball. After meeting Alice, he'd allowed the date for their marriage to slide toward the end of the season so that she might enjoy the parties and entertainments of London more freely.

That the Quartermanes were not entirely enamored of Miss Crewe's attitudes toward matrimony, even if they had been much together in London, no longer surprised him. Perhaps they thought they could reform Whitney by keeping her close. Everett doubted that was possible, and Alice's remark made him wonder how many other men had made it into Whitney's bed?

"Well, she is very pretty and generous to all," Alice murmured, glancing down at her fingers. "Everyone looks at her and remarks upon what she does and says."

Everett regarded his rather timid intended with a kind smile. Alice was beautiful, but pale where Whitney Crewe was vibrant. The pair of women had nothing in common on first glance, and he liked it that way. "There is no need to make any comparison. You are lovely, sweet and kind. You are the woman who will be my wife and countess."

Alice beamed, a blush rising up her cheeks. "I am, aren't I," she stated proudly.

"Well said, Acton. Well said, indeed," Thompson said approvingly. "It never does to compare one woman after another."

"She does have a considerable dowry that would make many a man overlook her flaws, especially her age and eccentricities," Mrs. Quartermane mused, looking closely at Thompson again. She tapped her husband's knee, waking the fellow from a doze. "What do you think, Mr. Quartermane? Is there anyone you know in need of a wife?"

Mr. Quartermane looked out the window. "I wouldn't care to speculate, Mrs. Quartermane."

Mrs. Quartermane tapped his hand again. "But don't you think the right man could turn Miss Crewe's head from this nonsense of traveling alone?" Mrs. Quartermane continued to pester her husband about it, and Everett tuned out the conversation.

If Whitney Crewe had ever wanted to be a proper lady, she had had ample examples of how to behave among her cousin's circle of friends.

If she'd been a proper lady, he'd never have met her twirling barefoot upon the grass of Lord Fairmont's estate.

He'd never have been seduced by her, lured to a quiet room and convinced to strip off his clothes for her pleasure. The heat in her eyes that night had produced many an erotic dream since.

He closed his eyes a moment and worked to banish the memory of Whitney Crewe that night.

"Here we are," Mrs. Quartermane murmured.

Everett jerked his head up as the carriage came to a stop, heartily ashamed that he'd spent nearly the entire journey lost in his thoughts about a woman he disliked.

Whitney Crewe *was* trouble. She made Everett forget he should only be thinking of his future wife.

He scooted out of the carriage before Mr. Quartermane and Thompson with the intention of being the one to assist his intended bride down the steps.

Alice was perfect for him. She'd never behave the way Whitney Crewe had, or would likely do in the future.

He aided Mrs. Quartermane down and the woman quickly grasped her husband's waiting arm. "Have you ever seen such a grand home as Twilit Hill, my dears? Why, Twilit Hill is almost as large as a castle."

"Without the battlements or the dungeon," Alice murmured for his ears alone. "I much prefer Warstone Manor, my lord."

He smiled down upon his intended bride. "I'm glad, because I tend to spend much of the year here."

"Yes, yes. There is no comparing Warstone to Twilit Hill." Mrs. Quartermane sighed as she looked around the shadowed front gardens.

"The woods can make it gloomy at first," Thompson remarked.

"It *is* such a shame that so much of the grounds are hidden from view because of all these trees."

"The woods are what I love most," Everett told his future mother-in-law proudly. "My great-grandfather had remarkable foresight to keep them, in my opinion."

Thompson bid them good night and disappeared inside, his hands shoved in his pockets. Thompson wasn't much for socializing with his other guests, and Everett doubted he'd see him again that night.

Mr. and Mrs. Quartermane bustled ahead and into the house, calling for Alice to follow. He watched them disappear inside with great excitement because Alice lingered.

At last, a moment alone with his future bride, and under the stars no less.

Alice smiled up at him shyly. "Warstone suits you."

He grinned. "As in a little weathered and rundown?"

"You are hardly rustic, my lord," she said but then frowned. "I mean, like the house, you have hidden qualities not easily discovered on first glance." Alice bounced on the spot as she rubbed her bare arms. "It is a little cold tonight though. Perhaps we could discuss the appeal of your home better when the sun comes out tomorrow?"

He held out his arm for her to take just as her mother's maid appeared, frowning at them. "Then let us venture inside. What do you say to a game of whist before you retire tonight?"

Alice winced. "I would enjoy a game very much, but I must see my mother to her room. She was complaining of an ache before dinner. I am not sure how long I will be."

"I am happy to wait until tomorrow night if it is more convenient to play then." Alice had such a tender heart and fussed over her family. He was looking forward to being the recipient of her attention once they married. But until then, he must be patient. "Of course, you must go and comfort her. Ask my staff for anything you require."

"I will, and thank you." She dipped him a curtsy and turned away, leaving Everett longing for some way to bridge the gap between proper decorum and some small degree of desire. He had not kissed Alice yet. There hadn't been a chance for any romantic interludes because her parents watched him and Alice like hawks or sent servants to shadow them at all times.

He scraped a hand through his hair. He felt he should have at least kissed her long before now, and the longer he left the first kiss, first embrace, the more he worried about it. And yet, wasn't there plenty of time to get to know each other after marriage? The banns had been called and he'd only have to wait three more weeks till they were man and wife now.

He raked his hand through his hair again. He had no reason to be discontent with his life, no cause to complain that it lacked certain pleasures.

And yet the fact that Whitney Crewe just happened to visit their mutual friends at such a delicate time irritated the hell out of him.

Alice would never have attended a bachelors ball where half the women in attendance were part of the demimonde! How was he to have known Whitney wasn't one of them? She'd acted so differently that night to how she behaved in polite circles now, even if that was often shocking.

Whitney Crewe *had* seduced him at the ball, without revealing her real name or asking for his. She'd then fled the moment he'd revealed his intention to marry—albeit someone else—taking his evening breeches away with her!

The ensuing gossip about that night could have threatened his marriage contract with Miss Quartermane, had her father learned of it, too. And when he'd discovered the identity of his *almost* lover, coming face to face with Whitney at a ball on her huge cousin's arm, he'd expected to be called out there and then. When no challenge had come, he'd tried to speak with Whitney privately, but had been firmly turned away, not even seen when he had called at her home the next day.

It was a great relief that everyone remained oblivious to their first real meeting. For weeks, he'd feared Whitney would launch some sort of revenge on him. The fact that she'd yet to say one word about their near-tryst bothered him. She'd greeted him with a polite smile at every public encounter, without a single hint she'd merrily taken his cock in her hand—with very clear intentions.

The proof of her lack of innocence was in her behavior that night, and that had slowly lessened his guilt afterward. He'd not been the first lover she'd lured away to a quiet room. He knew the signs of experience in a woman. A woman who had demanded his full attention and returned it threefold until she'd heard something distasteful of him. Whitney Crewe was a woman of unexpected passions. As eccentric as she'd claimed to be from their first encounter—and just as troublesome ever since.

"My lord," a footman called softly as he came running out of the house, coat flapping behind him like wings. "There's an urgent message from Rose Cottage."

Chapter Four

Everett snatched up the paper and quickly read the missive. Damn, not again. "Have my horse saddled. I'll leave from the stables as usual."

As the fellow raced ahead to do his bidding, Everett glanced up at the windows and checked for observers. Now was not the time for the Quartermanes to discover his secret. Relieved to see no one watching him, he dashed into the surrounding woods and, once beneath the dark canopy he sighed and slowed to a walk.

After Miranda's return, Emily *had* gone to Bath for a time. He had not lied to his friends about that, but he'd soon had a letter from her that she was ill, and then she'd arrived unannounced at his London residence.

He'd been horrified by the swift change in her health. He'd feared for her, despite the horrible things she'd done.

When she'd come to him in London, he'd brought her into his home and invited the best doctors to treat her. After being in her company every day for a week, he'd realized that Emily could not let go of her ambitions, and had become utterly unhinged over losing Taverham. Since Taverham and his family were in London, he had swiftly decided to remove Emily to the countryside to recover.

However, Emily could not be made to understand what she'd done in the past was wrong—and what she intended for the future was evil.

She *was* terribly ill, but she was also obsessed— sobbing over her unrequited love for Lord Taverham and vowing to make everyone involved in keeping them apart pay.

When Taverham and his family had unexpectedly returned a few days ago, he'd been forced to lock Emily away at a small cottage on his estate for the safety of everyone living at Twilit Hill.

Yet that was only part of the problem with Emily.

Only he, a pair of respected physicians, and a number of trusted staff were aware that Emily was dying.

He hurried into the stable and mounted a hastily saddled gelding. "I'll be back at dawn," he advised the stable master. "Say nothing of my whereabouts to my guests again."

"You can trust us to keep your secret safe, my lord. Do be careful tonight."

"There is a little moon, so I will find my way easily enough," he promised the man.

He wheeled the horse about and set his heels to its flanks. Riding in the dark across fields and winding lanes could be dangerous if he wasn't careful, but he would be on his own lands the whole distance. He'd made the trip to visit Emily many times by day and a few times by night already.

He kicked the horse to a fast trot as soon as he was beyond the woods and in open fields.

Emily had taken a bad turn *again*, and there was nothing he could do but wait and hope she might recover her health quickly this time.

He found the cottage without a problem and, given the gentle light glowing above the garden walls, knew everyone inside was awake despite the late hour. He drew to a halt at the garden gate and dismounted his weary horse. The head gardener who tended the grounds rushed out to greet him with a quiet welcome, taking his horse away immediately to be cooled down and housed in the nearby stall till needed again.

He approached the cottage gate quietly, listening for the screams and tantrums that had become part and parcel of past visits. Instead, the place was deathly quiet.

Stomach churning at the unnerving silence, he took out his key and let himself into the walled courtyard of the cottage, and made sure to lock the garden gate behind him.

Emily was waiting on a stool just outside the front door. Her face shone with perspiration, but her manner was devoid of all hysteria.

"Thank heavens you've finally come," she croaked as she rose to her feet unsteadily. "I feared you had forgotten me."

He hurried forward and brought his sister into his arms. He held her tightly, turning his face away in case she coughed over him. He'd been warned of the risk he placed himself in every time he called on her. "Of course I would come. You are my sister."

She sniffed his shoulder and then sneezed. "You were with *her*."

Her was always a reference to Miranda, Marchioness of Taverham, but he deliberately chose not to answer the accusation. Mention of Miranda tended to make his sister a little crazed, but the scent on his clothes could not be hers. It might be his betrothed's scent she detected, or perhaps it was wholly in her twisting imagination. Emily complained of a great many wrongs done to her lately.

"I came as soon as I could," he promised.

He had not told Emily that he was getting married, so he would not have to argue with her about his choice of bride. Emily had ambitions for *him* too, ones he disagreed with. She believed he was destined for a duke's daughter or some such nonsense. Money and prestige were all that mattered to Emily now, as it had been for their late parents. Emily wanted him to influence members of the *ton*, and making an advantageous match had always been her goal for him.

"What are you doing outside in the cold? Let me take you inside, where there's some light and we can have tea."

He took Emily's arm and urged her into the neat little six-room cottage on the far edge of his estate. The parlor was well lit and always warmest, so he turned her into that room. The two nursemaids hired to care for Emily startled at seeing them. They must have removed their face masks while Emily was outside and they rushed to retie them on.

He took his sister to a fireside chair, and chose the one opposite so a tea set could be placed on the table between them. Emily's hands shook as she poured.

"When will Kit come home," Emily asked suddenly.

"I've no idea." Everett pretended to drink his laudanum-laced sweet tea and said nothing of her fading strength. Instead, he talked of the weather and changes on the estate beyond Emily's walled garden, careful to avoid the topic that had led to her confinement.

"Lady Taverham is never away from Twilit Hill at this time of year," Emily remarked, studying him over the rim of her teacup.

The dowager Marchioness of Taverham and Emily had been as close as mother and daughter for years before Miranda's return. They'd not spoken since the revelation of her cowardly attack Taverham's son and heir. The dowager was furious and had readily agreed to keep a distance from Rose Cottage. The old and the very young were the most susceptible to disease.

"She is staying in London this year," he lied, sipping only a little. It was enough to fool Emily into drinking more until her cup was empty.

He chose to read to Emily, and after a few pages her head began to droop. He set the book aside, yawned widely, but was thankful he'd drunk very little of the laudanum-laced brew. Emily should sleep very peacefully now.

Her simple bedchamber wasn't far, so he picked her up, noting how light she'd become in recent weeks, and with the maid's assistance, tucked her into her bed. Then, on seeing her eyes flutter, he opened up the book again and continued reading until she was still again.

The nurses were waiting to speak to him in the next room when he stepped out of Emily's bedchamber. He took in their weary expressions with a heavy heart. "What happened this time?"

"The fever came upon her quick and she began to cough uncontrollably." One wrung her hands. "My lady became quite distressed and angry with us."

He nodded. These particular servants had been with the family for a long time, and he was grateful for their presence.

"You are doing me a great service putting up with all of that." He frowned to see their bare faces again. "I trust you are careful, and always wear the masks the physician provided you with when you are near my sister?"

"We try, my lord. But she hates when we do, and screams at us worse than ever in her fevered state."

"No matter what she says, keep wearing them." It was the only way to protect them. He waved them away. "It's been a long night for you both. I'll stay for a while and wake you before dawn. Go get some rest," he suggested before he returned to sit at the doorway to his sister's room for the remains of the evening, fighting the pull of the laudanum he'd consumed.

Chapter Five

Whitney turned her face up to the sun and basked in the freedom life afforded a single woman in possession of an unrestricted fortune. She was ecstatic to be rid of her last companion, an uptight woman in need of a stiff drink. Whitney had her affairs in order at last and blessed peace from being told what to do. She had the freedom to come and go at will in a way few women could claim.

It had always been difficult to enjoy herself in London, where tongues wagged constantly about what she did or did not do. It was next to impossible to move about without a chaperone, which was why she'd bribed the last one her cousin had hired to go away.

She walked through grass grown too long, all the while keeping an eye on the marquess' inquisitive son as he skimmed rocks across the water of a little stream they'd stumbled upon while riding.

"Time to turn back, Miss Crewe," Lady Taverham's servant called out from the ridge.

Whitney glared at the man. "You may go if you need to return to your other duties. I want to ride to the top of the next hill with Christopher before going back."

"It's the highest point on the estate, Landry," Christopher explained, making one more attempt to skim his rock so it bounced. "She has to see the best view."

Whitney patted his shoulder as his rock sank beneath the surface without one single bounce. "We'll try again tomorrow."

"I'm going to beat your three bounces if it's the last thing I do," he promised with the enthusiasm of a child without limits to his imagination.

She agreed, followed him up the hill, and turned to her own horse and the pair of grooms that had insisted on accompanying them that morning. They were waiting to assist her remount, as if she couldn't possibly manage the task alone. The largest one, Mr. Landry, seemed an obstinate sort of man, with a face only a mother could love, but entirely respectful. He also possessed the widest set of shoulders of any man she'd ever seen. There wouldn't be enough canvas to do this man justice unless it was life-size.

The second man said very little and seemed happiest when not forced to converse.

She mounted her horse effortlessly with Landry's boost and settled herself astride her horse. Whitney refused to ride sidesaddle except on Rotten Row in London. She'd had a charming riding outfit created for the express purpose of riding astride. Modesty and comfort assured. She felt safer this way, riding across unfamiliar terrain.

Christopher kicked his old pony on ahead of Whitney to begin the long climb to the top of the steepest hillside on Taverham's lands.

Landry scowled and glanced at the other groom first before speaking. "Begging your pardon, miss, but surely there are plenty of perfect spots to paint from lower down. You haven't seen the causeway yet."

"You fuss without reason, sir." The boy glanced over his shoulder, grinning as he urged his pony ahead at a trot. She offered up her most reassuring smile to each one of Twilit Hill's servants. "Can you not see that I am in danger of being beaten to the top? We came riding for the exercise and our mounts are far from winded. Never fear, I have more stamina than the marchioness. I promise you, Christopher and I are in no danger of fatigue."

Although they both appeared unconvinced, Whitney kicked her mount forward before they could think of more ways to protest, and pursued Christopher.

Lord Taverham had claimed they were free to ride anywhere on his estate, but his wife insisted Landry accompany her son at all times. Unfortunately, neither one had mentioned that Landry was such a stick in the mud, and overprotective, too.

Whitney reached the boy quickly and remained abreast with him up the steeper incline. Her horse surged forward, and so too must have Christopher's, because he burst out with a whoop of joy when they reached the summit at the same moment.

It was a glorious day, and the Twilit Hill estate was everything she was promised it would be. Rolling hills, green fields for miles around and a charming river that wound through the valley floor. The landscape was a painter's dream. She paused at the top of the hill to get her bearings then turned her mount in a slow circuit before stopping to admire the view.

"Oh, Christopher. Your home is very grand," she told him.

"It is, isn't it?" Christopher grinned, patting his pony's sweaty neck. "I used to try to imagine this place when I was little. I made Mother tell me of home each night before I went to sleep."

His brow furrowed, and then his smile slowly slipped away as he took in the spectacular view to the south.

"What is it?" she asked him.

"It will be all mine one day."

She brought her horse beside his, puzzled by his sudden change of mood. "And that worries you?"

"A little." The boy shrugged. "I know my father will teach me what I need to learn to run this place in his stead."

"But you are worried still?"

The boy nodded. "If anything happened to Mother or Father..."

"You'll be alone," Whitney finished for him.

The boy nodded quickly, biting his lip as he fiddled with the reins. "There's so much I need to learn."

"Don't forget you have your grandmother." Whitney squeezed his arm. "I'm an only child, and always longed for brothers and sisters. When my parents died, my aunts and uncles drew straws to decide who I would live with. Each new situation brought a new set of challenges."

Christopher gasped, eyes widening. "They didn't want you?"

"No, the problem was that they *all* did," Whitney reassured the boy with a soft laugh. "It was quite a squabble between them at first. To restore the peace, a ballot was set up and straws drawn. I went to live with Uncle Willard first, then when he died, another ballot was undertaken and so on and so forth. It all turned out quite well. By the time I was of an age to be taken seriously, there was only Uncle Nash left, and we both moved to live with my cousin, Lord Louth. Uncle Nash died last year."

Whitney had been to more than her fair share of family funerals, but she'd also experienced living in six very different but loving homes. She felt herself blessed to have lived such an extraordinarily diverse life. Christopher was blessed too, but in a way he couldn't imagine yet.

"I don't have any aunts or uncles," said Christopher in a worried tone.

"But you do have a cousin, and you do trust her, don't you?" The boy nodded quickly. "I am certain you can depend on Lady Carrington to smother you with love and support if anything should happen to your parents."

"I really miss Aggie and the others," Christopher admitted.

"The others are the children she took in from the orphanage?"

Christopher nodded quickly. "They were my friends. I haven't seen them in such a long time. I think they will have forgotten all about me."

Whitney clucked her tongue. "You were their leader, weren't you?" she asked him, already knowing that was the case. She had seen the children in action together in London, and knew they had all adored Christopher. They probably missed him, too. "They will not have forgotten you. Have you told your mother you'd like to see them?"

"She's always tired."

True, but the boy needed companions his own age to play with. Whitney remembered feeling very old around other children her age, since most of her time was spent with an older generation. Making and keeping friends though had been difficult when she'd moved homes so often during her childhood, too. She had many friends now, and wrote letters to them every day. But still, despite the shortcomings of her childhood, she wouldn't trade the love of her aunts and uncles for anything as fleeting as friendships.

"Your father promised me just this morning that your mama is much better than she once was," Whitney assured the boy. "Coming to the country and resolving their differences has taken away a great strain. Why don't you talk to your father about it first when we return and see what he thinks about extending an invitation to Lord and Lady Carrington."

The boy nodded. "I will."

"And in the meantime, I'm afraid you'll have to put up with my shabby company for games," Whitney apologized, pulling a long face.

Christopher laughed. "You'll do in the short term."

"You're sounding more and more like the marquess every day, you know," Whitney said, grinning from ear to ear. She glanced around, impressed with what she saw of the district. "As far as inheritances go, not bad, young man. Not bad at all."

Christopher began to point out features of the estate he recognized and a few moments later, the tension in him disappeared. She ruffled his hair affectionately, and thought she too might have a quiet word with the marquess about the boy's loneliness. He was much too serious for his age.

The grooms appeared suddenly, their mounts puffing and blowing. Landry seemed most upset of the pair. "Struth, Miss Crewe, have you no patience?"

"Some, but I refuse to let life pass me by while I wait for anyone's permission to enjoy myself," she told Landry.

She shielded her eyes from the sun and spied the roof of a distant manor house nearly hidden by an unending forest of trees. "Whose home is that?

"Lord Acton's," Christopher said quietly. "Warstone Manor abuts Twilit Hill on the southern boundary."

"Oh," she whispered, trying and failing to see more of the distant manor house. So that's where the naughty earl lived. The close growth of woods prevented her from noticing more than the roofline and chimneys of Warstone, but she thought it looked to be a peaceful place. At least from a safe distance such as this. It was closer than she'd imagined it would be. Perhaps an hour's stroll from the main house of the Twilit Hill estate.

Christopher turned his horse away, his smile slipping. "I'd like to return home now."

The grooms immediately surrounded the boy to urge him back down the path.

"Yes, of course. I'll join you soon," she called out to him, and watched as he disappeared from view.

Whitney turned her attention to the lands surrounding Lord Acton's distant home. Had she really expected to find ugliness surrounding his holdings? Yet there were dark woods crowding wide paddocks of rich farmland, roads no more than horse trails crisscrossing the landscape. The place seemed unfathomably peaceful for having been the birthplace of a scheming witch like Lady Emily Brighthurst.

She caught a glimpse of a figure on horseback galloping away from a distant cottage, and stood up in her stirrups. "What have we here? A lover fleeing a scandalous tryst?"

Landry spluttered and coughed. "No, miss."

Whitney frowned, noting the reckless pace the rider had set in his eagerness to leave the cottage far behind. "I thought you had gone."

"No miss."

She glanced at the man as she resumed her seat. "The boy is out of earshot, so there's no cause for false manners around me. What goes on in the countryside is the same thing that happens in London's finest homes, I assure you. Tell me that isn't a budding scandal?"

The man turned a fiery red, and Whitney raised one brow as she waited for her answer from him.

"Not a tryst," he spluttered at last.

She spotted the figure on horseback again, and concluded that the rider was headed directly for Lord Acton's manor house or stables. She was too far away to determine who exactly it might be. Only that he wore dark clothes. She glanced back the way the fellow had come. "Who is it that lives in that picturesque little cottage over there?"

"I couldn't say, Miss Crewe."

She stared at the walled garden and vast green field around the dwelling and felt drawn to see it in closer detail. "Well, if you won't tell me, I shall have no choice but to go down and introduce myself."

Landry wheeled his mount around and blocked her way. "You cannot, Miss Crewe."

"Why ever not? Lord Taverham said I can go anywhere I choose on his land."

"The cottage is not on his land, but on Lord Acton's."

"Ah." Whitney frowned. Although curious, she wasn't about to ask the scoundrel for his permission to do anything. And yet… "What he doesn't know…"

When she tried to ride around Landry, he placed himself in her path again.

She stared at him in consternation. "For goodness sake. What is so dangerous about that cottage that I cannot view it from a closer distance than this very high hill? I have it in mind to paint it as a surprise for Lord Acton's bride."

Landry set his hand on his hip. "I'm sorry, Miss Crewe. For everyone's safety, it is best that Rose Cottage not be reminded of the Twilit Hill estate or its inhabitants."

"Not be reminded?" she spluttered. "I've never heard of anything so ridiculous. How could anyone forget that gargantuan pile of rubble behind us?"

Landry glared at Whitney. "Turn back."

"Oh, very well. But you are being ridiculous. When I get back to the estate, I will have a strong word with Lord Taverham about these silly restrictions. I am sure Lord Acton would welcome my interest in painting any part of his home."

Perhaps that might be a stretch, she did not know Lord Acton well, but it wasn't as if she could do any harm painting a little cottage in an empty field.

"'Tis not his restrictions, Miss Crewe," Landry ground out. "The dowager marchioness ordered we keep a distance."

"Then I shall speak to the dowager directly this afternoon and clear up this problem."

Landry raised a brow. "You're a feisty piece, aren't you?"

"I prefer to speak my mind."

"Well, make sure you don't mention your intention to visit Rose Cottage around the young master. He will not be allowed to go with you, and we won't have him upset for anything."

Whitney stilled her restless horse, struck by the fierce and protective words Landry spoke. Such devotion. Such protection.

But why? There was no danger. Not anymore. Acton had sent his sister away to Bath.

Or had he lied about that?

Whitney glanced over her shoulder. Rose Cottage was on Lord Acton's lands and it was suspiciously off limits. Could he have been the figure riding from it this morning?

"Damn his black heart," she hissed furiously. "I should have known he wasn't to be trusted."

Whitney whipped her horse around and fled down the opposite side of the hill, intending to visit Rose Cottage herself.

Landry, caught unawares, cried out after her but she would not stop. She would see for herself if Lady Brighthurst was there—and if Lord Acton had it in him to lie to everyone he claimed to hold dear.

Chapter Six

Everett dismounted outside his stables, feeling weariness in every part of his body. It had been a long night and he was beyond exhausted. He needed to sit quietly for a moment and clear his head.

A groom took his horse away, leaving Everett standing at the entrance to the stables all alone, save for the old horses he couldn't bear to part with. He turned away as they acknowledged him, stepped into an area that had until last month been the stable master's private quarters and stripped off completely.

He placed his older clothing into a bucket near the doorway for boiling and dragged his feet across the room to the fireside. This daily cleansing routine was for his own piece of mind as much as anything. He couldn't bear it if anyone else was hurt unwittingly by contact with his sister through him.

He found the water heating at the range in the corner and mixed it in with the cooler bathwater already set aside in readiness for his return. He stepped into the lukewarm hip bath and scrubbed himself from head to toe with the new block of sandalwood soap, well aware his precautions might be for naught in the end.

There was no way to predict the spread of consumption, only its final result. Death.

Even without the threat of catching her consumption over his head, he felt better for cleansing himself after visiting with Emily, too.

It was not just her illness that troubled him, but the manner of her thoughts she often shouted out in her delirium. She was dark now, bitter and angry, seething with hate for Lady Taverham and her innocent son. Her sickness, fevers and dreams had affected her judgment, too. She wanted to rid the world of the pair. She still believed she could take Lady Taverham's place in the marquess' affections, if only Everett would let her go to him.

He refused.

He scrubbed himself again as he remembered her sudden awakening in the middle of the night, to rid himself of her vile words, but they were burned into his skull. She wanted Miranda dead. She wanted Everett to bring the boy to her.

Emily would forever be disappointed in him, because he could not agree to any of it.

He liked his best friend's son too much to allow him to be harmed. He'd not had much to do with children, but Everett found young Christopher curious, respectful, and often amusing. Christopher reminded Everett of the Marquess of Taverham as a young boy, full of wonder for the world and in awe of the estate he would one day inherit.

But Everett was aware the boy was uncomfortable when he was near, and only time and Emily's absence could change that.

Emily's actions had managed to make the boy wary of him.

He wished the boy no harm, and had been trying to smooth the boy's way into his new situation as best he could. It was not easy, but he was determined to one day call upon the boy and know he was not viewed as any sort of threat.

He redressed in finer clothes for the day then strolled out into the stables, stopping beside each stall to speak to the horses he owned. At the far end, Lion nickered a greeting.

He moved toward his favorite horse, scratched his nose and generally fussed over him.

"He's restless today," the stable master, Neals, complained.

"I thought one of my guests might have wanted to ride him by now." He had brought in his best mounts from the pasture, sure Miss Quartermane had professed to enjoy spending time in the saddle every day. But she had not once enquired after a horse to ride and his hints at an outing had been not outright dismissed, but certainly forgotten in the excitement of visiting neighbors like Twilit Hill.

"None have asked to," Neals said with a shake of his head.

Everett opened Lion's stall and the horse trotted out quickly, leaving him to pay a call on all the other horses in their nearby stalls.

"Lion," he called before the animal reached the farthest one, and the horse obediently trotted back to his side. He petted him, scratched him behind the ears, and then decided to take the old fellow out for a stroll while he checked on a few things.

Lion required neither lead nor saddle to make him follow Everett about. The beast was always content to walk alongside him like a faithful hound would, sometimes with his large, heavy head draped over Everett's right shoulder.

Lion nudged him.

"I know. I know. Walk faster," Everett said to him with a soft laugh.

He lengthened his stride, reaching the nearest outbuildings where workmen were repairing an old long-abandoned cottage on the edge of the woods. The workers, under Thompson's direction, were making better progress on repairs than he'd ever hoped for. The man himself was consulting his papers and marking off items as he joined him.

"Morning, Thompson," he called.

"Ah, there you are. I missed you at breakfast."

"Estate business," he lied once more. Thompson hadn't a clue about his sister's whereabouts. But the longer Thompson remained, the harder it was to hide where Everett went each day. "I see you're hard at work already on our project."

Thompson smiled and scratched Lion's nose. "I am eager to get the work done for you, so that next year's hunt is more comfortable than the last one for participants."

Thompson had a flair for architecture and design, and it had only taken half a day for Everett to agree to let his friend restore this building. It kept him busy and prevented him from dwelling on his family problems, too.

"Good," he agreed as he studied the cottage again, and the improvements underway with approval. Once completed, he would be able to house another dozen riders more than usual for the annual hunt he hosted. "Are you just about done here?"

"I'd planned to stay out a few more hours," Thompson confessed. "I want everything here complete before the wedding day arrives."

Everett smiled tightly at the reminder of his imminent nuptials. Everything seemed to hinge on that date. "Very well, I'll see you at luncheon then."

Thompson was good company and had asked many intelligent questions about the challenges of running the estate so far. The man's father was a fool to cut him off and not teach him more. Everett was toying with the idea of keeping Thompson around long after the wedding day to show him what his future might bring.

Everett turned toward the stables. Once he and Miss Quartermane were married, Everett would be distracted, but Thompson could be shown how to manage everything he had in mind for his estate. There were many other buildings in need of Thompson's expert eye, and then there was the possibility of adding modern plumbing to the family wing as well. Alice would be pleased.

His thoughts turned toward his future wife again, and his mood sank.

"Shouldn't I feel more for her by now?" he asked Lion.

Lion, ever ready for attention, rested his large head heavily on Everett's shoulder as they walked along. Everett wrapped an arm about his neck.

"Silly old horse," he said as he rubbed the great beast's nose. "You're not nearly as smart as you think you are."

Asking a horse why he wasn't more excited about his upcoming marriage didn't give him any answers. He cared about Alice's comfort, had made sure she had everything needed since her arrival, but there must be something wrong with him. He wasn't attracted to her as much as he'd hoped to be by now. And there was nothing to be done about that. He'd proposed, Alice and her parents had accepted, and the banns had been read for a wedding.

He walked back to the stables, secured Lion in his stall again and pondered the beast's future on his estate. He'd thought Alice might like him to ride, but now he wasn't so sure she liked being in the saddle as much as she had first claimed. Given he hosted a hunt each year, that disappointed him. He'd expected his wife to be an eager participant. He needed her to be at the least involved.

But if she wasn't a rider to the bone, as she'd claimed, they had one less thing in common. Perhaps he'd have to be more direct with his riding invitations in future. Lion was easy to manage for even a novice rider, easy to direct and be around, but his restlessness was because he was bored.

Lion needed someone to ride him each day, and that person had to be someone who would appreciate his playful nature, too, and want to spend time with the animal out of the saddle.

With Emily's health worsening, he didn't know when he'd find the time the beast needed.

The stable master drew close. "Do you want the grooms to take him out to the east field and gallop him for a bit today."

"No," he said, as a better idea came to him instead. "Would you deliver Lion to Twilit Hill, to the marquess' son, with my compliments."

The stable master grinned. "A fine idea. Lion will like the boy."

He grinned. "I hope so. Otherwise, he'll eat his head off here and grow fat and difficult."

"True," the stable master agreed.

He bid his horse farewell, knowing he'd be in good hands in Taverham's stables, and returned to the house and his guests.

Alice was in his study, standing at his open study door waiting and looking out upon the grounds. He took a moment to admire her. She was very pretty, her pale hair swept up in an elegant chignon. Today she was wearing another virginal white gown with a froth of lace at her bodice. One day he would peel her out of that dress and make love to her. The idea of it should appeal to him. "Good morning, Miss Quartermane," he called out.

Miss Quartermane yelped upon seeing him. "Oh, my lord, you startled me."

"Forgive me. I did not mean to." He drew closer. "You look lovely today."

"Thank you," she murmured, eyes lowering modestly.

He stepped into the room and looked about swiftly. No sign of her parents but they likely were not far away. He smiled down upon her. "Did you want me for something?"

"Not really. I was just admiring the views from all the rooms. What there is of it."

This room was closest to the woods, and he loved spending his mornings here. "I chose this room particularly for my study because I like the woods."

Her brow wrinkled. "Indeed you must. There is so much about."

"Please sit," he asked knowing time was short. It had always been difficult to speak with Alice without her parents hearing every word he uttered. "Don't be shy. Tell me what you like and dislike about the house."

Alice sank into a seat far from him, hands primly folded in her lap. "Warstone is very lovely, but the rooms are often so dark."

"Yes, the woods tend to cast shade on a great many rooms."

Her brow wrinkled again with a frown. "Why do you not cut down more trees?"

"Tradition. My great-great-great-grandfather chose this spot and removed over a thousand trees for the house and front gardens, and the northern fields that connect to Lord Taverham's estate. But no more than was needed for farming land. The forest was here first, so now we only remove what is needed and trees that are in danger of falling."

"And no one else has logged here since?"

"There hasn't been a great need."

Alice smiled. "My father believes you should cut the trees much farther back from the house. He says there is great demand for wood so tall and straight as yours are."

Everett was only too aware of her father's interest in his woods. Stripping the estate for profit sat ill with Everett, though. "Perhaps twenty years ago there was such a demand, but not now."

"Did you supply trees for the navy?"

He nodded. "For a few years only."

"Perhaps there is still a demand for lumber for other enterprises."

He shook his head. "I won't compromise the beauty, peace and tranquility of my estate for the few pounds offered."

"My father is a very shrewd businessman." Alice's eyes lit up with excitement. "He could make you a great deal of money."

He laughed at her enthusiasm. "I am well aware that his reputation for tough negotiation is a fact. No one strikes a better deal than Mr. Quartermane."

Her brow furrowed again. "But you would not make use of his expertise."

"As I said, I don't need the income, and after we marry I still would not agree to it." He smiled warmly. "There is no need to concern yourself with commerce on our behalf. I assure you, you will never need to pinch pennies as my wife."

"I was not concerned I would," Miss Quartermane stated somewhat stiffly. "My dowry is sufficient to provide everything you need, Lord Acton."

Lord Acton. My lord. But never simply Everett. He'd asked her to use his given name months ago, right after their engagement had been announced, but she hadn't yet done so. "Your dowry will benefit the children we will have together."

"Of course," she murmured, eyes lowering demurely again, and blushing.

It was a sad realization that Alice was as awkward with him now as when he'd asked for her hand in marriage.

She cast a look of longing toward the door when she heard a noise behind her, most likely her parents, by the sound of it.

He stood. "Shall we join your parents?"

"Yes, thank you."

They did not go far before they heard Mrs. Quartermane calling out her daughter's name in a whisper. Alice blushed, and hurried away to find her mother. Everett followed at a slower pace, wondering what he could do to make his future wife more comfortable before their wedding night. He did not like that she was uneasy with him. Although it was understandable. They were virtually strangers still, and had only three weeks to become better acquainted before they were bound together forever. A lot could happen in three weeks, he hoped.

Chapter Seven

---·◆·---

Whitney brought her horse to a stop just as the trees gave way to an empty, grassy field and threw herself out of the saddle. She stared across the field, glaring at Rose Cottage as it hid behind a high stone wall covered in climbing roses. It looked to be completely enclosed from her vantage point, but there seemed to be a drive of crushed white shell leading to it. The place appeared well tended, though she could see no signs of anyone about.

Taverham's groom burst into the open and he joined her quickly. "Lord, you're going to get me dismissed from my position."

"That will not happen if we say nothing about this." She shook her head. "See to our horses and remain here. I want to see for myself what he has done."

She'd not been introduced to Lady Brighthurst, but she'd seen her with Lord Taverham before Miranda's return. There had been something in her expression Whitney hadn't liked back then, and after all she'd heard since, she distrusted the woman. She had learned from her cousin that Lady Brighthurst was dangerous, and hated Miranda simply because Lord Taverham had married her. She doubted the woman could recognize her name, as they'd never been introduced, and prayed she may not know who she was friends with, or related to, either.

Whitney gathered up her skirts and marched across the grassy clearing and up to the wall. The pearl-gray stone was higher than her head and she could not see into the enclosure below the roofline and chimney stacks. She stalked the perimeter, searching for flaws, breaches in the stone that might allow her to peer through and know for sure that her suspicions about Lord Acton were correct.

At the far side of the structure, beyond sight of Mr. Landry, she came face to face with a man holding a pitchfork.

She shrieked, and took a hasty step back before she was impaled. "Oh, you scared me!"

"That was the point. What are you doing?" the man demanded.

Since he seemed to be a servant, possibly a gardener, she made herself smile. And since the pitchfork remained aimed directly at her face, she bobbed a hasty curtsy to show she meant no mischief. "How do you do, sir?"

The man sized her up, buried the handle in the dirt and leaned upon the pitchfork. "I asked what you were doing here?"

"Why, nothing untoward," she told him, fluttering her lashes as she decided the best way to approach him for information. He seemed very unfriendly very quickly. "I saw this charming cottage from a distance, and simply had to come closer and speak with the lady of the house. Such a pretty spot to live, don't you think? I was looking for a way inside so I might knock and make myself known to her."

She peered around his shoulder and saw a first break in the construction. There was a heavy looking garden gate set between the walls a little farther around.

"Never you mind who she is." The fellow scowled. "No one calls here."

"Is that so? How tragic. It's such a charming spot." She glanced around with wide eyes, looking for signs of other servants. Perhaps she could slip past this one man. "Does anyone come out?"

"No," he said bluntly, shifting the pitchfork from hand to hand. "And it's my job to keep busybodies away, so be off with you."

"Who's there, Thomas?" a woman asked in a tiny voice to Whitney's left.

From behind the wall.

Whitney faced the stone obstruction, looking for cracks or gaps to see through. Finding none apparent, she almost growled in frustration. She didn't recognize the voice, but then, she'd never heard Lady Brighthurst speak, either.

"Oh, hello there," Whitney cried to the lady. "How do you do?"

After a moment, the lady sneezed. "Not well, thank you. Who is it with you, Thomas?"

The gardener looked Whitney up and down. "A lady of quality, by the look of her fancy clothes, but she hasn't given her card as yet."

Whitney thought a moment. What harm could there be in giving her real information? She fumbled in her pockets, hoping she might just have a card with her. She came up empty. "I am afraid I don't have one with me, but I am Miss Whitney Crewe of London," she called out. "I am an artist of some renown."

It never hurt to speak well of your skills when speaking to other women.

"I don't believe we are acquainted," the woman inside said flatly.

"I am a friend of Miss Quartermane." Whitney waited for a positive response to that name and an invitation to come in.

"I am not acquainted with anyone called Quartermane," the lady claimed, which made it a certainty that she was not Lord Acton's evil sister.

"Oh dear," she murmured. For the first time, she began to have doubts that this was Lord Acton's sister after all. She might just owe the man an apology for her condemning private thoughts. Before she did that, Whitney had to be sure. "Might I have the pleasure of meeting you so that we might become known to one another?"

The gardener shook his head very quickly.

"I am not allowed visitors," the lady whispered.

"Not allowed visitors." Whitney adopted her most scandalized expression solely for the benefit of the gardener's keen eyes. "Why ever not?"

"I—" The woman began to cough violently. When the horrible sound continued for a good many minutes, Whitney pressed her hand to her chest in sympathy. The lady did not sound very good at all. "I think you must go away now," the woman eventually gasped out.

She heard other voices with the lady, murmuring soothing words to lure her back inside to a warm bed and glass of wine, and was glad she had someone to care for her during her illness. "Goodbye then," Whitney called out. "I do wish you a swift recovery."

Whitney glanced at the gardener without bothering to conceal her concern. But she still needed to know who that woman was. Unfortunately, she suspected the gardener, judging by his cold expression, would not be forthcoming in that respect. "I've never met so many unfriendly people in my life in one place. Very well, I shall depart with my curiosity unsatisfied and a bruised heart. Perhaps I will also go to another district for inspiration for my art and meet nicer people there."

She gathered up her skirts and made slow progress around the structure. The gardener did not follow more than a few steps and, after he turned away, she slowed, listening to the people move about the enclosure closest to her.

"Wait," the lady inside the walled garden called out suddenly. "Did you say you were an artist?"

"Yes, I am indeed. I came to Worcestershire in search of inspiration."

She was also here to teach Taverham's son, but kept that to herself for now. If the woman was Lady Brighthurst, she'd rather not announce the connection for now.

The lady gasped behind the wall. "I should like to see your work. I am a great patron of the arts. Do you sketch, too?"

"Yes, quite often. I find it soothing." Soothing, and awkwardly arousing when her subject was male. That, she never confessed to anyone.

"Will you come back tomorrow?" the lady asked

Whitney grinned widely but kept her voice unconvinced. "For what purpose? To be threatened by that awful fellow with the pitchfork again? I think not, madam whoever-you-are."

"Thomas would never harm you if I ask him not to," she promised. "I need someone drawn for me. But I must speak to my brother first."

Brother.

Whitney shivered with a sudden chill. "Tomorrow, but only if you honor me with your name and your brother's today."

"Emily. My name is Emily. I desperately want a sketch of my brother, Lord Acton. Are you acquainted with him?"

"I am not." Although she had feared Acton was hiding his sister here, the confirmation he had lied rocked her more than she imagined possible. She would not return tomorrow, and she certainly wouldn't sketch Lord Acton for Lady Brighthurst. "Unfortunately I am engaged elsewhere tomorrow," she lied. "I would come back another day if I have time."

"Thank you." The lady resumed coughing, and then other voices could be heard behind the wall, demanding Emily return inside to rest. Although Lady Brighthurst protested that she wasn't tired, they all moved away, possibly inside the cottage until Whitney could hear nothing more.

Whitney snarled silently. Acton had let his sister come home. There was simply no excuse possible to forgive his behavior. How dare he go back on his word and put that dear, sweet boy in danger!

Chapter Eight

—— ◆ ——

Miss Quartermane shielded her eyes as they emerged from the shadows cast by a tract of dense woodland and blinked in the bright sunlight that burst over them. "How soon until we reach the village?"

Everett gestured to the small cluster of neat thatched buildings directly ahead of them. "We're already here."

The village closest to his estate, nestled against the forest edge, was full of people he cared about deeply. He wanted Alice to know them well too. He brought the carriage to a halt and jumped down outside the smithy, where he'd leave his carriage for the hours they strolled about.

"Oh," Alice cried out with a laugh, but as she looked about, her happy expression softened to one of confusion. "I thought the place wasn't so small."

"Close enough to visit easily," he promised, "far enough away not to hear the church bell unless the wind blows up hard from the south."

He raised his hands to assist Alice alight. He caught her about the waist and drew her down, close to where he stood. He held her only a moment then reluctantly released her. Her parents were following them in another carriage, a larger covered barouche, so this moment of privacy was only to be fleeting. He intended to make the most of their short time alone together however in conversation.

Alice walked ahead a few steps, looking about her. "I thought Lady Taverham mentioned the village boasted a pretty set of shops? A seamstress, a bakery."

"She was talking of the town on the other side of the marquess' estate, no doubt. Traveling there and back from Warstone would take the better part of the day, I should imagine. It is a trip I rarely make. How about we stretch our legs for a bit? There's a pretty spot at the other side of the village chapel where I used to fish as a boy."

Alice glanced over her shoulder. "We should wait for my parents."

He glanced at her in consternation. "I wasn't going to take you very far. It is just down the road a ways."

"Mother is very keen to see the chapel where we will marry," Alice told him with an apologetic smile.

"Of course. The vicar is looking forward to meeting you all, too." As were the rest of the nearby residents. He noted Noah Blake, the village smithy, approaching in the periphery of his vision, and smiled. Perfect timing for a quick introduction to be carried out. "While we wait for your parents, I'd like to introduce you to my oldest acquaintance in the village. Someone you can depend upon should you ever find yourself to be in need of assistance."

Blake nodded to him. "Lord Acton."

"Mr. Blake," Everett said as he gestured to his future bride. "Miss Quartermane, may I introduce Mr. Noah Blake. He runs the smithy and the tavern. You'll meet his wife, Nancy, at luncheon."

Alice gaped at Blake as he touched his cap.

Once upon a time, Blake may have been bullied for being a sickly child, but thanks to his life of labor at the dirty forge, he was impossibly large now and perhaps a little intimidating, given Alice's expression.

She eventually dipped a very small curtsy. "How do you do?"

"Very well, Miss Quartermane," Blake said with an easy smile, then he gave Everett a sly grin. "Very pleased to meet you at long last, as will everyone in the village be."

"Oh, thank you." She glanced over her shoulder, and then

sighed as her parents' carriage emerged. "There they are. Do excuse me, Lord Acton. Mr. Blake."

Alice backed away and turned to walk swiftly toward the approaching conveyance. She waved enthusiastically to her parents and then waited for them to disembark.

Blake took up the reins of Everett's carriage. "Your lady is pretty, and a right proper one."

Although it pained him to admit it, Alice was not a bold creature. She was much too formal for the countryside. "She'll warm to you eventually, Blake."

He hoped that wouldn't take long, because he had a great deal to do with the men in the district, and their wives.

"I would have thought…" Blake began but then shook his head.

"What?"

Blake scratched his jaw. "I thought you preferred redheads?"

Everett ignored the question. "I have a feeling the visit will be a short one," he warned.

"Right you are, my lord. Will you be wanting luncheon from the tavern still?"

"Indeed, we will," he promised. The Blakes would have gone to a lot of trouble for him today, and he would not disappoint them. He thumped Blake's back. "Did I hear you and your wife were at odds again? What was it this time?"

"It weren't my fault," Blake protested. "The marquess' new guest got Nancy's hackles up a bit."

Everett turned slowly to face Blake. "Do you mean Miss Crewe upset her? What has that woman done now?"

"Sounds like you are acquainted with Miss Crewe."

He hid a grimace. Too well acquainted. "We are."

Blake's grin widened.

Everett shook his head, knowing Blake was thinking about Everett's supposed preference for redheads. "Miss Crewe's cousin is the Earl of Louth, a very great friend of Taverham's."

"Redhead, about so tall," he said as he set his hand at chest height. "Wore a pink coat. Only saw her for a moment. She jumped down from driving the carriage and four, whistled, and then two weary groomsmen scrambled out from inside the carriage to take her place at the reins."

Everett pinched the bridge of his nose. Was this typical of Whitney? He'd heard all sorts of nonsense about her in London, but driving herself across the countryside was a new one. No wonder she'd seemed rather untidy last night. "What in particular did she do to upset Nancy? Her driving or whistling to the grooms sleeping inside the carriage?"

"Neither. I made a mistake of admiring the lady a little too obviously." Noah winked. "She seemed a very energetic redhead, and I told Nancy she'd be a handful. That's all it took to make my wife's temper soar to match her own red hair. My woman knows my weaknesses too well," he said, laughing as he turned the horse and curricle toward the village stables. "Never fear, I chased Nancy round the bed this morning, so she's forgotten all about it for now," Blake promised. "She'll be completely merry by the time your wedding feast arrives."

Blake moved away, leaving Everett shaking his head.

Really, someone ought to straighten Whitney Crewe out. Put their foot down. Make her consider the damage she was doing to her reputation by flouting the conventions of society so openly. Not that Whitney Crewe would ever be his problem to worry about.

Everett hurried forward to meet his future in-laws and strolled around the village with them for an hour. He took them as far as the causeway where he once fished as a boy. They returned to the tavern a little early because when he suggested a stroll through the edge of the woods, they appeared disinterested in further exercise.

"Ooh, I have never seen so many trees," Mrs. Quartermane exclaimed as she beat the air with her fan quite unnecessarily. "Doesn't those woods give you chills, my dears."

"Oh yes," Alice murmured.

"It is cooler in the woods' shade," he suggested, but he suspected Mrs. Quartermane was not referring to the temperature. Some people were uncomfortable in the woods about his estate. They craved open spaces rather than the comforting surrounds of nature.

"I'm surprised not to see more signs of woodcutters plying their trade," Mr. Quartermane said with a keen eye for their surroundings.

"They wouldn't dare cut down one single tree beyond what is needed without my consent," Everett insisted. "Those trees are all on my land."

Mr. Quartermane's eyes lit up with interest. "I tell you again, we could make a fortune delivering those trees into the right hands."

There were many who pestered him to lift his restrictions on logging the woods on his estate. Mr. Quartermane wasn't the first nor would he be the last to try to strike a deal. However much it might appeal to others, Everett would always refuse. But he didn't want to give offense by being too curt about it right now. "Mr. Quartermane, perhaps this discussion could wait for another day."

"Yes, yes. Business must indeed wait," Mrs. Quartermane agreed. "Alice and I are already bored to tears with the topic."

It was not a hot day, but the woman was gasping, and as he glanced at Alice, he noticed she too seemed flushed now. Everett led his group toward the tavern and the promised luncheon he'd arranged for Blake's wife to prepare. There was no one else about in the tavern, so he settled his guests and went in search of Nancy himself.

"Good morning, Mrs. Blake," he called out when he reached the base of the stairs.

Nancy rushed down from the private rooms above, clearly flustered.

"My lord." She dipped him a deep curtsy.

He looked the woman over and noticed she had made an effort to smarten up her appearance. Not that she wasn't always handsome, but her gown was a soft shade of blue and her hair was intricately twisted about her head. He only ever saw her wear this particular dress on special occasions. "You look lovely," he whispered.

She preened a little and then laughed. "Don't let my Noah hear you flirting with me, my lord."

At one time, he'd thought himself half in love with this fiery redhead, but she'd chosen better in giving her heart to Noah instead. "He'd agree with me."

She stretched to look past his shoulder at his group and then shrugged. She turned back to him with a wide smile. "How soon until your betrothed is joining us?"

His grin stretched to painful. "She's already here."

"But she's not… I thought she'd be a redhead." Nancy looked at his bride again, eyes narrowing, and then back at him. She blushed red from the top of her gown to the roots of her red hair and bit her lip, looking up at him with embarrassment. "Forgive me. I should know better than to listen to Mr. Blake about matters of the heart."

"Of course." He gestured for Nancy to precede him and hid his annoyance. "Let me introduce you to Miss Quartermane and her parents."

The introductions were brief and somewhat stilted, and then Nancy rushed off to stir up the cook to bring their luncheon out, her color still high. He pondered her embarrassment as he made small talk with Mr. Quartermane until an array of dishes was set before him. Was his past preference for redheads that well known that people talked about him when he wasn't around?

"Excuse me, my lord. May I ask a question?" Alice said suddenly.

"Of course," he promised. He glanced at her parents to see if they were listening, and they were. "You need never ask permission again," he whispered.

"Thank you." Alice smiled quickly. "It concerns Mr. Thompson."

"What about him?"

"Do you not worry about angering Lord Clipson by keeping company with his disowned son," she asked.

"Truthfully, no." He frowned at Miss Quartermane. "Thompson has been my good friend for many years, and just because his father has cut him off does not mean I must do the same. He is a brilliant man, and an honest one."

"I see. So he did not ruin that woman?"

"Which woman?"

"That poor woman who fled from the Fairmont Ball with her face covered. Surely you have heard the stories about the gypsy?"

He didn't need to hear the stories to know how stretched the tale had become since that night. "I'm sure the situation isn't quite as grievous as gossip suggests."

"But she was heartbroken."

"Heartbroken?" Everett didn't think that was possible. Whitney had never given him any indication that she'd expected anything from him, not even an apology. She'd refused to see him.

"They say she was inconsolable," she whispered.

He considered that. Yes, Whitney had been upset with him that night—angry, but not inconsolable. "Who said that?"

"Well, everyone. Although I do wonder if Miss Crewe could be correct."

"In what way?"

"She said the lady probably was grateful for her narrow escape from such a despicable man."

For some reason, that suggestion stung.

"Lord Acton, why didn't you call on me," an old voice called.

Everett recognized the voice behind him and grinned as he swung out of his chair. Mrs. Jennings may have been his old nurse once, but he was very fond of her still.

He quickly stood and inclined his head to his old nurse. "Mrs. Jennings, how lovely to see you."

"Posh," she chided. "None of that gentlemanly nonsense. Give us a kiss, sweetie."

"It is so good to see you on your feet again." He grinned and pecked her on the offered wrinkled cheek, despite Mrs. Quartermane's horrified gasp. Mrs. Jennings had raised him, loved him as if he were her own. Now that she was older, it was his turn to look after her. She'd taken a bad tumble a month ago and only now seemed to move about easily.

He brought her forward. "This dear lady is my old nurse. Mrs. Jennings, may I present Mr. and Mrs. Quartermane, and their daughter, Miss Alice Quartermane."

"A pleasure," she told them, eyeing Alice boldly. "You must be his lady."

"We are engaged to marry, yes," Alice corrected her.

He smiled at Alice. "Would you excuse us?" he said to her, and then drew Jennings outside, away from the taproom she lately frequented for medicinal purposes.

He took some coins from his pocket and pressed them into her hand. "How is the knee, really?"

"Aching like the devil, but I still intend to dance at your

wedding feast." She clasped her coins tightly. "Thank you for the coin, my lord."

"If it's not enough for your needs, send Black to me for more."

Mrs. Jennings glanced around him. "I thought she'd be different. Does she look after you? Make you happy?"

He laughed softly. "We're not married yet."

"That's just a few little words. It's the love that counts, in the end," Mrs. Jennings murmured.

He felt his face heat.

Mrs. Jennings scowled at his silence. "Didn't I tell you to wait for love?"

"I couldn't wait forever," he warned.

"That's always been your problem. Rushing in rather than letting the good in life come to you." She patted his hand. "Patience is all you need."

"Forgive me if I have my doubts about that," he chided. "I made my choice."

Mrs. Jennings face fell. "I hope you'll not live to regret it."

"I won't." Everett sighed. "Do you need me to send a cart to fetch you for the feast?"

"Such a good lad. I'd walk if only this leg would mend faster."

"Now who is impatient?" he chided.

She pushed him away, "You'd best get back inside before they think you've run away with me."

"No chance of that." He kissed her cheek again and escorted her as far as the crossroads.

She hobbled down the lane to her little home, leaning heavily on her cane. When he returned to the tavern, the Quartermanes were ready to leave. They filed out to climb into the carriages in silence.

Alice sat straight-backed at his side as they followed her parents' carriage all the way to Warstone Manor. Coming home usually made him happy, but today, Everett couldn't think of a single thing more to say to the woman who would soon share it with him.

Chapter Nine

Whitney threw herself from the saddle and stalked toward the marquess, leaving her horse behind for the eager groom to take away to the stables. "My lord," she called out.

Kit smiled. "Ah, you're back at last."

"Indeed." She glanced beyond the marquess to where Christopher rode atop a different horse now. He looked happy, and as she had no wish to upset him, she strove to calm her temper. She had hoped the boy had gone in to his tutor by now. "More riding lessons?"

"Another gift from Acton," Kit murmured. "He sent the old boy over earlier today."

Whitney snorted. "Buying the boy's affections with horseflesh, is he?"

"That's it. Keep your heels down," the marquess called out to his son as a groom led the boy and tall horse around the enclosed paddock. The marquess glanced her way. "Noble is quite old. Long past the age of riding to hunt or galloping or any other nonsense. Acton was kind to consider that having Lion to ride might help Christopher become accustomed to being so high off the ground. He is a little timid yet around the taller higher-strung horses I have stabled. This one, though, Chris could crawl under him and he'd barely twitch."

Whitney watched the pair and conceded the older mount was

a very good idea. Sensible. Safe. She remembered her first ride on a larger mount quite vividly still. Her first horse had belonged to Uncle Isaac. He'd won the beast at cards, and he had not been calm or as steady as this one appeared to be. She'd had the devil of a time controlling him, and her reaction to being so high for the first time hadn't helped. She was lucky she hadn't been thrown, and it had taken her a while to feel confident enough to remount that same horse again. "He seems comfortable up there," she conceded reluctantly.

"Acton is a good judge of horseflesh." The marquess nodded. "Between our two stables, I think there will be enough variety for Chris to learn upon without needing to visit the horse markets. Acton has been quite generous."

She narrowed her eyes. Was it guilt driving the earl? "Does Acton own many horses?"

"A dozen hunters, and another dozen older ones are eating their heads off in his stables and fields. It's high time he did something about them, but he can barely part with any. It's about time they earned their keep, in my opinion. He's a bit too sentimental about some."

"That's surprising," she grumbled.

"Not really. You don't know him like I do," the marquess told her. "He's a good friend."

"Not to Miranda," she complained.

The marquess straightened, and then scowled at her fiercely. "That is no one's business but theirs."

Scolded, Whitney could only nod. Kit would learn soon enough that his so-called friend wasn't to be entirely trusted with the truth, or his family's happiness. But with Christopher drawing near, perhaps now was not the best time to mention what she had discovered that morning.

She looked away, and her eyes landed on the Dowager Marchioness of Taverham on the other side of the stable yard. The older woman was watching her grandson from the shade of a beech tree, making no move to come closer to the marquess or her grandson. The dowager rested with her two hands on the head of her cane and appeared to be leaning upon it as she watched the lesson.

"Your mother is here," she whispered to the marquess.

He kept his attention on his son. "Yes, I know."

Whitney nodded politely to the older woman and then regarded the marquess with suspicion. "How long has she been standing there alone?"

His jaw firmed. "An hour or so."

An hour? "Why are you not standing together?"

"I have my reasons."

Whitney glanced between the pair again. The older woman wasn't exactly the warmest, but as she had learned earlier that day, family was extremely important to Christopher. If his father was rude to his own mother, might he not notice and do the same one day to Miranda when they disagreed? "You risk setting a bad example for your son by ignoring her," Whitney murmured. "Christopher looks up to you."

The marquess pursed his lips and said nothing to her criticism. But as he glanced toward his mother, a frown line appeared between his eyes. At least he appeared to be thinking about what she had said.

Whitney bid him goodbye to let him stew on her words a while.

She strode toward the dowager quickly, and dipped a curtsy. "Good morning, my lady. I was just on my way to see you this morning."

The dowager spared her the briefest glance. Her attention was fixed on her grandson. "It's nearly noon."

She smiled. For all the dowager's prickly nature, Whitney admired her consistency. She had never been one for small talk. "I imagine it must be. I've been out riding for hours."

"Yes, I saw your return, and that you rode astride, too," she huffed indignantly, her eyes flicking over Whitney's cleverly made gown.

Whitney had found the most ingenious dressmaker who understood Whitney's needs perfectly. This gown was in fact wide-legged trousers, concealed by an overskirt split up each side. She was perfectly covered when mounted astride, and when standing, her attire gave no hint that she was wearing anything out of the ordinary.

Whitney turned to view Christopher as he rode now at a slow trot. A groom was still leading him, but he looked very happy with his new horse. "I prefer to be careful when in the country, and particularly when riding unfamiliar fields."

The dowager, unconsciously perhaps, swayed forward on her cane as her grandson spoke to the marquess. She smiled briefly and sighed. Whitney couldn't hear them and she wondered if the old woman could read lips.

"Where did you ride to?" the dowager asked.

"Christopher took me to the peak," she admitted.

"The peak, you say?" The older woman glanced her way again as Whitney nodded. "My grandson came back alone some time ago."

"Hardly alone. He had a groom with him."

"And you had but one with you, and no proper chaperone, either."

"I tried to send Mr. Landry back too, but he refused to leave me when I rode down the other side of the peak," Whitney confessed. She met the dowager's gaze directly. The groom had hinted the dowager was aware that Acton was keeping his sister at that cottage. The dowager would know what views Whitney would have seen from up there, too. "I have never enjoyed being coddled. I also do not appreciate being deliberately kept in the dark about certain risks to my friends. I wished to ride farther and investigate *all* the hidden mysteries of the district, so I did."

The old woman swallowed. "And were there many mysteries to be found to the south?"

"One," Whitney said, and then said no more. She would let the old woman decide if they would discuss Lady Brighthurst or not today.

At her side, the marchioness stirred, finally giving Whitney her full attention. Lady Taverham hobbled around with the use of her cane and stood before her. "And," the dowager demanded irritably.

Whitney met the woman's gaze and saw anger in her old eyes. The dowager had been much around Lady Brighthurst in past years. Learning the woman had tried to harm her grandson must have angered.

Whitney nodded slowly. "I spoke to her."

The dowager exhaled sharply. "You saw her."

"No," Whitney said as she noted Christopher was

dismounting. "I only spoke to her through the wall, but she does not sound at all well. Have you not visited her?"

"No, and if you value your friendship with my son and his wife you will not do so again," the dowager warned. The older woman took a few steps toward the distant dower house and then turned back slightly. "I believe it will rain soon, Miss Crewe. Good day."

"My lady," Whitney said. At the sound of running feet, Whitney turned and discovered Christopher racing toward her, hat in hand. She smiled at the boy's happiness. "How was your lesson?"

"Smashing," the boy said as he grasped her hand. "He is so tall I was afraid I'd fall off at first."

"Most horses are tall. But you didn't fall and you will get used to him soon enough."

"He will indeed." The marquess agreed as he joined them.

Christopher tugged on her sleeve urgently. "Did you ask?"

For a moment, she hadn't a clue what the boy meant. She was still thinking of Acton's deception.

"Not yet." Whitney ruffled Christopher's hair. "Shall I ask now?"

He nodded.

She faced the marquess. "Forgive the impertinence, my lord, but I was wondering if you might consider inviting the Carrington children to visit in the near future. Perhaps next month."

"Can they come, Father? Please. I'd very much like to see them all again."

The marquess frowned at Whitney, but then leaned down to his son's level. "Next month sounds like a long time to wait. How about they come now instead?"

The boy whooped. "Tomorrow?"

"Not quite tomorrow. In the next few days perhaps." The marquess nodded. "I have already invited the Carringtons to visit for the next month, and also some other friends of ours. Your mother and I thought to surprise you, but the first guests arrive soon."

"It is still a surprise. The best one." Christopher threw himself around his father and the pair hugged for a long moment. "Thank you, Father. I cannot wait to see them. I have to tell her."

Christopher bolted after his grandmother, who hadn't gone very far at all on her cane.

The dowager turned at the sound of his approach. Christopher stopped at the dowager's side, and clearly told her his news in great excitement, given the way he waved his arms about. She smiled too, which was nice to see. But by the way the dowager suddenly looked back at the marquess, and then shook her head, Whitney knew that she'd been excluded from any discussion of guests coming to the estate.

How much of what went on here was now hidden from the older woman out of spite? That did not seem fair when she lived here, too. "He's fond of her."

Kit shrugged. "He's fond of everyone."

"No, he's not," Whitney disagreed. "Your son is very selective about who he befriends."

"You are right, he is careful," the marquess conceded. "More careful than I ever was. What did my mother have to say for herself today?"

She glanced up at Kit to see him watching his mother and son make their way slowly toward the dower house just as the rain began to fall lightly over them. The dowager leaned heavily on her cane and the boy slipped under her other arm to support her, helping her along at a quicker pace. Judging by the frown he wore, Kit *was* concerned about his mother too, but would not admit it.

"Families should not squabble. Time together is short and should be treasured," Whitney murmured, thinking of her own parents. They had died when she'd been too young to understand how great their loss would be. "If you want to know how your mother does, you should ask her directly."

Kit frowned at her. "It's complicated."

"For Christopher's sake and happiness, perhaps you should un-complicate things before it is too late. She's not a young woman anymore. Traipsing about the estate in all kinds of weather just to see her grandson will wear her out."

"She's as fit as a fiddle," he protested.

"How could you possibly know that is still true when you won't talk to her anymore? You could hardly expect her to confide in you if she wasn't feeling her best when you keep secrets," Whitney argued, as the rain came down harder. "If I still had my mother around, or my father, I would never let a day pass without speaking to them. No matter how angry I was with them. Excuse me."

Whitney hitched up her skirts and made a dash for the nearest shelter. She had meant to say something about Acton's lies and Emily's location, but decided against it for now.

If Kit and his mother had been talking, would the dowager have brought the matter up on her own? But then Kit would have even more reason to be displeased with the dowager for keeping Emily's location a secret from him.

She bit her lip, debating with herself. What Whitney knew could cause further trouble between the pair, but she decided there and then to stay out of the situation.

However, when it came to Acton, she was not ready to let his actions slide so completely. She would give him a piece of her mind the next time she saw him, and give him a chance to volunteer to set the record straight himself.

Chapter Ten

Acton reined in his horse and stared up the grassy slope at an unexpected sight. High above him on one of his hills sat Miss Whitney Crewe, pink gown spread about her, red hair shining like a beacon in the sunlight after a day of dreary rain.

Alarmed by her presence on his land, and this field in particular, he turned his mount toward her.

"I'll return shortly," he called to Thompson, who'd been helping him drive his cattle into this very field.

He urged his mount up the steep incline, intent on removing Miss Crewe immediately.

Whitney was sketching in a large book, obviously without thought to her surroundings. He had not spoken to her since the night of her arrival. Whitney Crewe had been keeping to herself—painting the portrait of their mutual friends.

He tied his horse to the twisted branch of a nearby tree and rushed toward her. This high up, the views were breathtaking and Whitney appeared enthralled. The lower part of the field, however, was full of his hungry cattle grazing on lush, fresh grass and doing the usual things cows did. Whitney did not look around, but the slight hitch to her posture suggested she knew he was there.

He crouched down a few feet away, keeping one eye on the herd, and waited until she lifted her hand from what she was sketching. "Good morning."

She scowled. "How have you managed to hide what you do for so long?"

He blinked. "I'm not hiding. I am moving the herd."

She huffed. "I spoke with Lady Brighthurst a few days ago," she told him, frowning at her drawing. "She invited me to visit her again and take tea. Should I go?"

Acton was on his knees before Whitney the next moment, pulling the sketchpad from her hands and looking closely at her appearance, her pretty face. She did not appear sick or fevered yet. Of course, he could not check her temperature without first removing his gloves, which he absolutely would not do. "Are you mad, woman?"

"Good God, no," Whitney said, finally meeting his gaze with displeasure written all over her face. She pulled away. "But *she* must be by now."

He backed away slightly. "Where did you say you saw her?"

She looked down her nose at him. "At Rose Cottage, of course!"

"Damn," he muttered. "What the hell where you doing on my land?"

"Oh, I don't know," she said as she smoothed her page. "Perhaps I wanted to know how far to trust you. I had to discover if my friends are safe or not. Shame on you!"

"They are safe," he promised. "Emily cannot leave the garden unless someone lets her out. And no one should have let you enter." He drew back a little more, worried that his instructions had been ignored. "Did she cough on you?"

"Of course not." Whitney scowled again. "Your servants followed your instructions to the point. A very sharp and pointy pitchfork, actually. I was warned away. Your sister favored me with conversation but we only spoke through the wall."

He slumped in relief. Whitney was safe, but that did not excuse her for trespassing. He jabbed his finger at her. "I apologize if you were frightened, but never visit her again."

"Concern, Acton? It's a little late to worry about me after the way you behaved the first time we met."

Her remark set him aback, and he stared at the woman he'd lost his head over one wild night. He'd often wondered what she thought of what had happened between them, but this was the first time she'd ever alluded to it. It might be unwise, but he wanted to get the topic out in the open at last. He was tired of waiting for her to reveal his indiscretion to his future bride. There was no one to hear them today. No one to know if they argued about it, should the conversation go that way.

"I recall the terms of our first meeting were quite openly discussed," he said quietly. "You wanted me that night, and I wanted you."

"True, and then I discovered your plans for matrimony. Now it is an encounter best forgotten," she promised. She began packing things away in her little painter's box, and then frowned at him again. "But do not change the subject. Surely you have a heart. How frightened will young Christopher be when he discovers your sister is living so close to his home? My cousin has let enough slip for me to know she tried to harm the boy."

Everett closed his eyes in a bid to be rid of his family shame. He'd hoped no one else would learn what his sister had tried to do to Christopher, but of course, Lord Louth must have told his cousin. He could barely believe Emily capable of such villainous acts himself, except he'd seen Christopher's terror with his own eyes. Emily's feeble attempts to explain had only convinced him it was entirely true. She'd tried to kill the boy. It was only because of Taverham's kind heart that she'd not been put on trial.

Lately, though, she'd given up any veneer of innocence on the matter.

"He will not find out, and it will only be for a while."

"A day or a year will make no difference to the boy. He is still afraid," she protested, and then narrowed her eyes. "Does Lord Taverham know she's there?"

"No," he admitted, hating that he was lying to his best friend. If Taverham and Miranda had stayed in London, as he'd expected them to, Everett wouldn't be in this situation. Emily was too weak to be moved now. It was safer all around if she came into contact with as few people as possible, which was why she was confined.

"His mother does."

"The dowager knows everything that goes on here," he told her. "I used to think she had the sight."

Whitney snorted, an inelegant sound that strangely set him at ease. "Then why is Lady Brighthurst still here? Miranda told me the night of my arrival that Lady Brighthurst had gone to Bath."

"Emily *was* in Bath, and then she returned to me."

"Do your promises mean nothing?"

"I am well aware of the promises I make." He slumped in defeat. "I do not wish to talk about the matter."

"Well, I gave you a chance to explain." Whitney began to get up. "I have no choice now but to warn my friends about your sister, and let them know they have been put in danger."

"Don't!" Everett unwisely caught her hand and prevented her flight. A shock of sensation shot up his arm at the contact. He pulled her back down to sit close to him. "Wait."

Whitney lifted her chin, and when their eyes met, he was filled with an unreasonable surge of yearning for this eccentric woman. She was so fierce in her loyalty to their friends. Passionate about everything that mattered to her. But it was the unexpected rush of desire for her that nearly took his breath away, reminding him of the way they'd been together at the Fairmont Ball. His attraction to her had been instant and overwhelming that night.

Whitney must have felt something too, because her expression softened. "Wait for what?" she whispered.

"I want you to understand." He forced away his desire ruthlessly. "Something has happened to my sister, and that is the only reason I keep her at Rose Cottage."

She blinked. "What reason could there possibly be to explain your lies?"

He released Whitney. "Emily is ill. I'd hoped she'd improve in the country air and familiar surroundings but...they say it is consumption."

Whitney stared at him in horror then scrambled away. She flipped open her box of paints one-handed and removed a black cloth. "You fiend! Are you trying to harm *me* now?"

She held the cloth across her nose and mouth.

"Of course not." He winced and put his hands back into his lap. "I am very careful. My London physician explained what steps I might take to protect myself and others. I bathe after each visit with Emily, scrub my hands with lavender and rosemary oil, and never wear the same clothes around other people. These gloves are entirely new, too."

"There are other ways it spreads," she warned. "A breath, touch, intimacy." Her eyes widened in horror.

Was she thinking they had been very close the night they first met?

He winced. "I believe you are safe. She was not ill when we first met, and it was your wish that we did not kiss."

Her eyes narrowed. "And what of Miss Quartermane, then? You would have certainly kissed her a dozen times by now. What have you told her about your family?"

"I've not kissed Miss Quartermane, so she is safe," he promised quietly. Given Whitney's reaction just now, he decided it might not be wise to risk trying to kiss his bride for a while, either. He had not considered that when he'd announced their wedding date. "How can I tell her about Emily's crimes when I barely understand how *I* could not have known what she was doing?"

Whitney slowly lowered the black cloth, sitting back on her heels as she faced him across a greater distance. "You must tell her. You must tell everyone to take precautions."

He nodded, knowing she was right but dreading the confession. Emily wasn't getting better. If Whitney had stumbled upon Emily, then it was possible Miranda and her son, or one of their gossip-loving guests, might too one day. Consumption was said to be easy to catch if one was young or unwell. He didn't want anyone to suffer a similar fate to Emily. "I will."

"Today," she insisted.

He scowled her. "You go too far, Miss Crewe."

She shrugged, shook out her black cloth and began rolling it up.

He stared at the material without realizing what he was seeing for a long moment. "What is that?"

Whitney shook out the material again and waved a pair of paint-smeared black silk breeches under his nose. "Have you missed these, my lord?"

His lost breeches. He reached for them, but Whitney was quicker. She packed them away in her little box. "You cannot have them back now. They've come in quite handy."

"You shrew," he whispered in horror.

"If I was a shrew, I'd have already told your intended what you were doing the night before you met her," she warned.

He looked away, feeling guilty and ashamed. The one night he'd been incautious of his honor in society was the one time he'd truly felt free. Having the woman turn out to be Whitney Crewe, cousin of an earl, an acquaintance of his intended bride, was a source of embarrassment to him. If he'd known her name, connections, he'd never have touched her. "Why haven't you?"

"I've never particularly enjoyed sharing my mistakes with the world," she admitted. "My cousin would have locked me up and thrown away the key if he'd learned of that night."

"I don't doubt it," he replied.

He stood quickly, glancing down the hill as he suddenly remembered why he'd rushed to Whitney's side.

The herd was meandering up the hillside now, cropping long grass as they went. He scanned the herd for the bull and saw him sniffing round one of the females. For now the beast was distracted, but soon…

"You have to leave."

He glanced down, just as the pages of Miss Crewe's sketchbook fluttered, revealing glimpses of her art. He focused on that. A hand, an eye, the line of muscle down a long leg. From this angle, she seemed quite accurate. He twisted to see more. A man's leg, perhaps, thigh bare and knee bent.

Whitney snapped up the book and tore out a different sheet. "Here. You might as well have this."

He stared at the sheet in shock. It was a portrait of a naked man without a face. "Are you mad? Who is this scoundrel?"

She laughed. "It is funny that you don't recognize yourself. I thought it a fair likeness."

He glanced at the sketch, noting certain private parts were drawn in great detail. It did look a bit like him, but she'd flattered his figure quite a bit, he felt. "Why would you draw me like that? When did you draw it?"

"I drew it today. I'm unfortunately cursed with an excellent memory, and sometimes I must draw what is in my head and not my heart, in order to move on to other things." She pulled a face. "Like all expectant brides, Alice seems nervous about the wedding night. Perhaps a sketch of what her future holds might calm her anxiety about the future."

He choked. "Any gently reared young woman would faint to be shown such an image of their intended before marriage. It couldn't possibly calm Alice."

"It should," Whitney murmured, and then straightened, holding her box to her chest. "The human body is a thing of beauty and grace, and you have nothing to be ashamed of, my lord. Anyway, give it to her whenever you like or do not. It makes no difference to me."

Everett tore the drawing into tiny pieces and threw them to blow away on the wind. "Do not draw me again."

"Believe me, I never want to."

He raked his hand through his hair, hoping she meant it. "How can you call yourself her friend and draw that sketch of me? We don't even like each other."

"True," she said with a soft laugh. Whitney stood, tucked her paint box under her arm and clutched her sketchbook. "Goodbye, Lord Acton. I expect to learn you've confessed your sins to Lord Taverham by the end of the day, or I will do it for you."

He heard the bellow, and shouts of alarm from his men, before Whitney had moved out of range. "Damn. Come here."

He caught her arm in a tight grip, urged her to his horse, and then tossed her up into the saddle before she had time to protest his rough handling.

"Is that sound what I think it is?" Whitney immediately swung her leg over the horse's neck so she could ride astride. She looked around as he set his foot to the stirrup. "Why didn't Taverham warn me his bull had been put out with the herd?" she complained, eyes wide on the approaching animal as it began to run up the hill toward them.

Everett mounted behind Whitney and settled her closer against his chest before urging his mount around. "Because that is my bull, my herd, and you've mistakenly wandered onto my land. I came to warn you."

"Took you long enough to tell me," she grumbled. Whitney leaned into him, holding her belongings tightly to her chest. "Can we please go now? He looks very cross."

"He always is," Everett murmured as he kicked his horse to a gallop, swept down the other side of the hill facing the Taverham's estate. The bull would tire long before half a mile had passed, but he headed for the nearest boundary, a high stone wall and ladder gate through which Whitney could use to return home safely.

When he finally saw the boundary, he risked a quick glance over his shoulder. The bull hadn't pursued them far, as his own men had managed to cut off the beast and were driving it in the other direction.

With the danger past, he slowed to a walk and loosened his hold on Whitney.

He grinned as she tugged her gown over her bare knees.

"There," he said. "Safe again."

Even as he said the words, he knew he was stretching the truth a bit. He hadn't noticed when it had happened but he now sported an erection. The movement of Whitney's shapely derrière against his crotch was the most maddening sensation. He tightened his grip around her waist to hopefully lessen the friction.

Whitney stiffened. "I must admit, I don't feel very safe in your arms right now. Is that…?"

"Yes. My apologies," he said, cursing his body under his breath. He stopped when they reached the ladder gate, swung off the horse, and lifted his hands up to Whitney. "I promise to behave."

His wayward organ twitched again at the very sight of Whitney riding astride his horse. It made him imagine other things, pleasures and positions he'd never share with her.

He bit his lip, determined to hide what he was thinking.

A ghost of a smile twitched over Whitney's full lips, then she fell into his arms. Everett lowered her gently to the ground and stepped back. Whitney immediately started smoothing her skirts.

"Are you all right?" he asked.

"I'm fine," she said, then wrinkled her nose. "I always seem to look a little rumpled no matter what I do."

He considered suggesting she shouldn't drive a carriage and four in the dark as she had the night of her arrival, if that was so, but he suddenly didn't want to ruin the peaceful moment between them.

"You always look lovely," he promised.

Whitney punched her hands to her hips. "That sounds suspiciously like a compliment, Acton."

"It was sincere." He blinked in surprise that he was not helping himself by revealing he might find her attractive. What was he doing, saying nice things to her anyway? He shouldn't be complimenting Whitney Crewe. He should save that sort of business, flirting and such, for his future bride.

He felt his cheeks heating and fiddled with the reins as guilt filled him. Whitney may occasionally look a little windblown, especially when compared to Alice's pristine perfection, but such untidiness suited her, particularly in the countryside. "Walk up that rise and you will see the main house not far away. I'm sure you can find your own way home now."

He mounted his horse.

"Acton," Whitney called. "Thank you for your aid today."

"A pleasure," he promised. He tipped his hat. "Until we meet again, Miss Crewe."

Reluctantly, he glanced her way and saw her smiling up at him, a pair of distracting dimples on full display. "Until our next misadventure, my lord," she promised.

Chapter Eleven

------- ◆ -------

Whitney trudged up the hill alone, her step light and a feeling of peace filling her soul. She didn't look back to see if Lord Acton watched her go because she suspected he was still there, making sure she stayed out of harm's way.

She smiled and pulled a stem of wild grass to twist between her fingers as she walked along. She was terrible, wasn't she? Flirting, just a little, with an engaged man. She should be ashamed, but all she felt was intense relief to have been mistaken about his reasons for keeping Emily's location quiet.

He was conflicted, and that was not an easy feeling to reconcile.

He wasn't a monster. Yes, his sister had been scheming to make trouble for her friends. And yes, he had dallied with Whitney when he ought not to have given her a second glance. He was marrying an exquisite woman, the perfect bride. Alice was everything a proper gentleman could want in a wife.

Acton was charmingly protective, and it surprised her that she did not mind it in the least. He had spirited her away from what would have been certain injury, perhaps even death, from a misadventure of her own making.

And he was clearly upset that his evil sister was dying of consumption.

He suffered no weakness of character for showing compassion for the woman. He should have told his friends about Emily, but she could understand he was hesitant to upset them or make them live in fear again.

He might be a good man after all, though still far too handsome to completely ignore. She liked to look at him a little too much and too often. But she would draw one last sketch of him tonight and then tuck it away in her private collection. She would draw him on his knees, holding her hand as he asked after her health with such fear in his eyes it had made her heart skip a beat.

She had been happy today with him, if only briefly.

Lord Acton wasn't the heartless scoundrel she'd made him out to be in her own mind, but she could not allow any further lapses of propriety to happen between them. He was marrying Alice Quartermane and that was the end of it.

The hub of activity in the Taverhams' country home revolved around the kitchen garden, and Whitney made her way there. There were a few servants out and about in the garden, and she greeted each one as she made her way to an open doorway. Upon arriving at the estate, Miranda had taken over a chamber closest to the garden—for the view of the activity, she said—and Whitney could see her poring over her ledgers in the sunlight.

Whitney picked a sprig of rosemary and bruised it with her hands, making the scent wrap around her in soothing waves.

"We need rain," Miranda complained as Whitney joined her inside.

"It will come," Whitney promised, seating herself near Miranda and opening her sketchbook to a new page. Miranda looked lovely with the sun behind her like that. She began to sketch the marchioness' face as she worked. "It always does."

Miranda frowned at her ledger, tapping her pencil against the pages briskly. "Forgive me for worrying out loud. I'm not used to these matters, or living here yet. Managing an estate of this size is quite a lot of work."

Whitney sat in a nearby chair and smiled at her friend. "What does the dowager have to say?"

"Nothing."

"Have you asked her for advice?"

"I've thought about it, but she is as warm to me today as the day I returned."

Whitney looked up. "Is that a surprise, given the marquess is avoiding her?"

"Not really." Miranda rubbed her brow. "Damn it all. I cannot concentrate today."

"Is there something on your mind?"

"Oh, everything. The weather, the harvest, the state of the wine cellar..." She laughed as she left the desk and sank into a spot beside Whitney. "Tell me you are enjoying your visit."

"I am enjoying my visit very much," she promised, twisting to rest her arm across the back of the chaise so she could still sketch the marchioness. She leaned upon her free hand, and talked as she moved her pencil with the other. "I've never been to this part of the country, and it's lovely. Green and lush. Just the way I always imagined. My uncle Yardley would have said even a dead seed would grow here in a drought."

"I've been meaning to ask, just how many homes have you lived in? You mention so many uncles and aunts I can barely keep track."

"Seven homes in sixteen years. Four uncles, two aunts, and then I lived with my cousin, Martin."

"I wonder that you were never eager for a home of your own? My years of wandering about have made me appreciate what I have now more than I might have done as a younger wife."

"I managed some of them, especially for my unmarried uncles. They always employed terrible housekeepers," she said with a fond laugh. "But now, how could I commit to managing a home, my husband's estate, and still hope to see something of the world? If I married, my husband would control my fortune. He would control my future, too. I don't imagine many would allow their wives to paint scandalously unclad gentlemen for the sake of her art."

"Oh, I am sure you are correct on that score. Many men would find that sort of thing an embarrassment and an attack on their masculinity." Whitney giggled but Miranda continued. "Responsibilities can put a damper on travel, but I would hope for your sake that there might be one man with an open mind who could fall in love with you and let you see the world, too. For me, it is such an effort just thinking about returning to Town next year for the season, with all this yet to understand." Miranda sank back with a weary sigh, took up Whitney's free hand and squeezed. "You know, Martin once claimed you'd never married because you were disappointed in love in your first season."

She burst out laughing. "Does he still believe that? I never said anything of the sort to him, but it is not my fault if my cousin chose to latch on to the only thing my aunt Thomasina said that made sense."

"Have you ever been in love?" Miranda's eyes lit up with curiosity. "Been swept away by a gentleman and thought maybe, maybe he's the one for me."

Whitney winced. "Well, if I had, you can tell that I've never received a proposal of marriage from him. Love and marriage have never been issues I had to decide upon one way or the other."

Miranda studied her closely. "Whoever he was has no sense, and therefore could never deserve such a woman in their life."

For a response, Whitney laughed rather than agreed.

"So, tell me more about this trip you wish to take," Miranda asked. "When exactly does your adventure begin?"

Whitney told the marchioness her itinerary for the journey, her hopes for the adventure on foreign soil, and dreams of mingling with like-minded individuals. "What I've learned from my time in London society is that I'm not suited to doing the usual thing expected of proper young ladies."

"I think you fit in with some people we know well," Miranda suggested.

"But not with the majority, and that is a mark against me. Even Alice thinks I'm strange. She is so fixed upon making a good match, but doesn't understand that having a husband could mean putting her dreams on hold forever if she had any others. I haven't the selflessness to give up everything I've longed for the way she has."

Miranda nodded, as if she understood. "Does it frighten you to think that you will be so far from everything you've known? And everybody you love?"

"A little, but I intend to write often."

"I'm glad, because you know I won't sleep well—"

"They're here. They're here!" Christopher bellowed as he burst through the door from the garden and then rushed away toward the entrance hall of the house, screaming about it at the top of his lungs.

Whitney grinned at the marchioness. "I think you have more guests."

"Shall we go and greet them too?" Miranda asked with a laugh.

Whitney nodded and followed after Miranda, listening to the rush of feet in all parts of the house. New arrivals meant more work for everyone. A trio of carriages were coming along the drive at a sprightly pace and by the time Whitney gained the front steps, the carriages were drawing to a halt before them.

Whitney curled her hands over Christopher's shoulders to hold him still as he bounced on the balls of his feet. "Wait. It may not be them."

Just then, small heads popped out of all the carriage windows, and then more hands than the heads should owned began to wave frantically.

"It is them!" Christopher promised.

"I think you must be correct," Whitney agreed, happy for the boy that he would have playmates his own age at last.

The family disembarked, a melee of children and servants and luggage around a pair of very rumpled parents.

Having met the couple before in London, Whitney held her arms out for baby Elliot even while pressing a kiss to the sagging mother's cheek. "How lovely to see you again, Lady Carrington," she murmured. "Let me give your arms a rest."

"Oh, thank you." Lady Carrington immediately turned to her cousin and hugged the marchioness tightly.

After a moment, Miranda began to squirm. "Agatha, my dear, a little air?"

"Sorry," the woman said with a laugh as she drew back, her eyes shining with tears of happiness. "I'm still astonished every time I see you."

Miranda cupped Agatha's cheek, and then looked about them at the gathering children. "My word, you've all grown so much I barely recognize you all."

Lord Carrington backed away and shook hands with the marquess, who was late arriving to greet the newcomers.

Whitney looked about for Christopher, and saw him standing

with his arm draped over one of the children's shoulders. The pretty little girl was nattering to him nonstop about their trip, from what she could tell.

Lady Carrington eased closer. "Mabel was so excited to be coming to see him that we had to sing songs for the last half hour."

"Was that painful?" Whitney asked out the side of her mouth.

"You have no idea. My head is still ringing from the sound," she confessed. "The joy of travel with children."

"We should get you all inside for tea, and a little respite, too, wouldn't hurt anyone, I think," Miranda said, looking toward Whitney with a hopeful expression she interpreted quite easily.

"I'll see to the children, shall I?" she offered.

Lady Carrington clutched at her arm. "If you could help them get settled, I would be forever in your debt."

"I might just collect on that one day," she said with a sly wink. "I'll return when they are settled upstairs."

"We'll be in my parlor overlooking the kitchen garden for the afternoon," Miranda called as the cousins made a fast retreat.

Whitney gathered the noisy children and servants with Christopher's help and urged them all upstairs to unpack and claim their beds. There were many small side excursions, led by Christopher himself unfortunately, so the trip took some time. The Twilit Hill servants stepped in, redirecting the enthusiastic children, who wanted to see everything at once. They eased the way, and soon the children and nursemaids were taking tea in the nursery very happily.

Whitney returned to the marchioness' office and discovered Miss Quartermane and her mother had arrived in her absence, taken over her favorite chair, and were idly flipping through her sketchbook.

She felt a twinge of annoyance as they shook hands. "How lovely to see you again," she murmured as she retrieved her possessions. Alice and her mother had no right to touch her things, even if she had left them behind.

"We saw the carriages from the village and rushed to greet the newcomers," Alice exclaimed.

She glanced around. "Is Lord Acton with you?"

"Oh, unfortunately not. You know how men are. He's gone

off to do something with Mr. Thompson. I think he said it had something to do with cattle."

"Yes, of course." She smiled quickly. "By all accounts, the earl must be very involved with his estate. It is a busy time of year for farming."

Alice winced, and then glanced at the marchioness. She received a subtle nod and then drew Whitney to the far side of the room. "Actually, it is you I've come to see today. Since our time together is painfully short I was hoping you'd agree to my proposal."

"What proposal?"

"You are my dearest friend, and you must know that I value your presence here at such a critical time in my life."

Drat it. More talk of the wedding was in the wind.

"Alice, my plans cannot be changed," Whitney said gently. "I have already booked my passage, and my travelling companions will be waiting to meet me at the docks. I won't delay to attend your wedding."

Especially when it was a marriage she didn't support.

Alice rolled her eyes. "I wish you did not have to go. Out of all my new friends, I so wanted you to witness my triumph so you could tell everyone about it."

"I am sure the day will be perfect." Whitney stifled a groan. Friendships within the *ton* were so complicated. Being talked about were necessary and frequent activities if one wanted to be known and admired. Alice cared a lot about her reputation.

"I hope so. Given it will be here, beyond the reach of so many of my acquaintances, I was hoping you might be persuaded to stay for my sake."

Whitney shook her head.

Alice pouted. "You don't understand. It is the most important day in my life. We may not feel the same about marriage, but I want you there."

"For what purpose?"

"We both know that a ladies standing in society is important and depends so much on the worth of her connections."

"True."

"Imagine what a coup it will be having you there, beside the Duke of Exeter and Lord Taverham's guests for the ceremony when I speak my vows."

Whitney considered Alice's fevered expression. "I would think having Lord Acton beside you speaking his vows was more important."

"Well yes, of course." Alice's smile dimmed. "He'll be there too. I know you constantly deny that you don't wish for a husband, but surely you see my dilemma."

"I'm not sure I do."

"You are much older than I, wise in ways I cannot imagine being. You could have already been married by now, a leader in society, given the size of your fortune and connections. They are far better than mine, and we both know it. You could have married anyone, duke or commoner. You always know who is worth encouraging."

"Marriage should have nothing to do with fortune or connections," Whitney protested.

"Of course marriage has everything to do with those things. They are what matter most in society," Alice claimed with a shake of her head, making the ringlets bob and sway. "Why is it so wrong to marry and gain the respect of your peers? Carving out a place in society is important for women."

"Such superficial desires are *never* more important than love." Whitney clenched her jaw, noting Alice's astonishment at her claim. She softened her voice. "Look, it is none of my business how you live your life, so long as you are happy."

"That brings me to my reason for speaking to you today." Alice grasped Whitney's hands suddenly. "Do you think he really loves me?"

"I cannot answer that," she told the woman, astonished at the question. "Men are very good at hiding their emotions from strangers, but if he tells you he does I would believe him."

Alice worried at her lip. "He hasn't said he does, but I think you can help me decide if it's possible."

"What?"

"I want to know if he loves me and if he's worthy of *my* love." Alice sighed deeply. "I mean, you can help me decide if he is capable of loving me before we marry."

Whitney gasped. "How do you expect me to do that?"

"By flirting with him to see if he can resist you. You are very pretty for your age, you know, and men always clamor for the attention of popular women. No one will notice if you pay Acton a little more attention here in the countryside."

Whitney could only stare at Alice, because she suspected throwing herself at Lord Acton wouldn't bring about the confirmation of fidelity Alice hoped for. There was something between herself and Lord Acton still, desire and curiosity, and try as she might, she had been fighting those feelings for the sake of this friendship. "No!" Whitney protested. "What sort of friend would I be if I even considered it?"

"The very best friend I have. I trust you completely," Alice promised, her eyes wide. "I know you wouldn't ever try to steal him for yourself."

"Of course I would not." The idea was absurd. Acton was a man of his word. He was marrying Alice. She took a deep steadying breath. "You're just feeling nervous about him. I'm told every bride feels this way at some point before they wed. It was *you* Acton asked to marry. You will be Lord Acton's wife."

"Lady Acton," Alice said in a dreamy tone.

Listening to Alice whisper the name with such reverence filled Whitney with annoyance. Alice was marrying the title, not the handsome devil who owned it. Alice didn't even seem aware of Lord Acton's physical appeal. Whitney couldn't do as Alice wished, but she could still guide her friend to discover the love she should want more than the title of countess. "Alice, if you want to know the state of Lord Acton's heart, you're going to have to find out on your own."

Alice's eyes lit up. "How do I do that?"

Whitney's mouth grew dry, and she had to swallow a few times before she could get the words past her lips. "I recommend you seek out Lord Acton privately, alone, and see what happens next."

Alice looked at her with a worried expression. "Are you suggesting I allow him to kiss me before the wedding takes place?"

Whitney had actually meant a little more than stealing a single kiss, but a kiss was a good place to begin. It was *romantic*. Acton would like that.

She glanced toward Alice's mother, who was rising from her

chair to join them. Alice's mother would never approve of Whitney's suggestion, and would probably lock Alice in her room if she suspected anything untoward was going on before the wedding.

She grasped Alice's arm and forced her to walk about the room to delay Mrs. Quartermane from joining them. "If you want to know what he feels for you, seducing him is certainly a way to determine it," she advised.

For a moment, Whitney feared Alice would faint—but then she nodded quickly. "I'll do it. Tonight."

Chapter Twelve

Everett drew to a halt and dismounted before the Twilit Hill stables as the sun was setting on a frustrating day. Chasing after his betrothed across the two estates seemed to be his lot in life. He'd returned from his visit to Emily, only to discover Alice had suddenly taken herself off to pay a call upon his nearest neighbors again. It seemed her plan to become acquainted with the residents of the district was bearing fruit, given the number of invitations delivered that morning. Her popularity had left him at something of a loose end, so he'd finally come to Twilit Hill to call upon Taverham, and keep his promise to Whitney.

He handed the gelding off to a groom with a fond pat and headed for the main house. He wasn't accustomed to using the front door any more than Taverham used his, so he cut through the formal gardens, heading for the nearest set of open doors.

"No, no, no. Stop!"

Everett recognized Simon's anguished voice instantly, and he took flight for the boy, running as fast as he could toward the walled kitchen garden ahead.

If Emily had slipped her guards, he always feared she'd come straight for the boy first.

He barely registered two servants lingering by the garden gate as he rushed inside to save Christopher.

But the boy was fighting off Whitney Crewe, not Emily.

He stopped in shock but still pulled the boy toward him, out of harm's way. "What the hell are you doing to him?" he roared at Whitney.

She gaped at him, and then glanced down at Christopher.

The pair then looked up at him at the same time, and only then did he notice they were drenched from head to toe and happy. Christopher's hair was plastered to his skull and the boy wiped away the drips as he started to laugh.

Whitney's gown was soaked completely in the front, and she too was laughing at him.

"Did you think I was in real danger, my lord?" the boy asked. "From Whitney?"

Both held teacups full of water rather than tea.

"I'm not sure. I'm still not quite certain what is going on," he admitted.

He released Christopher quickly, confused as hell as the boy's laughter grew louder.

He felt a tug on his coat and he looked down.

A little girl stared up at him. "We're making it rain for the rhubarb," she said with an adorable lisp.

She smiled widely despite her hair hanging in sodden ringlets around her face, or the fact that her little white smock hung limp from her shoulders to her knees, like that of all the others.

As he took the time to notice more of his surroundings, including seven children of varying ages, he noted that they were similarly disheveled. There was a horde of children standing about laughing, along with Christopher.

Taverham had said the Carrington children were to come and visit for a month soon. Apparently, they had arrived since his last visit.

He looked about again and belatedly realized that they were in fact making some attempt to water the kitchen garden, but getting most of the water on themselves.

They were *playing*, and Whitney was at the heart of it.

Embarrassed by his overreaction and their laughter, he took another step back. "My apologies for the interruption to your game. I have only just arrived and didn't understand what was going on. Please continue."

Whitney peeled her sodden gown from her sides to curtsy deeply, her smile widening. "Thank you, my lord. We were going to anyway."

She took a step toward Christopher and quickly dumped the contents of her teacup directly over the boy's hair. Christopher yelled and flung the water from his cup straight into Whitney's face. The splash made no difference to the woman's countenance. She laughed and ran away.

So did all the children, and once they had rearmed themselves, the fight resumed in earnest around him.

Mabel ran to the gate, took water from a new pail set upon the ground by a pair of timid servants hiding just out of sight, and flung it haphazardly about her. More than half hit his legs but he couldn't move. He'd never seen such madness as Whitney Crewe had provoked.

She dashed about the walled garden—being chased or chasing the children. She gave no thought to decorum, no credence to restraint. She did whatever the hell appealed to her at any time of the day or night, apparently.

And Everett couldn't look away from her face.

She *enjoyed* battling with each child until it was clear that they were running out of ammunition. Water was growing scarce and the tubs were almost drained.

He glanced back and noticed the pail of water little Mabel was using. He hefted it, and cautiously approached an emptied tub.

Christopher grinned. "Thank you, my lord."

Everett nodded as he poured it out. "I'll fetch more."

He turned—and water slapped into the back of his head. The droplets slithered over his neck and a few even reached his face.

He brushed them aside, fetched another bucket and returned.

Whitney watched him closely as he poured out the water slowly, an impish smile playing across her lips. He would bet his favorite horse that she'd been the one to throw water at him.

Impudent wench.

He'd get her back for that.

Before the pail was drained completely, he flung out the remainder at her.

Most hit Whitney squarely in the chest, but she only laughed and scooped out more water to throw back at him.

A new battle began.

One between himself and Whitney Crewe.

The woman shrieked as he chased her with the remaining pail of water. She fled to the far gateway and bent to collect a new pail.

Everett stopped immediately as she turned, eyes flashing.

"My turn," she threatened, brushing back fallen strands of her flaming-red hair.

He eyed the pail. "There is a lot more water in your pail than I've thrown at you."

He took a pace back but was captured from behind by Christopher.

"I've got him, Whitney!"

She sauntered forward with a saucy sway of her hips. "Well done, lad."

She flung her water but it mostly missed him, flying over his shoulder to hit the ground beyond. Still, enough water slid down his legs and into his riding boots to make him shiver.

"You'll pay for that," he promised with a sincere smile, and once Christopher let him go, he rushed back to the gate. "We need more water," he told the laughing gardeners. "A lot more."

They rushed away to do his bidding, he hoped, and Everett returned to the battle.

He probably looked foolish chasing the children about, but he couldn't remember the last time he'd had so much fun. The play might have been meant for the children but he was enjoying himself as he hadn't for a long time, or at least not since he'd been their age.

He put a wall at his back as the youngest children rushed past, chasing one another during a brief respite. They were happy children, for all that they were orphans. He could see why Christopher spoke of them so often. He was their leader. They did everything he suggested without question and without complaint.

Everett folded his arms and smiled as the screaming grew louder. No wonder the boy's spirits had been so low until now. He'd been lonely, and clearly used to a different life before returning to his father.

Everett knew what that was like. Just lately his home had felt so empty and cold. Unlived in, even with guests underfoot. He was still not used to Emily's absence, not that he wished to bring her back into society with him after what she'd done.

Water suddenly cascaded over his head, and he cried out in shock, spluttering to catch his breath.

He turned to look behind him and noticed the tips of a ladder disappearing behind the wall he'd been leaning against. Infuriated, he jumped to catch the edge of the wall to see who had snuck up on him.

His assailant, of course, was the only person who'd ever be impertinent enough to attack him.

He hauled himself over, as he'd done many times as a boy, and dropped to his feet on the other side. He shook the water out of his hair. "That was terribly underhanded, Miss Crewe."

Whitney backed up a few steps, her hand extended, an empty pail lying between them. "Now, my lord. Don't do anything you'll regret later."

He advanced. "I rarely regret anything when it comes to you."

"Then do your worst, my lord. I'm ready," she said as she beckoned him to follow with her fingers. "Catch me if you can," she dared him.

He pursued her, pail at the ready, but as she backed up another step, her heel caught on a tree root and she started to fall. Everett dropped the pail and darted forward to catch her before she hurt herself.

He jerked her into his arms, staring down at her merry face and flashing eyes. His breath caught at her triumphant expression. She was so open. She was happiness through and through.

He suddenly wished he had kissed this woman. "I have you."

"Do you?" she challenged. Whitney grasped him by the shoulders, eyelashes fluttering. "Or do I have you?"

Her grip firmed, and Everett, eager to win, pulled her tighter into his arms.

Her fingers drifted up into his hair and he shivered. Whitney felt so good against him. He lowered his lips toward hers, but turned away at the last minute. He held his cheek against her bright hair and breathed in her scent again. He remembered too well the night he'd lost himself in wickedness with her. Despite the lack of kisses that night, Whitney claiming to be unromantic, he'd never been more aroused. And he was excited now with her pressed against his body.

Whitney made a little sound, half gasp, half moan, as he held her close.

He backed her up against the nearest tree, eagerly exploring her curves once more.

She pushed against him weakly. "Acton, do you make a habit of seducing women?"

Her question startled him more than words could say. He *was* seducing her, and he'd never meant to. He drew back to stare at her, cheeks warming under her scrutiny. "No."

She stared at him too, her breasts rising and falling fast beneath her damp gown. "Probably a good idea, since you are to marry," she warned, but then a smile teased the corners of her mouth upward. "But I do feel special."

He didn't know how to respond to that but he fought his own smile. At least she was not offended by his manhandling. "What the devil am I doing following you again?"

"I am asking myself the same question. You don't want me."

"And you've made it clear you don't want *me*." He was engaged to marry, and yet he was filled with doubts about himself and pretty much everything in his life. The only certain thing was his attraction to Whitney. He cleared his throat. "I do not regret what just happened."

"I'd be offended if you did," Whitney promised, eyes flashing. She gestured toward the gateway. "I have to go back to the children. I promised their mothers I would watch over them."

Confused by the abrupt change in her manner, he fell into step and stopped at the archway when she did. In their absence, the children had settled down to watering the plants at last. They crisscrossed the walled enclosure, working together to get the job done. Each one appeared half drowned and vastly untidy, but all seemed very happy.

He leaned against the wall, away from the temptation of Whitney Crewe. "What brought this on?"

Whitney leaned against the opposite arch, her eyes fixed on him. "The long journey had made them quarrelsome, so…a little chore disguised as a game…and Lady Carrington has an hour or so of peace now, and will have seven very sleepy children by bedtime."

"You're very good with children."

Whitney laughed. "My cousin would claim that is because I still am one."

"I am not surprised by that," he said. But when she frowned, he quickly clarified why. "Louth seems a very serious fellow. I don't think he'd have joined in."

"He's a good man but not much like me, I am sorry to say."

That he easily believed. "What is the rest of your family like?"

Whitney glanced down at her bejeweled fingers, and then clasped her hands together. "Louth is my only living relative. My mother and his were cousins."

"I'm sorry. I didn't know."

"I am, was, an orphan. Just like these children." She shrugged. "My parents died when I was quite young, I barely remember them now. I went to live with my aunts and uncles. None of them had children, so it was a lonely life, even if they doted on me."

"I'm sorry."

"Don't be. I was well loved, but they're all gone now." She held out her hands, displaying the odd collection of rings on her fingers. "This is all I have of them."

He counted the array of mismatched rings she wore, and his heart squeezed painfully, especially with the way she played with an incomplete one. "You have lost a stone," he noted.

"A casualty of my carelessness." She winced and turned the empty setting into her palm. "I keep hoping to discover it somewhere."

He frowned. "What was it? The stone?"

"It was an emerald," she told him. "My uncle Willard traded gems sometimes and he told me it was the best he'd ever come across."

Everett had found an emerald among his clothing the night he'd met Whitney. Without knowing her identity, he'd tucked it away, hoping to meet the owner again and return it. But later, because Whitney would never agree to see him alone, he'd not been able to confirm if it had been hers. "I have it, Whitney. I have your emerald."

Whitney blinked. "You do?"

"When I called to see you in London, it was in my pocket to be returned to you."

"Oh." Whitney surprised him by not asking for it immediately. Instead, she smiled and said, "I'm glad to know it was not lost after all."

He'd almost lost it to a thief the night his engagement had been announced, though. Probably wise not to mention that and worry her unnecessarily. He searched his pockets, finding it tied into his handkerchief. "There."

"Thank you," she whispered. "It means the world to me."

"It's very valuable," he agreed.

"I always assumed it was, but that is not why I wanted it back." She clenched it tightly in her hand. "I could easily buy a new stone."

Curious, he dared ask about her situation. "Your parents provided well for you?"

"Yes, and my aunts and uncles made me their beneficiaries, but I'd rather have my family back than have their money," Whitney confessed.

He caught her hand and squeezed. His glove squelched and dripped water onto the ground between them.

She shook off his grip with a soft laugh. "Are you here to see Taverham or your bride?"

He flinched. "Are Alice and her parents here?"

Guilt filled him because, once he'd seen Whitney, all thoughts of his bride had vanished from his mind. He hadn't given one thought to what he was doing, and to whom he was doing it with.

"Not now. They must have left, oh, a mere half hour before you arrived." Whitney bit her lip, her smile growing pained. "The children were too noisy for the Quartermanes to tolerate, I suspect."

He glanced toward the children again. They were loud, but it wasn't intolerable. "So you brought them outside to play."

She nodded, but given the way her smile fell, he sensed there was something more on her mind. He was slowly beginning to understand this woman. Too late perhaps, but he felt better for it. Right now, given the silence and her tense posture, she was holding back her thoughts from him, and he suddenly wanted to know them. "What is it?"

For a moment, he didn't think she would answer him, he was

being terribly nosy today, but then she tipped her head from side to side and sighed deeply. "When you leave today, be sure to return home straight away. Alice is very keen to see you."

"For what purpose?"

Whitney straightened her shoulders. "The usual conversation between betrothed couples, I imagine."

Wedding talk again? Gods, he'd rather not have to endure that conversation. Mrs. Quartermane was still hinting it was not too late to return to London for a marriage at St. George's by special license. "I am on my way to speak with Taverham."

"He was in the rose garden with Carrington last time I saw him. Smoking cigars." Her nose wrinkled with distaste. "You should hurry and join them, and then leave to go straight home."

"If you think I should," he said slowly as he held Whitney's gaze a long moment. "But I had intended to visit my sister after I speak with Taverham. Emily is lately complaining about my nighttime visits."

"How often do you go to her?"

"Most days, unless there is work to be done. She's become despondent in her solitude." He winced, knowing Whitney had no reason to care about Emily's state of mind. "I intend to take her out into the garden and enjoy the sunshine with her for a little while today, to see if that lifts her spirits."

"It is a good idea. It is also good of you to care so much, after the embarrassment she must have put you through," she murmured.

"She is my sister. I cannot turn my back on her now when she needs me," he said, throat growing tight.

Whitney's expression softened a little more. "It's a nice day for a stroll."

"Within the garden walls, not without," he promised her quickly. "She's not strong enough to go far without my support."

She nodded slowly. "I am very sorry to hear it. But don't forget to seek out Alice after that," she reminded him.

When she smiled again, he felt uneasy because it was very obviously forced. "I won't forget Alice," he murmured, wondering if that would always be true.

Chapter Thirteen

---◆---

With one last glance at Whitney, Everett took his leave of her. The business with Taverham couldn't wait. He passed through the kitchen garden, dodging the occasional flick of water aimed at him with a laugh, and looked ahead to the formal gardens. The rose garden stood more or less directly between Twilight Hill and Warstone Manor. If Taverham had been there at the time he'd passed this way, Everett would never have spoken to Whitney today.

He was glad he had.

His heart felt lighter, and it was nice that she accepted his determination to be a good brother. She was a good listener.

He tugged down his damp waistcoat, beginning to feel chilled in the breeze that curled around the ornamental trees on the manor's southern side. At his home, where no tree stood less than twenty feet tall, it took a gale blowing for him to notice a change in the weather.

Twilit Hill had been designed, cultivated, with no allowance made for natural growth. A series of garden rooms, full of clipped hedges, garden beds and checkered paths, led visitors away from the manor and eventually to wide-open fields.

He was halfway through the rose garden when he spotted the marquess and viscount sitting in the shade together in a cloud of cigar smoke.

"Your mother will throw a fit," Everett warned as he joined them.

Taverham blew a perfect ring of smoke and watched it float away. "I'm a grown man. I can do whatever I want."

Viscount Carrington agreed, drawing on his cigar without a word.

Everett hadn't had much to do with Viscount Carrington. He was related to Taverham through his marriage, but with Miranda gone for so long, encounters with him had been few and far between.

And this year, there'd been a scandal around the time Carrington had married, a broken engagement and breach-of-promise suit, that had become quite a messy and expensive affair. Since his marriage, viewed as unpopular by many, Carrington had rarely been seen, eschewing society for the company of friends and family and the children he'd taken in.

Hostesses had dropped him from their guest lists immediately and the loss of popularity had to hurt. But for all of that weighing on him, he seemed in good spirits now.

"You must do as you like, but within reason, surely. I'm positive your wife has opinions on many things," Everett suggested, hopeful that his remark would not sound the least bit disparaging of the marchioness. It was a delicate line he walked, always taking pains to never unwittingly give offense. Not that Everett had found fault with the marchioness since her return to her marriage. He could not say he and the lady were friends yet, but she had chosen not to make him an enemy. He appreciated that she'd not believed he should be punished for Emily's behavior. "I take it Miranda has no objections to cigars?"

"None as long as I air my clothes well and don't kiss her straight after I return to the house," Taverham confessed with an easy smile. He dug in his coat pocket.

"Agatha is much the same about cigars. I keep my smoking to the out of doors, too." Carrington squinted at him. "I say, did you run afoul of my children on the way here?"

"How can you tell?" He was still uncomfortably damp. "But in their defense, it was my own fault I am in this state. I misunderstood the reason they were screaming and ran right into the fray."

"And suffered for it." Taverham came close, staring at his coat. "You could be wet enough to the skin to create your own puddle, I think."

"Very likely." Everett relaxed and declined the offer of a cigar from Taverham. He glanced around with a fond smile. "Emily always loved this garden."

Taverham inhaled sharply. "I'd prefer you not mention that name to me again."

"I must." He glanced at Viscount Carrington. "Would you mind leaving us? I need to speak privately with the marquess."

Carrington glanced between them and then nodded. "I'll take a walk about the grounds while I finish this, and then head inside to help settle the children down for their dinner."

The lanky viscount wandered off with an easy smile and jaunty wave.

"That was unnecessary," Taverham warned when he was gone. "He's family."

"I know he is part of your family, but I'd rather what we talk about remain between us. It is about Emily that I wish to speak, and the garden she loved so much seems an appropriate place."

"I cannot forgive her," Taverham warned sternly. "She kept Christopher's existence from me."

"Yet, you still acknowledge your mother, and she knew about the boy, too, didn't she?"

"That is entirely different," the marquess claimed as he jumped to his feet. "Why do you think my mother moved to the dower house?"

But Taverham still spoke of the dowager marchioness, whereas Emily had been erased from any and every discussion. Everett understood why, but still, she was his sister. He was as appalled as anyone at her behavior, but that was the past. He only had the energy for the present. "Emily is here."

"What?" Taverham roared.

Everett cringed at the fury in Taverham's eyes. "Not here on your estate," he hastened to add. "But she is at mine."

"Since when? The ladies haven't spoken of her."

"They haven't seen her," Everett promised. "I moved Emily into Rose Cottage."

Taverham advanced angrily, and Everett took a pace back,

maintaining a distance between them for Taverham's sake. They had never fought, not physically, and now was not the time to start over a situation he couldn't change, even if he desperately wished to.

Taverham followed him. "How dare you put my son in danger?"

"Just listen to me," Everett warned, his face heating. Bringing Emily home put everyone in danger, but not for the reasons Taverham assumed. Consumption was contagious, especially so for the young, old or infirm. Taverham had a son, an aging mother and a wife with a weak heart. "The boy is in no danger if he keeps to your lands, I promise you."

Taverham turned away, ripped a rose bud from a vine and crushed it in his fist. "If she even looks twice at my boy, I will turn her over to the magistrate immediately and offer up all the sordid details of her behavior. I trusted you!"

Everett gritted his teeth. "I said he was safe, and I mean it. There is no excuse for her behavior. None," he agreed.

"And yet you brought her within three miles of where we live?"

Taverham dug his fingertip into Everett's breastbone so hard he winced.

"For God's sake, listen," he protested, and Taverham drew back, frowning. Everett turned away to gather his excuses into a coherent explanation. There were a group of gardeners gathering not too far away, so he lowered his voice to a conversational pitch. "I thought you said you would remain in London longer than you did. She was here when you first arrived, and I cannot move her now. She does not even know you have returned to the estate, and I don't intend to tell her."

"Someone is bound to tell her. Your fiancée will certainly mention us being here when they speak." Taverham's eyes widened. "I promised Miranda she could trust you. You promised to keep that bitch away from my family, and I thought she would travel as she always wished to."

"She will remain at Rose Cottage for the foreseeable future."

Taverham stared. "Have you lost your mind?"

"The garden gate is always locked."

Taverham rocked back on his heels and raked a hand through

his hair until it stood on end. He knew Rose Cottage well, having consulted on improvements in past years. The fact he'd locked the garden gate was an important point in his favor, as it ensured the boy's continued safety. "You really confined her?"

"It is as much for her own safety as anyone else's," Everett confessed, his voice thickened. "She is dying."

Taverham shook his head swiftly. "Nonsense. A ruse. She's after sympathy, as she always did as a girl. You could never see it. I will not fall prey to her pretty little lies again."

Everett lifted his chin. He'd been fooled without a shadow of a doubt in the past, but Emily's days of twisting him around her finger were well and truly done. "She has consumption. The doctors in London, and here, confirmed it. She is in a very bad way."

Taverham took several paces back, his skin leeching of color. "Consumption?"

Everett took a steadying breath before he bared his soul further, hoping some good could come from total honesty about Emily. "She came to my house in London, sick with it, and, after speaking to the doctors I consulted, I drove her directly to Rose Cottage in my own carriage myself."

"Is that why you left London without warning me?" Taverham appeared stunned. "That was weeks ago."

"It was. I took her away before she could make any attempt to call upon you and your wife and son. That could have been disastrous, given Miranda's fragile health and the boy's fear."

Taverham's face colored red. "What do you expect me to do, now that you've told me about her? Wring my hands and wish her to get better soon? Weep at her bedside?" Taverham gestured to the gardeners who hovered at the edge of the garden and started pointing to the roses around them. "Take them all and burn them."

The gardeners came with axes and shovels in hand and began to remove the rose bushes one by one, tossing them carelessly into barrows.

Everett's chest tightened with sorrow at the destruction they wrought in such a short time. Emily had tended this part of Twilit Hill's gardens as if it were her own. She'd spent hours here, coaxing the buds to bloom so that the man she loved in vain always had beauty around him. Seeing her act of hopeless love wiped from existence hurt more than he'd imagined it could.

Taverham's men were quick and efficient, until only bare garden beds surrounded them. "Perhaps after this is gone, Miranda will feel inclined to venture here at last."

Everett frowned. "Why wouldn't she come to this part of the garden?"

Taverham turned on him. "This is the place my new wife saw Emily in my arms the night we married. This is where Emily kissed me."

"What?!"

"Your sister was intoxicated, and I carried her home to Warstone rather than let her embarrass herself before the wedding guests. Because of that kindness on my part, Miranda was led to believe I was unfaithful to her, and always would be. I cannot care about Emily if I wish to keep my wife happy."

He gasped, shocked completely. Taverham hadn't ever given him a full explanation of why Miranda had gone away, only that Emily had played a part. He had thought her actions toward the boy were bad enough, but this too…

He raked a hand through his hair. "I had no notion of any of that."

"Now you know everything," Taverham insisted. "Emily deliberately set out to wreck my marriage, sowing the seeds of doubt and mistrust in Miranda's mind early on, and later attempting to poison my memory and faith in her return, so I would declare her dead and marry Emily once I was free. All so she could take Miranda's rightful place as my wife. Emily is dead to me already."

Everett gulped. He couldn't expect sympathy for Emily. Not after this too. Taverham was well within his rights to be furious, but Emily was Everett's only family. He couldn't throw her out to fend for herself. She might return to Twilit Hill and cause even more trouble. "She is not long for this world."

Taverham scowled. "I don't give a damn."

Everett nodded. In truth, he understood this reaction from Taverham better now. "If the idea of her death gives you pleasure, so be it. If you had anything left you want to say to her, you know where to find her. The gardener there will only open the gate to you, and no other."

"I wouldn't waste my breath," Taverham said. "Leave as soon as it's polite to do so, and do not breathe word of this near my wife, son, or anyone at Twilit Hill. I will not have Christopher afraid of her shadow ever again."

He winced at the dismissal, and bowed formally. Whitney knew about Emily, of course, but he suspected she would say nothing, now he'd spoken to Taverham. "Of course, my lord. I do beg your pardon for the intrusion."

Chapter Fourteen

———◆———

Nights at Twilit Hill were long and normally quiet. At least they had been before Lord and Lady Carrington had arrived with their exuberant children. It was growing late, but the older imps showed no signs of being weary or ready for bed. Lady Carrington was hesitant to leave them and return downstairs to her waiting husband.

"You can leave them to me tonight, my lady," Whitney assured her.

"Are you sure?"

The woman remained dubious, even after Whitney promising twenty times at least that she would be fine with them. "Absolutely. I've been looking forward to this all afternoon. I'll keep the maid company until the last one is deeply asleep."

Lady Carrington beamed. "Has anyone ever told you that you are remarkably kind?"

Whitney thought about that a moment. "That's not the usual compliment I receive, but I'm happy you think so…and to help you. I'd only be awake and sketching alone in my room anyway."

Lady Carrington hugged her quickly. "You are my savior. I cannot thank you enough for giving up your time and the peace you had."

Whitney looked around the nursery and grinned as the children smiled up at her. They were only still because they were waiting for Lady Carrington to go so they could play again. "It's my pleasure." Whitney nodded. "Enjoy your moonlit stroll with your husband, my lady."

Whitney was certain they'd be doing more than strolling in the dark, and the delicate blush climbing Lady Carrington's cheeks confirmed it. "I will. Thank you again."

Lady Carrington took one last peek at her sleeping youngest child, and then slipped out the door, shutting it very quietly behind her.

All of the children leaped up to kneel upon their beds immediately.

"You may get up, but absolutely no running about will be allowed."

"Yes, Miss Crewe," they murmured as they slipped off the beds to play with Christopher's many toys.

Little Mabel came across the room and lifted up her arms for a hug instead.

Whitney indulged the girl a moment before carrying her to a distant corner of the room, where the light was brightest, and depositing her on a cushion on the floor. She sat, too, pulling a drawer she'd borrowed from the housekeeper closer to her side. It was full now with paper and charcoals, and topped with thin pieces of timber, about the size of a large book, to place paper upon while they sketched.

"I should have enough for everyone," Whitney said as she began to pass them around.

The slower children rushed over and collected theirs. They jostled each other in their bid to sit as close to Christopher as possible, and Whitney had to hide a smile at their antics. Christopher's fears he'd be forgotten had been for nothing. They had definitely missed him.

She glanced out the nursery window, noting the darkness outside, and sighed as her thoughts quickly turned in another direction.

Night was the perfect time for a seduction. She rubbed her hand around her neck and then shook her head to herself. Tonight, Alice would seduce Lord Acton and ensure the wedding went off without a hitch. She could not imagine him resisting Alice. What man would deny a seduction, especially if he was about to wed the woman seducing him?

Acton was a lusty man, although he hid that side of his nature quite well.

She scolded herself for feeling uncomfortable about suggesting to Alice that she should seduce him. Whitney believed in love and marriage, and particularly in faithfulness and desire. Alice apparently did *not* share those opinions, to have suggested Whitney participate in her devious little test on Acton.

It was another difference between them, and something that troubled Whitney a lot. She had always thought Alice was a good person through and through. She hoped it was just pre-wedding nerves getting the better of her good sense. Alice had nothing to worry about when it came to Lord Acton. He was a man of experience and very passionate.

She collected her papers and started to pass one sheet to each child, determined to put that whole conversation from her mind.

"What should I draw?" Mabel asked immediately.

"Draw whatever you want. Something that you like."

"I like everything," she promised, and received nods of agreement from the other orphans.

"Let me see," she murmured, wondering if the children were afraid of disappointing her with their choices. She'd never met a group of children more eager to please than Carrington's orphans. Little did they know she had been an orphan once, too. She had turned herself inside out to please each aunt and uncle she'd lived with. To be what they wanted so they wouldn't send her away again. It was a terrible way to live and to think. She was very glad she'd acquired the courage to be herself at last. "We could all draw Christopher—if he can stay still long enough, that is," she suggested.

They all giggled at that.

"I'm going to draw his nose," Mabel proclaimed, staring across at the boy.

"I'm going to draw his ear," another, sitting right beside Christopher, exclaimed.

"His feet," a boy to Whitney's right decided.

"His eyes," Whitney murmured. Sketching them now as practice would help her complete the family portrait she was painting.

"His hands."

"His big fat tummy," another teased.

"I am so going to get everyone for this," Christopher threatened in a menacing tone.

Everyone laughed.

"Actually, this is a good idea and could be an interesting exercise." Whitney decided, ignoring Christopher's bright blush. "If everyone draws one piece of Christopher, we can put the pieces together tomorrow and we will see how he looks."

Christopher rolled his eyes. "I'm going to draw you instead, Miss Crewe," he warned before rolling onto his tummy and beginning his sketch.

Whitney reclined against the wall, watching the children at work and trying again not to think about the activities Lord Acton might be engaging in at that very moment with Alice.

She began lightly sketching the outline of Christopher's brows, and then the shape of his eyes, but her mind soon returned to what other people were doing elsewhere. She paused sketching as she scolded herself silently.

She shouldn't feel upset under the circumstances, but the truth was she felt more than a little envious.

It was not as if she wanted Lord Acton for herself, but she remembered too well now how it felt to be with him today. He was interesting, and constantly surprised her, although not always in a good way. The thought of him making love to Alice made her stomach unsettled.

She forced her attention to the page again and added new lines. Across from her, Christopher was trying to draw her and hide his efforts at the same time.

"I'm done," Mabel exclaimed before jumping to her feet to show Whitney her sketch.

The nose she'd drawn was huge and not at all like his. But from the perspective of a smaller child, perhaps it would seem that way. Whitney quickly hid it from the other children so there could be no discussion tonight. "That is lovely, now off to bed with you."

Mabel kissed her cheek and then slipped into her bed, but peered at the others as they continued working.

One by one, the children brought her their drawings and went to bed, until it was just Whitney and Christopher sitting on the floor all alone, with the yawning maid for company. She smiled at the boy and whispered, "Are you about done?"

"Almost." He made a few more marks but then rolled up his paper up before Whitney could see his work.

"Are you not going to show me like the others have?"

"Oh no, I'll show you tomorrow, after everyone else has embarrassed me," he said with a grin.

"All right, if you must." She stood and went to check on everyone. Christopher did the same, pulling up blankets, tucking toys in more securely around the Carrington children.

She stood back and watched him fuss over them. "Did you always tuck them in at night?"

"Aggie and I did it together most nights, but that was before I left to live with father and be his son. There was no one but me to tuck in there."

Whitney's eyes misted with tears, but she brushed them aside. "I'm sure Lady Carrington misses your help very much."

"They're all asleep now." He got into his bed, the one placed closest to the door, with one final glance over his shoulder. "Whitney, can I ask you something?"

"Anything."

"Why are you sad tonight?"

"I'm not sad," she promised.

He sat up, his frown deepening. "Mother used to wear that same expression at night when I was young. She always said it was nothing, too."

The boy was too clever by far. She went to him, kissed him on top of his head, and tucked him firmly into his bed. "Your mother was probably thinking of your father, so far away. But if I am sad, it is because my time here is almost over, and that is because I want it to be."

Christopher caught her hand before she could escape. "I had fun today. With Lord Acton, I mean. I didn't think he'd like to play with us."

"Neither did I." Today, Acton had revealed a great deal more than the boy had noticed. He still desired her, even though they had no future or plans for one. He was going to marry someone else. He was probably being seduced at this very moment. Whitney's stomach churned anew. "He was a good sport about it and came to protect you. Remember that in the future."

She collected a chair to sit upon.

"You don't have to stay until I fall asleep," Christopher suggested.

"I promised I would."

"You promised Aggie to stay until *her* children were asleep."

"I naturally included you along with them," she said softly. "But if you don't want me to stay, I'll wish you a good night's sleep, young man. Pleasant dreams."

"Until tomorrow," he said, and then yawned widely.

Whitney nodded to the maid, slipped from the room, and only took a few paces into the hall before she sagged.

By rights she should seek out her hosts, if only to say good night, but she knew she couldn't bear to spend another minute pretending she was happy.

She *was* sad, and she wouldn't be good company for anyone.

As she undressed without the assistance of a Twilit Hill maid, she glanced about her bedchamber at the traveling trunks waiting for her adventure to start, and thought of the few mementos from her life she had tucked away in them.

Only once in her life had she had a room of her own, a home she could call her own. It had been so long ago now that she could barely remember the wallpaper pattern in her parents' house, much less the color of it.

What she did remember best was the doorway to her parents' bedchamber. There'd been a gouge in the doorframe from when the door had become stuck and her father, anxious to reach her trapped mother, had taken up an axe break it down. His desperate destruction of the barrier between them, the kiss when they were together again, had been so very romantic.

That was real love.

Love was what Whitney had craved all her life, but never dared count on.

Whitney curled up on her bed, but sleep wouldn't come as she remembered all the little gestures between her adoring parents. After an hour of tossing, she lit her lamp, drew her sketchbook onto her lap and began drawing a scene that came from the deepest recesses of her heart.

The woodland she drew featured heavily in her imagination

quite often, although she'd never set foot in such a beautiful place. To Whitney, the setting felt magical, charged with possibilities and hopes and dreams. She'd been drawing this scene for many years, though she was unsure when exactly she'd first started sketching it. Most likely the place existed only in her imagination, but it felt so very real to her tonight.

A gentle bubbling stream wound through trees and rocks, narrow enough to step across in certain parts. There were great towering trees overhead that blotted out all but the odd shaft of sunlight. The woods were warm, inviting, filled with sounds that soothed Whitney in her loneliest moments.

Only tonight, there was a gentleman in the scene. Lord Acton's face peeked at her from between the trees.

She blinked back tears and held her work at arm's length. Each time she drew the scene, it seemed a little different. Alive in a way most sketches could not mimic, but it had always been hers alone. Having drawn Acton there changed it and made her wish things might yet be different. That he could have been anyone else.

An impossible wish, perhaps.

She quickly tore up the sheet into little pieces, slipped from bed to consign the image to her cold hearth. Tomorrow morning she'd burn them, and she vowed never to draw him again.

She turned down the lamp and climbed back into her rumpled bed. But as so often happened, her thoughts turned to the events of the day, and tonight she remembered Acton, sunlight surrounding him, too handsome when he smiled with drips of water running down his handsome cheeks.

Almost too endearingly sweet to turn him back toward his future bride for the affection he sought. But she'd done it for the sake of his marriage. He should be faithful to Alice, not luring her to fall in love with him.

She hugged her pillow, trying valiantly to forget how easy it had become to be around him. They had more in common than she'd ever suspected. He was amusing when he stopped worrying what others thought of him.

He'd been gallant, too, in his own way. He'd caught her as she'd fallen today, and she feared it might already be too late to forget him.

Chapter Fifteen

———— ◆ ————

"**O**h, you cheated," Emily complained as she threw her cards away to fall to the floor of her little bedchamber.

"I'll have you know, I did not," Everett warned her as he bent to scoop them up. "My honor wouldn't allow me to be so dishonest."

She pouted a few minutes and then narrowed her eyes on him. "Why do you not visit me more often in the daytime?"

He collected all the cards and sorted them out. "I have an estate to run, and sitting at your bedside gossiping will not ensure the work is done properly."

"You don't gossip with me anymore, either," she complained.

He shuffled the cards. "I've nothing new to share."

She pulled her shawl tighter about her chest. "Have you had no letters from him?"

"Nothing," he promised. Kit hated writing anyone, and probably wouldn't ever speak to him again, either. "Cousin Howard wrote and invited me to spend Christmas at his estate though."

"You always spend Christmas here with me," she protested. "You cannot abandon me."

No, he would not accept the invitation, but would Emily even be here at Christmas to spend it with him? Her doctors had warned him she might not last that long. Her swift decline continued to alarm them all. "I know, which is why I declined immediately."

Emily fussed with her blankets. "Has Lady Taverham asked after me?"

"The dowager?" He looked down at the cards. "She's still in London."

"And Taverham? Is he very unhappy, do you think?"

It may be unkind, but he would not give his sister false hope where Taverham was concerned. The man loved his wife very much. "He's happy, I'm sure. He always loved Miranda. He was always faithful, wasn't he?"

Emily had once hinted to him that she and Taverham had been secret lovers, which had been quite untrue. He'd been shocked discover how far back in time her scheming had begun. Emily had not the power to claim the marquess' heart, only the desperation to make others think she had.

"Out of duty," she complained.

"Out of love," he promised, knowing now that it was true. Despite Taverham's anger at Miranda's disappearance, his friend had always loved his wife. He'd been faithful and had always hoped for her return, he'd said.

She waved her hand. "What do men know of love?"

Emily suddenly turned her face away and gave in to another wretched bout of coughing. His sides ached at the tearing sound before she was halfway done. When she finally recovered her composure, she fell back against her pillows, gasping raggedly, her handkerchief wadded up in her hand. "Continue," she croaked.

He dealt her a new hand of cards, but had to wonder if they shouldn't stop altogether for the day.

"I know love when I see it," he promised. "Our parents were in love when they wed, and all through the years of their marriage, too."

Of late, so many of his acquaintances had found love, which made him wonder about his future.

Could he feel it for Alice? A woman he'd given his word to marry? A pretty young woman he knew so little of even now. He shuffled his cards, wondering if he could ever know anyone well enough to love them as his parents had each other. He hoped to love Alice one day. But his preoccupation with Whitney Crewe—

what she was doing, what she would say next—were a constant reminder that he was torn.

It was ridiculous that he looked forward to Whitney's company more than he did Alice's. He liked Whitney more and more each time their paths crossed, and he did not mind that she put him in his place occasionally. But it wasn't love he felt for her. It couldn't be as strong as all that.

It was desire, a result of one disastrous, glorious night of interrupted passion and a little lingering curiosity on his part.

He allowed Emily to win their next game purely to keep her from another tantrum.

"I want to go home," Emily said quietly.

"You know that is impossible. Peace and quiet is what the physician recommended for you. At Warstone, you would become busy managing the house, and any visitors might overly excite you into another coughing spell."

"You have imprisoned me. I want to sleep in my own bed again, to look out my own windows to the woods of home. Is that too much to grant a dying woman?"

He looked her way, stunned. Her color was high, cheeks flushed with the light sheen of perspiration. "You are not dying, but you have become fevered again. You should have said something."

He called for her nurse.

"I've always known I was," Emily whispered. She lay back limply, listlessly rocking her head on her pillows. He moved back to let the pair of nurses press cold compresses to her brow and fevered cheeks. "I am not getting better. I am getting worse."

The far nurse gave a tiny nod as she came toward him with a crystal dish in her hands. A peek inside revealed Emily's handkerchief was dark with her blood.

His gut tightened in dread at that. He'd been warned her lungs would weaken and she might begin to spit up blood near the end. The little hope he'd harbored that she might still recover fluttered and died. Emily would die, soon, and only he would mourn her.

He steadied himself to give nothing of his feelings away as he returned to Emily's bedside.

"I think you're getting better," he told her with false optimism as the second woman left the room. He had lied to Emily more in the past month than he had in his entire life, simply to avoid upsetting her. The nurses had told him earlier that she was sleeping more and more each day when he wasn't around. He sat next to her bed again, caught her limp hand in his and squeezed her fingers. No matter what she'd done, he didn't want to lose her. He didn't want any of this to be real.

Emily pulled away. "Must you always wear those horrible black gloves when you touch me?" she complained. "I hate them."

"It is what the physician advised. I apologize again for taking such precautions," he reminded her. "I want to be able to see you."

"I want to see you too," Emily agreed before she lapsed into silence, studying him. After a time, she tossed him a brief smile. "You must marry, Everett, and have a son to continue the line," she told him in a complete change of subject. "Our family will die with you unless you marry soon."

It was on the tip of his tongue to promise he had that situation well in hand, but if he told Emily about Alice now, she would want to meet the woman immediately. He couldn't have that. "There is always Howard Lynch to succeed me."

"Dearest Howard, such a lovely, biddable boy when he was young. He has not visited us in such a long time. I must write to our cousin and enquire after his wife. You must have a son before he does or there will be talk. Everett, fetch me my writing desk and you can post my letter tomorrow."

Howard's wife had delivered a healthy son a month ago. He kept that news to himself, as well. Worrying for the succession, for the future of the family, would do Emily no good. Everett kept so many secrets from Emily now that he sometimes had trouble keeping track of what she did not know. He'd never told Emily about the night he'd met Whitney Crewe for the first time, either. Emily would not have been kind if she had ever learned the identity of his seducer.

"You should rest, sister."

"All I do is rest and wait in this dreary place. I swear I have more conversations with strangers than I do with anyone I know, and you know how uncomfortable I find forward women."

He stared at Emily as she bit her lip, wondering if finally,

Emily would confess to meeting Whitney Crewe. She hadn't said anything so far, and he was suddenly worried that Whitney had returned after she'd promised not to visit again. "To what woman are you referring?"

"Oh, just a traveler, I think she was," Emily said dismissively. "She accosted our gardener and claimed to be an artist, of all things. You know, one of those uncouth people so prevalent on the fringes of society. Of course, she came at a time when I was not fit to receive anyone, so I sent her on her way immediately."

"Did she return?"

His breath caught as Emily took her time answering.

"Thankfully not. I would have had her sent on her way if she had."

He relaxed. Whitney was in no danger. At least he could count on her to take care of herself once she understood where the real danger lie.

"Besides, I'm still waiting on my new season's gowns from London to be delivered."

He laughed softly. "When did you have a chance to order new gowns when you were in London?"

"When I was there last. I told you about them. I'm sure I did."

He stared at her, doubting her word. "Before you came to see me?"

She rubbed her brow. "Well, it couldn't have been after, since you've confined me here ever since," she accused.

He smiled quickly, but he was troubled. Had she gone to see the seamstress or merely imagined she had? Some of their conversations of late had been very confusing. "I will send for them immediately when I return to Warstone."

If the gowns had actually been ordered, he would have his man in London collect them.

He saw Emily was tiring, he gathered the cards and set them aside. "I won't be able to see you tomorrow."

"Why not!" she pouted.

"They are finally ready to put a roof over the newly repaired cottage. I want to be there. You know how dangerous that sort of thing can be."

"True," Emily said, and then smiled up at him and offered her cheek. "Be careful, too."

"I always am." He nodded to her instead of pressing his lips to her fevered skin. Emily did not always make it easy for him to keep a distance. She sometimes forgot the danger she was to his health.

Emily sighed heavily and snuggled down in her bed as Everett slipped out the door, leaving her to the care of servants he trusted to do what was right where she was concerned.

He rode back to his home. For a change, Emily had been more or less herself again. The sister he knew and loved, not the brokenhearted schemer angry with the world at large. He did not expect the peace to last of course, but he'd gratefully take any respite.

It was very late by the time he was changed into fresh clothes and returned to the house. He was fit to mingle with his guests again, but only a few lamps were lit at this hour. He checked his pocket watch for the time as he stepped through the morning-room doors that had been left unlocked for his return.

"Where have you been?"

He glanced up in surprise at Alice Quartermane's demand. He put his pocket watch away before he answered. "I've just come from the stables," he said carefully, determined to give nothing away as to where he'd really been.

Her brow furrowed. "But I went there."

He smiled quickly but was surprised she'd gone looking for him. "We must have only just missed each other then."

He looked for her ever-present parents, but they were nowhere to be found or heard in the distant halls. "Is anything wrong? Are your parents all right?"

Alice smiled. "My parents are very well. They retired some time ago, my lord. I wasn't sleepy, so I thought you might like to keep me company."

"Ah," he said, then smiled and headed for the door. "We can finally play that game of cards we spoke about. Let me fetch my housekeeper to act as chaperone."

"I don't want a chaperone," she said, quickly moving to intercept him.

He came to a halt, and slowly turned to stare at her. "You don't?"

That was quite the turnabout. Usually Alice was the bastion of propriety and decorum. The rules stated that unmarried men and women shouldn't be alone, and she had stuck to them like glue until now.

As if reading his thoughts, Alice shook her head. "We are to be married."

"Indeed." But he swallowed down sudden nervousness at the thought of that future, and surprised himself by taking an awkward pace back. "You've never sought me out before."

She brushed her palms against her legs and then moved toward him. "Are you not happy to see me?"

"Of course I am," he promised, nervousness turning to genuine alarm. In all the time Alice had been promised to him in marriage, she'd always hidden behind her parents' protection, never giving him a moment to even steal a kiss. That she sought him out now seemed highly out of character. He wondered at her motive, her sudden change of heart.

But then he recalled his last conversation with Whitney Crewe. What had she said about Alice and tonight? *Don't forget about Alice?* As if he could. "You are going to be my wife soon."

And that event seemed much too soon all of a sudden.

"I am looking forward to beginning my duties as your countess," she promised him. "That is why I thought it best that we talk together in private now."

Duties? Whitney had mentioned Alice would be waiting for him, but hadn't hinted at what the conversation might entail. He had assumed it to be about the wedding day festivities, not their future life together.

"We don't need to wait to be alone to talk to each other about the future."

"I know this must seem forward," she began, drawing closer. "But if we are to be man and wife, I think the rules could be bent a little, don't you agree?"

She settled her fingertips on his arm, looking up at him with a rather bold stare for the first time ever. As she slid her hand upward to his shoulder, he realized talk was the last thing on her mind tonight.

"Yes, but..." He suddenly felt the need to scramble for the door and shout for a chaperone—any person would do—and it had very little to do with protecting Alice's health.

He took a steadying breath to calm his panic, but he was very curious about why Alice would approach him in such an eager manner so suddenly. "Tell me why you agreed to marry me?"

Miss Quartermane looked lost. "I don't understand, my lord."

He smiled quickly to hide his dismay. "It is as straightforward a question as it could be. Why marry me?"

"Because you asked," she murmured.

"Is it only because I am an earl that you accepted without knowing a thing about me?"

"My father vouched for you. He said I could not do better, and he was right. We met, and I liked you very much."

Was Whitney correct? Was this marriage bound to disappoint him?

He wasn't attracted to Alice. Not even half as much as he was to Whitney Crewe. Alice Quartermane professed to only liking him so far, and he'd secretly hoped for so much more.

He forced his smile to grow wider, even if inside he was desperate to find an excuse to leave the room. "Miss Quartermane, I am glad you accepted my proposal, but I have no wish to tarnish your reputation."

Her face fell.

"Your parents speak very highly of your virtue and would become very angry with me if they ever found out we were alone together before we were married," he said gently, hoping to ease the sting of his rejection. He could never behave with Alice the way he had with Whitney. They would share a bed on their wedding night, and not before. "They might become disappointed in you, and I cannot have that. I want to be on good terms with them, for your sake particularly. I know they mean the world to you, and I hope they will visit us often in the future. I would not like them to feel you had been compromised before we wed."

"They do like you," Alice promised. "They would indeed be angry with me for seeking you out like this. I should have considered their feelings, too."

"We'll keep this to ourselves then," he said, then Everett gestured Alice to an armchair beside a card table and hurried to ring for the housekeeper.

He sat opposite her, but his stomach was in knots at the

prospect of future encounters when they were man and wife. Forming an intimate connection with Alice didn't seem so appealing anymore, when that was all he should be wishing for. There was nothing wrong with Alice. The fault lay within himself. The fire, passion, wasn't there when he looked at her. He'd only ever felt it once in his lifetime.

With Whitney Crewe.

It made no sense that he could still want the eccentric, opinionated, frustrating woman he'd once dallied with instead of the *proper* young woman he'd offered for.

He fought to keep his expression clear of the shock and hopelessness of his discovery as he shuffled the cards. What was he to do? He was engaged to marry the friend of the woman he yearned for, and there was no escape if he wanted to be considered a gentleman. Only a woman could end an engagement, and he had no reason to believe Miss Quartermane would suddenly change her mind about marrying him.

Unless you give her a reason to be dissatisfied before the wedding day.

His head cleared of confusion. If he no longer desired to marry Alice, although he still liked her very much, he had to do something—and now. He was no monster, but he wasn't being fair to her, or even faithful in his private thoughts. They were ten days away from marriage. He would have to act swiftly if he had any chance of escape.

He would have to find a way to make her dislike him enough that Alice would want to call the whole thing off. He'd have to become very disagreeable, something that went against the grain and might sabotage the inroads he'd made with his best friend's wife if she learned of his behavior later.

When the housekeeper slipped into the room, he had her sit near Miss Quartermane. After tonight, he would make sure they spent even less time together.

Alice studied her cards and then glanced his way. "Have you had any word from your sister yet?"

He winced. "No, none."

Chapter Sixteen

———◆———

The nearest village to Twilit Hill was a warm and wonderful place, nestled at the edge of a large woodland area. Small and somewhat rundown, it reminded Whitney of the place that had become her first home after her parents' deaths. She'd gone to live with Uncle Willard when she was only nine. He had been a man of few words, but strong and proud and unfailingly honest. A blacksmith by trade, he'd had little idea of what to do with a weeping orphan girl of limited strength except put her to work around the workshop.

She smiled at the sounds emanating from the distant smithy and turned her feet in that direction. She had not minded the work she'd been put to by her uncle. The distraction of being busy had lessened her grief somewhat. Her uncle had given her the task of tallying his accounts when she proved capable later, sweeping floors and keeping his house in order, and even performing some of the delicate work his customers expected of him.

She had become quite adept at pouring molten metal to fashion nails, too, a job that required a very steady hand and patience.

She paused at the doorway, lost in the rhythmic sound of the blacksmith's strikes on the anvil, and sighed. She missed her uncle very much. He'd been a good man who'd made her feel safe and loved and wanted.

She took a few steps into the workshop, curious to see any differences between her uncle's old establishment and this one. As far as she could tell, the two places were much the same. Heat blasted from the forge, and an untidy and oddly comforting array of tools lay scattered about. The smell of hot metal strong in the air. She felt instantly at ease and waited to be noticed before venturing farther inside.

The blacksmith was a great hulking fellow, who clearly knew his work well and focused solely on what he was doing. He wore a thick leather jerkin over his clothes, and his forearms bulged with the force of each strike upon the anvil.

She sighed again. Such a man, such a physique.

She jerked her gaze from him as a tiny red-haired woman hurried in through a distant door, two tankards of ale in hand.

The woman froze when their eyes met.

"Hello," Whitney said in her friendliest tone, eyes darting to the blacksmith, who'd finally noticed her, too. "I didn't mean to interrupt."

The lady set the tankards down and gave the blacksmith a pointed look. He quickly went back to work and ignored Whitney's interruption.

The woman drew closer, eyes hard as she took in Whitney from head to toe. "Can I help you? Are you lost, my lady?"

"Lost in the past a little bit," Whitney confessed, smiling as she looked around. "I once spent a lot of time in a place like this."

The woman's brows rose in surprise. "Did you now?"

Whitney nodded, aware the woman was scrutinizing her fine clothing quite closely. Nowadays, Whitney did not dress as if she'd spent a year and more stoking fires. "My uncle was a blacksmith."

The woman's eyebrows rose even higher, as if she could not believe that. "Where is he?"

"He passed away, a number of years ago now, I'm afraid." Whitney shrugged. "I thought of him as soon as I heard that strapping fellow over there."

"My husband," the woman said, folding her arms over her chest—claiming the fellow in a way that said "hands off my man." "I'm Nancy. Mrs. Nancy Blake."

Whitney immediately liked the woman for her obvious possessiveness.

"Miss Whitney Crewe." Whitney grinned as she held out her hand. Mrs. Blake took it with obvious reluctance. "He has excellent taste. Redheads always make the best wives."

"But they are the most troublesome of creatures at every other moment," a deep voice added from somewhere behind her.

Whitney whipped around and stared into the shadowed corners, recognizing the owner of the voice at once. "Acton, is that you?"

The blacksmith's wife hurried around Whitney, carrying one of the tankards toward the earl she could not see clearly yet. "There you are, my lord. Sorry to keep you waiting."

"Quite all right, Mrs. Blake," he said kindly, but Whitney detected a faint slurring of his words.

Whitney took a few steps in his direction, squinting until she saw him clearly. She hadn't seen the earl today, but she had been thinking about him—a lot more than she should. Only Miss Quartermane and her parents had called at Twilit Hill since the day of their water fight. Miss Quartermane had been out of sorts today, but hadn't explained what had upset her. She hoped her advice to seduce the earl the other night had not gone awry or made trouble between them.

"What are you doing here?"

"Drinking," he said, before taking a very long drink to prove his point. He sank back into the straw with a groan, as if he'd no intention of standing to greet her...or of ever moving again.

She flashed him a quick smile. "I expected to see you with Miss Quartermane when she arrived at Twilit Hill today."

He scowled, and Whitney gulped at his expression—most definitely out of sorts today. Had something gone terribly wrong between Acton and Miss Quartermane the other night?

She pushed aside the selfish burst of hope that filled her heart and focused on him.

On closer inspection, Lord Acton appeared rather terribly presented. His clothing was wrinkled, his usually clean-shaven jaw was dark with the beginnings of a beard, and if she wasn't mistaken, he was quite foxed.

She narrowed her eyes on him in disapproval. It was only nine in the morning, far too early for him to be in this state, no matter the reason. If she had erred in her advice to Miss Quartermane, she would make amends and do her best to set things right again. "I trust you and Miss Quartermane have not argued?"

"Of course not."

Whitney was relieved, and not a bit surprised by that. Alice was lovely, so whatever was going on with Acton may not have anything to do with his relationship with his betrothed. It was just a feeling she had, based on Alice's cool mood earlier that day. It really wasn't any of her business…and yet she couldn't help but poke and pry into the reason for his current unhappiness. "Then what is wrong with you?"

He studied her, scowling anew. "What's it to you?"

"I'm not sure, but that is a good question, isn't it?" She didn't approve of his impending marriage, or keeping secrets, but that did not mean she wished him ill. "I am interested, so tell me what I want to know and I will cease bothering you."

"You like meddling in my life, don't you? Going so far as to put scandalous ideas in my future bride's head." He scowled, and then finished off the tankard in one long guzzle. He wiped his mouth with the back of his hand and belched in a rather rude manner, quite unlike the man she'd come to know.

Whitney rocked back on her heels. She'd never seen him act so strangely; this was completely out of character. "I did not think you would object."

"I object most strenuously," he claimed.

He struggled to stand, and Whitney caught his elbow when he seemed in danger of toppling over. "Acton," she chided. "Be careful."

He shook her off violently. "Stay back," he warned.

The consumption.

Whitney put her hands behind her back but planted her feet, placing herself directly in his path. She was far enough away that his breath couldn't strike her face, and close enough that she could see every emotion play across his handsome face. "I've never once seen or heard you be anything less than a gentleman."

He scowled at her again. "Now that's a lie."

She almost laughed. She had seen him solemn, flirtatious, aroused and naked—all in one night. She was trying, fairly unsuccessfully, to do the right thing and put that night firmly from her mind, but he made it so difficult.

"You can keep your clothes on today," she whispered. "I meant that you are being a bit of a beast and very rude. I hope you are kinder to Alice than you are to me."

He pushed past her, and Whitney followed him at first with her eyes. Perhaps she shouldn't have mentioned Alice Quartermane—the lovely and proper debutant that would soon be his wife. They were so different, and of course Acton had chosen her. Still, it stung a little to be rejected when she was only trying to be his friend. Whitney was not always so wicked, but she'd acted it with him, and he couldn't forget it, either.

The blacksmith and his wife had drawn close together and were staring. She grinned at them. "Do you happen to have a water trough outside?"

"Indeed, I do," Mr. Blake confirmed, but then his eyes narrowed. "What do you want it for?"

"I may need it for medicinal purposes," she confessed, and then slowly followed after the drunken earl. "Nothing sobers a man faster than a good dunking," she murmured.

As luck would have it, Acton stopped quite near one.

When he saw Whitney, he groaned and pressed his hand to his face. "Kill me now," he mumbled.

"You're not going to be that lucky. You'll probably live forever." She nudged his shoulder in what she hoped he understood was a playful manner. "What has gotten into you today?"

He shook his head then grabbed a fencepost to steady himself. "It's all your fault."

"My fault?"

He looked at her sternly but then looked away again.

"Acton? Is it your sister? What is wrong? Tell me, please."

He glanced her way slowly and stared at her. She grew warm under his close inspection, and suddenly the stirring of desire filled her, along with the need to wrap her arms about him and promise everything would be all right. She tried to smile but that only made her more aware of her awkwardness around him now. He didn't want her. Not really. He wanted a good woman. A better woman than Whitney could ever become.

She let her eyes fall but Acton reached out and caught her arm. When she glanced up at him again, she saw his desire—as clear to her now as the night they'd first met and flirted. A soft smile played about his mouth, drawing her in.

She leaned a little his way, but he released her and stepped back.

"Damn," he muttered, before raking his hand though his hair. The gesture made him seem vulnerable and uncertain, so Whitney waited patiently, determined to learn what was wrong and how she could help.

"Please tell me what I can do," she whispered.

He straightened. "Taverham reacted worse than I expected him to when I mentioned Emily."

"Worse," she whispered. "Oh, dear. I'm sorry."

"I am no longer welcome at Twilit Hill," he stated, squinting at her. "That is one reason I am not squiring Miss Quartermane hither and yon."

"Oh." She sighed. "I had no idea Taverham had taken the news as badly as all that, but he's been a bit of a bear to everyone, too, when I think about it. He didn't harm you, did he?"

"No." Acton grunted and sank down on the edge of the trough. "Can't even blame him for being angry. Stupid thing to have done, not to explain the situation as soon as he arrived."

"As far as I can tell, no one has been told. Christopher has been riding or leading Lion all about the estate very happily," she promised him. "Miranda hasn't said anything about Emily to me either, which leads me to suspect she might not know yet. She would have warned me to watch over Christopher more closely if she knew."

"It's only a matter of time then."

Once the rumors spread, Acton would have a hard time keeping Emily's condition from other members of the *ton*. Friends might wonder why she was locked away too. "Have you told Alice? Have you told Mr. and Mrs. Quartermane?"

"No," he confessed. "Only you. Alice and I…"

Whitney gritted her teeth. "If you and Alice are to have a happy marriage, you must tell her about Emily and the difficulties you could face. No relationship can withstand secrets such as these."

"If I told her all my secrets now, she might not consider you her friend anymore. Have you thought of that?"

Whitney swallowed. "I imagine that may become the case anyway."

"Because you've seen me naked?"

She smiled quickly at the pleasant memory. "Because I will not be around to amuse her when she is out of sorts."

"That's right, you're leaving the country." He bit his lip. "In five days?"

"Yes."

"Why the rush?"

So she had no chance of being delayed and remaining to witness the day Acton wed, of course. But she wouldn't confess that. Instead, she trotted out the most reasonable excuse she'd concocted and shared already with others. "Because I have an appointment with my banker, to discuss financial matters for my trip and the liquidation of my investments."

He gave her a strange look. "I would have thought your cousin managed your affairs."

Whitney shook her head. "I am more than capable of managing the inheritances my aunts and uncles left to me."

"I did not say you couldn't, I just thought Louth might have been of help while you are away."

"You assume I am returning."

His eyes widened. "And you're not?"

"I plan to thoroughly enjoy myself, and if I find a place I love, there really isn't any reason to ever return to England, is there?"

He gaped at her for a long moment, but then he put his head in his hands with a groan.

Whitney still wasn't sure if he was upset over Emily, telling Taverham about it, or simply feeling the effects of his intoxication right now.

Whitney considered what to do if it turned out to be the latter. Her uncle had sworn that drinking a concoction of garlic and rosemary steeped in hot water aided clearing the head. She was reluctant to recommend such a vile-smelling concoction to anyone, even if it had seemed to do the trick for her old uncle.

Yet, Acton sounded miserable, and it was unlike him to show himself in such a state. He'd known about Emily for some time, but losing the respect of Lord Taverham might just have upset him a great deal more than he'd want to let on.

She carefully placed her hand on his bent head and stroked his hair. He had nice hair, pale and straight, but he reeked of the ale he'd been drinking, so much that she wrinkled her nose. "Surely falling into a barrel of ale isn't the way to mend fences with your friend."

Acton froze as she continued to tease her fingertips into his hair. "Wasn't trying to get drunk because I'm a disappointment to him. He's every right to be angry. This is for…another reason entirely."

"You're not a danger to everyone you meet, you know," she promised. "I'm not scared of being near you."

"You should be." He stood suddenly, and because Whitney was standing so close, they bumped into each other. For one surprising moment, Acton was as close to her as he'd been the night they'd almost made love.

But then he windmilled his arms and toppled backward, catching Whitney's arm and dragging her shrieking into the mucky waters of the horse trough behind him.

Chapter Seventeen

——◆——

Everett came up spluttering, attempting to lift Whitney off of him to get out of the water. Unfortunately, it wasn't easy, as the slippery woman had fallen into a fit of giggles unlike anything he'd ever heard from a proper lady. As her gown grew sodden, it seemed even harder to separate themselves.

"Oh, lud!" Nancy screamed as she raced toward them. "My lord. Miss Crewe. What happened?"

"An accident." Whitney finally got her hands on the sides of the tub and heaved herself upright. Mucky water cascaded over him again, and he covered his face to avoid the worst of the deluge. "That wasn't supposed to happen to me too," Whitney promised.

She was helped out, and then stared down at her skirts in disappointment. "Oh no, and this was one of my favorite gowns, too."

"I'm sure it can be saved," Nancy Blake promised. "Are you all right, Everett?"

Blake pulled Everett out with one strong jerk, and he stood dripping water from every inch of his clothing and skin.

"Perhaps consider your wardrobe before you attack me next time," he muttered, flicking his arms and sending a shower of water droplets everywhere.

"Next time?" Whitney asked, all innocence and teasing

curiosity.

He shook his head, but smiled. Of all the women to become drawn to, he'd never expected Miss Crewe to crash into his life, and for him to like the disruption to his orderly and proper existence. "Becoming entangled with you seems inevitable."

Her smile grew wide. "It is not deliberate, I swear."

He snorted and flicked his hands again. Whitney sidestepped being struck, still grinning. It was remarkable how a quick dunking had cleared his head of the drink, too. He was feeling rather good now, much better than the pleasant buzz the ale had delivered earlier that day.

He hadn't been drinking because of Taverham. The marquess would calm down—eventually—and they'd go on as neighbors and friends probably forever, most likely.

He'd come here to avoid Miss Quartermane and to set tongues wagging about his drinking. Getting Whitney Crewe mixed up in his endeavors to make himself appear poor husband material wasn't part of his original plan, but unwittingly, Whitney had helped in ways he hadn't imagined. Out of the corner of his eye, he spied a few villages peering at them from a distance. Tongues would definitely wag now—and none of it would be good for Whitney, though.

Blake gestured to the smithy. "You two had better come and dry off inside before the gossips see you."

Too late, Everett feared, but he'd not planned this encounter.

"A very good idea," Whitney agreed, struggling to walk toward the smithy in her wet gown. "Hurry up, my lord, before you catch your death."

Although tempted to walk home as he was, mucky and dripping wet to add to the gossip, he followed her inside. It wasn't his intention to tarnish Whitney's reputation or friendship with Alice, but they did have Nancy and her husband to act as chaperones.

Once inside, she moved swiftly to the blaze and stood as close as could be considered safe.

Even so, Everett warned her back. "Be careful of your gown."

She held out the sides from her legs. "I think I'm too wet to catch alight."

He stared at her, at how her damp gown revealed every curve

of her body in front of the blaze. There wasn't much left to the imagination after his quick perusal. Whitney pushed her hair back from her cheek with the heel of her hand.

"Your hair isn't wet." Why wasn't she angrier with him for ruining her dress? Nancy would have been furious. "Are you really all right?"

"Oh, yes. A bit of water never hurt anyone. Your body saved me from a full dunking, I suspect. I do hope this sort of thing doesn't become a habit for us though. Getting drenched when I'm around you is sure to become tedious."

Her cheeks colored a little with a blush, and his mind strayed to other ways to warm her and get her wet.

Blake choked on laughter behind him.

Everett scowled at the man and turned around. "What are you laughing at?"

"Nothing, my lord. I'll give you privacy," he suggested with a wink, and then, eyes averted, slipped out the back door.

"Thank you," Whitney called after him as she began to peel off her short spencer. The garment was very soiled and dripped dirty water in an unending stream onto the dirt floor, even before she started to wring it out. She glanced his way, frowning. "You should remove your coat, and waistcoat, too, before you become chilled through."

He hesitated. Stripping off in front of Whitney Crewe again was the last thing he should do if he wanted to be considered a gentleman. "I don't think that's a good idea."

"I can control myself, you know," she told him with a heavy sigh.

"I beg your pardon?"

"If you fear removing your clothes will incite my passions, I can assure you, I'm too uncomfortable to contemplate any seduction right now." She glanced his way, and then winked. "It *is* possible to resist your manly appeal, my lord."

He snorted. "You have already done so."

"You are engaged, so I must." Whitney sighed. "It was fun though."

"Fun?"

"How we met."

He scowled at her. "Hardly the right word to describe that

scandalous night."

That night had been one he couldn't forget, despite trying so hard for so long.

Her chin dropped and she turned her face away. "Then how do you describe it?"

He frowned at the uncertainty her question suggested. He eased closer, making sure his breath would not strike her face when he spoke. "Hell."

Whitney laughed softly. "Was that before or after I took away your breeches?"

"Definitely hell afterward."

"And before?"

Her eyes grew wide, vulnerable, as she met his gaze, and he couldn't summon up his former irritation over her hasty departure. Meeting Whitney had been unplanned and definitely a shock to his senses. "Some meetings defy description and are unforgettable," he promised.

He set his bare hand to the curve of her back and traced a circle on the damp material over her spine. Her breath hitched, and he drew back quickly, afraid of what that reaction might lead to next.

Whitney fell silent as she wrung water from her skirts, flashing him a glimpse of her slender legs as she did so. He hadn't seen very much of Whitney the night they'd met, but he wanted to now. Damn it all. He was supposed to have put this woman behind him by now, but nothing he tried had ever managed to purge Whitney from his imagination. Would he ever forget her?

She straightened suddenly and offered her hand. "Friends?"

He'd never had a female friend, only a sister. He wasn't entirely sure he could be a friend to a woman like Whitney and not desire her, but he nodded and shook hands with her. He'd rather have Whitney as an ally than an enemy any day. "I'd like that."

"Why did she call you by your first name?" Whitney asked suddenly.

"I've known Nancy and her husband since I was a boy."

Her brow rose. "Yes, but why does Nancy use your first name when her husband does not?"

He laughed. "First girl I ever kissed," he confessed.

Whitney's face lit up with amusement. "So you've always been drawn to red-haired women?"

"Apparently," he admitted with another laugh. "They tend to cause me trouble though."

"We are never boring," she said, grinning widely.

Nancy Blake returned, arms full of fabric, and Whitney cooed in pleasure. "Dry clothing."

Blake returned too, carrying a blanket.

"Oh, this is so pretty," Whitney gushed as she was presented with Nancy's best blue gown to wear. She glanced at the Blakes and about the chamber. "Now, how are we to do this?"

"Do what?" Everett asked.

"Change my clothes. I'd rather not trudge water inside their home if I can avoid it. Besides, its warmer here by the forge than anywhere inside could ever be."

His mind blanked. Whitney naked in such a setting should not excite him. Even if it did.

Everett swallowed hard. He grew hard, too.

Blake handed him the edge of a blanket, still smirking, and keeping Whitney on the side nearest the fire. He and Blake turned away while the women chattered as Whitney stripped off her wet clothing and donned Nancy's best dress.

He peeked once or twice, catching a glimpse of pale skin and one luscious breast as she raised her arms high.

"Oh, the material is so deliciously soft against my skin," she said with glowing approval to Nancy. "Thank you so much for the loan of it. I'll have it returned straight away."

"There's no hurry," Nancy promised. "I'll next wear it on Everett's wedding day."

Everett's stomach dropped at the reminder that he had still to prove himself unworthy of Miss Quartermane's hand in marriage. He had to do more than get drunk and fall into water troughs to make that happen, and as he was finally allowed to lower the blanket, he considered what else he might do to speed the end of his engagement.

"Are you not changing?"

"I will be fine as I am."

Although she appeared unconvinced, Whitney did not argue with him about becoming chilled again. She left her soiled gown with Mrs. Blake, acquiescing to Nancy's desire to launder the garment for her. "I'll return for that later in the week, shall I?"

Nancy nodded, stroking her fingers over the fine garment possessively. "It will be ready."

When Whitney said her goodbyes, Everett followed her outside quickly. Perhaps Whitney might have some ideas on how to sabotage his engagement, but then he dismissed his thought immediately. He could not ask her, his newest friend, to help him with this. "I cannot go all the way, but I would like to walk you as far as the boundary fence."

"In case I stumble upon another bull in the field?"

"There is another body of water you could fall into along the way." He grinned and gestured to a narrow trail leading into the woods. "No point another gentleman getting himself drenched, should you catch another man's attention. It's much shorter to go this way than walking the long road."

Whitney agreed, and he led her onto a corner of his land that many of the locals and servants used to reach Twilit Hill from the village. As they passed into the woods, he heard the sounds of a well-sprung carriage traveling through the village behind him. A quick glance revealed the Quartermanes were finally returning to Warstone, and he was glad to have missed them.

He pulled Whitney on when she would have stopped to wave at them, steadfastly turning his back on all he'd thought he'd once wanted.

They stepped into the woods, and at once a sense of peace swept over his skin.

Beside him, a soft gasp left Whitney's lips as she looked around with wide eyes. "How beautiful and peaceful."

She was not afraid; she was enthralled by her surroundings.

He caught her hand and tugged her along at his side.

They didn't have long to be friends. Just a few brief days and then she would be gone. "Tell me more about your trip."

"There's not much more to say."

He frowned. "Will you be traveling with friends?"

"Yes and no. I have engaged a married couple to travel with me. We meet in Dover next week but they come highly recommended. They have made the trip before as companions to an acquaintance of mine. They each know enough language to help ease my way though most countries."

"My sister always wished to travel, and if Miranda had not returned, we would have spent last summer traveling in foreign lands, you know."

"I hadn't heard about that."

"Once Miranda came back, Taverham changed his mind about going, of course, not that I hold his decision against him."

"You must be so disappointed. How did your sister take the news?"

"As badly as you can imagine anyone in love would."

She winced, but then wound her arm through his. "My cousin always promised that he'd travel with me, but when I saw how much in love with Iris he was, I knew he'd change his mind, too, and not join me."

"Love does strange things to people with plans, doesn't it?"

"Yes, indeed it does," she agreed with a soft, sad sigh.

He drew her a little closer, as close as he dared as they passed beneath two towering birch that leaned toward each other, forming an arch. "Here, look at this. There is a local legend that claims that when two unattached people pass through this arch, they will have love and prosperity forevermore. Many carve their initials in them."

Whitney slipped from his grip, glancing up quickly. "Did you bring Alice here?"

He shook his head. "No, and I probably won't. Alice dislikes the woods, and has no room in her heart for myths."

"She's a practical woman."

"Unlike you," he noted.

"I'm practical," she protested.

"Practical isn't the first word that comes to mind when I describe you."

Her eyes widened with what he suspected was fear. "How do you describe me, and to whom?"

"To everyone I meet, I say you are an agreeable young woman with impeccable connections," he promised. "But to myself, I say Whitney Crewe is a woman of remarkable intellect, frighteningly impulsive, and as passionate as the wilderness surrounding my home."

He saw her gulp. Saw her dismiss his honest compliment as

ridiculous flattery, and his heart melted a little more. He should never have been alone with her, but he could not regret that he was finally coming to understand the woman who'd seduced him was not confident in her appeal now. She was not a brazen flirt with everyone, but she had firmly caught his attention, as he had caught hers he suspected, and he wanted more of her than he could let her know.

When he smiled at her, Whitney turned away. "We should go. Miranda will be wondering where I am," she whispered, as she hurried ahead of him toward a fork in the path through the forest. There were many paths to take, and she could easily become lost without his help.

"Then let us not disappoint the marchioness," he said as he ran to catch up with her. He held out his hand, and she reluctantly placed hers in his again. He drew her down the proper path toward Twilit Hill, and not the one that circled back toward the village. "Now, tell me, where are you lodging before you depart on this ship of yours?" he asked, simply for the pleasure of hearing more of her upcoming adventure.

Chapter Eighteen

———◆———

Painting a portrait took time and concentration—the latter of which Whitney had very little today. Her subjects were without fidgets, except for Christopher, who always seemed too full of energy no matter the time of day. His parents were happy together, although the marquess wore the occasional frown sometimes.

Whitney was struggling to bring this family portrait to life and longed for an outside distraction or visitors to put an end to this torture for a little while. There was nothing wrong with the portrait but, for the moment, she couldn't put her finger on what distracted her today.

"Christopher," Miranda murmured out the side of her mouth. "Don't wave your foot about like that."

"Sorry," he said quickly, and his eyes drifted toward the window again.

Whitney had already decided that the boy should be painted looking off toward the window, because he never stopped looking for his friends. Lord Carrington had taken them all off for a long walk this morning while Whitney painted.

She set her paintbrush down. "Perhaps we should take a break. Everyone may stand and move about."

Christopher shot off the chaise he'd been perched on and immediately headed for the French doors that looked over the rear of the property. Miranda followed, warning him not to go far.

Despite the necessity of ending the session, Whitney was disappointed with herself. She had never been so distracted as she was this past week. Perhaps it was the change of location upsetting her focus, but whatever the cause, she had no choice but to return to her work shortly. She'd made a promise, to the family and to herself.

She had to finish this one last painting before she could leave for the continent.

She had promised to meet her traveling companions on a certain day, which would allow them to meet their ship with a day to spare.

She could not understand why she wasn't in the mood to paint. She always painted. In London, there had been a steady stream of new bodies and views to capture. Even in the never-changing countryside around her cousin's estate, Whitney had painted every single day.

She was almost as distracted as Christopher. Her mind far away, beleaguered by images of a man she shouldn't think about.

The marquess approached Whitney. "You're frowning. Is something the matter?"

She did not want to answer that. "So were you."

He grunted. "It's nothing. Did I hear that you returned yesterday wearing the blacksmith's wife's gown?"

"I had an accident with a puddle of water."

His brows rose in surprise but he did not laugh. "And that required you to change clothes?"

"I fell in a horse trough," Whitney confessed, believing confession now was better than trying to hide the truth from him. The details of the encounter with Acton would eventually reach his ears.

The marquess appeared shocked, though. "How did that happen?"

Ah, so he didn't know that Acton had caused it. Not yet, anyway. "An accident. Nothing to worry about. Why are you in a bad mood?"

"As I said, it's nothing of importance."

She did not believe that. "You have been looking toward the windows all morning."

"So have you," he countered.

Whitney turned away as a blush climbed her cheeks. She hastily cleaned her brushes. She'd not realized she'd been looking out the windows, too, but she knew what she'd been searching for outside.

Acton still had not put in an appearance. She had not thought the marquess would banish his oldest friend forever because he'd shown compassion to someone who didn't deserve any.

When Whitney had a problem, she always faced it head-on, head high, and without regret. Today would be no different. She was concerned that this estrangement could go on too long if she didn't speak up. "Why has Lord Acton not called with Miss Quartermane these past few days?"

The marquess' jaw firmed. "I've no idea."

Even now, he would not admit that he had *banished* the earl. "You and I are only children."

The marquess frowned. "What does that have to do with anything?"

Whitney smiled sadly. "Do you ever wonder what it would be like to have a brother or sister to be responsible for? I wanted a family quite desperately when I was young."

Taverham's eyes narrowed. "I didn't."

"You had the advantage of having neighbors, Acton and his sister Emily, to play with, I hear. After my parents died, I lived with my aunts and uncles until their deaths. None of them had children, so it was an adjustment for all of us."

"I'm sorry," he murmured.

"Everyone says that, but I consider myself very lucky," she mused. "Each one of them were different situations. Some of my family were easy to get along with, others more difficult. Aunt Thomasina never let me out of her sight. She smothered me, nearly kept me her prisoner because she was afraid I'd be seduced and ruined, or taken away from her. She lived in fear of everything, I later learned."

"That must have been difficult for you," he said, wincing in sympathy.

"When Aunt Thomasina died, I moved to Uncle Nash's home, and there I had a chance to make some friends." Whitney smiled broadly. "Uncle Nash had a very active social life, and he was very handsome and well informed. But he often secretly entertained female acquaintances after I'd retired for the night. Some of them were married, I'm ashamed to say, and from influential families. He made his living being agreeable, and I loved him regardless. Even though he never intended to, he broadened my knowledge of romantic entanglements and love, quite a bit, let me tell you."

Taverham frowned. "What are you getting at, Trouble?"

"What I am trying to say is that I don't imagine it is easy to turn aside a sibling in need when they are the only family you have left. They will always be a member of your family, even when they are evil to the bone."

Taverham sucked in a sharp breath. "You're talking about that woman?"

"No. I am talking about your friend."

The marquess turned away. "You don't know what he's done."

"Actually, I do," she confessed quietly. "I discovered the lady's whereabouts quite by accident, and I spoke to her to be certain it was her."

The marquess stared. "Do not go near her again."

"That is almost exactly what Acton said, too, but with much more panic and concern in his voice than yours."

"What do you mean?"

"Can you not see that he is terrified?" Whitney shuddered. "Consumption is a horrible way to die."

"You've seen it before?"

She nodded. "My parents."

"I'm sorry."

"I am, too. I knew they would die, everyone said so. Aunt Thomasina came and tried to take me away from them for my own protection. I ran away from her, of course. I walked three miles in the dark, just so I could nurse my parents in the last days of their lives because I loved them."

Taverham lowered his face.

"What he's done is understandable. Reasonable. She's all he has left. He's taken all the precautions he can to protect everyone."

"What precautions?"

"Emily is locked behind a wall. There is a servant with a pitchfork patrolling the grounds to keep the unwary at a safe distance. No one goes in without his permission. Acton seems to wear gloves at all times, he says he bathes after every visit, never wears the same clothes around other people after he's seen her. He acts with more caution than I ever did."

"How do you know so much about him?"

"Artists pay attention to people around them." She laughed softly. "Also, I bullied it out of him, and he couldn't resist me."

Taverham chuckled, too. "That would be a first. He's usually much more inscrutable."

"You underestimate my skills at uncovering secrets." She licked her lips, thinking of the man again. "He probably didn't want to tell you because he imagined you couldn't possibly care what became of her after all she's done. I can understand your anger with her may never end, but why punish *him* for something he cannot change? Will you truly turn away from a lifelong friend in his time of need?"

"You don't understand." He checked the room. Miranda and Christopher were on the far side of the room still. "Christopher barely trusts Acton as it is. I don't want to make things worse between them. And there is Miranda's health to consider. I cannot lose them."

"Then explain the reasons you sent him away, but please clear the air so he knows you don't hate him. It doesn't even have to be in words. Invite him riding or ask his opinion. You told him to leave and he went…and hasn't returned, has he? Did you mean forever?"

Taverham's eyes widened. "No, of course not."

"But he's done exactly as you asked and expects nothing more." She had an idea. "If you are so worried about the risk to Miranda and Christopher, invite Acton to luncheon in the open gardens, where there can be no danger to anyone else."

The marquess fell silent for a long while. Eventually he nodded. "That is actually a good idea. We'll have a party tomorrow when the other guests arrive. The children can come and go at will and be as noisy as they like. Thank you, Whitney. I know you don't care for the man, but you've a great heart and courage to speak up."

Whitney sighed. She might like Everett more if he wasn't marrying someone else. "We can continue with the portrait later today when you have time."

When Taverham announced the idea of an outdoor luncheon to his wife and son, the pair were greatly enthused and they all went away. Whitney straightened up the room, repositioned pillows on the long chaise the family had been sitting on. She returned to cleaning her paintbrushes on Lord Acton's breeches, covered the canvas from idle viewing, and tried not to think about what might happen tomorrow.

Lord Acton was full of unexpected surprises lately. He had made her feel quite good about herself. They were friends now, and Whitney always took good care of her friends.

Whitney had a lot of male acquaintances, but her friendship with Lord Acton felt different. But then again, she'd not almost shared a bed with any of the others.

That made her reasons for offering friendship with Acton complicated. She liked looking at him. She liked talking to him, but his impending marriage cast a pall over every conversation. He was making a mistake marrying Miss Quartermane. Couldn't he see the woman was wrong for him?

Alice only cared about being a countess. Gaining a title and the distinction that came with it for her family had always been her goal. She didn't even like or want children, which was of course a common reason any man took a wife.

Whitney had trouble believing now that Acton only wanted a wife for the size of her dowry, but there was every chance she didn't know him as well as she believed. He was quite introspective here in the countryside, and kinder to those with less distinction than he seemed to be when in London.

His friendship with the Blakes, a rough-looking blacksmith and his hotheaded wife, was proof of his good heart. He deserved more.

Chapter Nineteen

---◆---

Everett spread the map of the continent across his desk and traced the journey from England to Florence with his fingertip. So far to go for a woman alone with two strangers for protection.

Emily had initially been nervous about leaving London society behind at first, but had quickly changed her mind as they'd made firmer plans that included Taverham.

His new friend Whitney Crewe was boldly enthusiastic, and seemed to take the potential challenges she might face in her stride.

At least for now. Who knows what might happen to her?

He rooted around in the trunk, rediscovering all he'd once packed in readiness for a similar journey. Compass, letters of introduction, money hidden away everywhere he could think of. If Miranda had not come back to her husband, he would be on the continent right now—drinking wine in foreign taverns, sleeping under different stars, seeing a world beyond England's shores, like many of his friends had already done in their youth. Like Taverham, he'd inherited the family estate as a young man and, with no brother to succeed him, he'd lived a dutiful life in the countryside.

Until now, he'd accepted that such a trip would be denied him forever.

But what if it wasn't?

He shook his head, dismissing the idea as fantasy, and packed everything away, slid the sea chest back under his desk and dropped into his chair. Perhaps he could consider traveling one day, but when that might be possible, he didn't know. There were too many uncertainties in his future to make any plans for himself.

There was Emily to care for.

And perhaps Alice Quartermane to marry still.

A tap at his door broke him from his brooding. "Come," he called.

Thompson stepped into the room, a hesitant smile on his lips. "May I interrupt?"

"Certainly," he promised, gesturing the man inside. "What can I help you with?"

"The repairs are finished," Thompson stated as he shut the door.

"Excellent," he exclaimed. "I must confess, I had a look early this morning and thought it must be almost done. Congratulations."

"So that's everything."

Everett smiled. Not everything. He had a proposition to discuss now. "Sit down, Thompson."

Thompson did, and looked at him expectantly.

"We've been friends for a long time and it pains me that you're in this situation, but I would like to offer you a position."

Thompson's brows rose. "Employment?"

"Indeed. Warstone could use a man who knows how to get things done."

"Such as?" Thompson regarded him warily.

"Improvements, estate management, and the like. Duties of a steward. The position comes with a generous income and a newly repaired cottage to live in rent-free."

"Why would you want me for your steward? I know nothing of managing an estate. My father—"

"Your father is a fool to not see your potential. Your work on the cottage is proof of that. Everything ran smoothly and ahead of schedule. You are a man who knows how to make things happen. I know your finances right now do not allow much room for ambition, but one day, perhaps not too far away, things might be different. I want you to remain at Warstone and learn the ropes of managing an estate such as this."

"Because you'll be too busy being a doting lapdog while your wife shops in London," Thompson smirked.

Everett shifted in his chair, uncomfortable with the suggestion. He'd already escorted Alice to the shops a few times in London and had found it the most boring of pastimes. "I'm offering you a chance to discover your strengths and to make something of yourself one day. Here, you will be far away from your father's criticisms and your brother's scorn."

Thompson said nothing to that, but Everett was certain his friend was giving the matter serious consideration. Allowing Thompson to return to his family, begging for scraps, was unthinkable to him. "The matter of your employment could remain between us and my servants, if you like."

"You would let me pretend?"

"Yes," he said firmly. Taking a position as his steward could cost Thompson more of his standing in society, and he had precious little left. Thompson must find an honest way to support himself soon. His father had cut him off without a penny, and the burden of living on the charity of others must be wearing him down.

"I'll do it," Thompson said, looking him in the eye, shoulders and back straightening. "I'd be proud to have anyone know that I worked for you."

Everett grinned. Thompson was a brave man. "Excellent. Shall we discuss your duties?"

Thompson nodded. "I have some ideas for improvements, too."

"I rather thought you might have something extra up your sleeve after your weeks here."

"Rose Cottage?" Thompson asked.

"Is not to be touched or discussed," he said quickly.

Thompson nodded slowly. "As you wish."

"Now, what I want from you is—"

A rapid knock sounded on the door before he got any further.

"Yes, what is it?" he called.

The Quartermanes' maid edged into the room. "Miss Quartermane is ready to go calling."

"Please wish her a pleasant outing," he told the woman

immediately.

He would not go. Alice only wished to visit the Taverhams, where he was not invited anymore.

He shooed the woman out of the room when she lingered. "Off you go. I am very busy today."

The woman backed out of the room reluctantly, worrying her lower lip.

"Now, where were we," he said to Thompson. "Firstly, we need to hire loggers to cut wood for the coming winter months. Speak to Blake in the village first. He'll round up some local lads to assist, who'll take payment in lumber or coin. The head gardener can provide an estimate of what must be cut for the estate."

Thompson nodded, quickly making notes in his pocketbook.

"Now about the cattle. The bull was put to the herd, so there is nothing to be done now but wait for the inevitable outcome. About nine to ten months for that. You'll find several books in the library you can use as a reference. After that—"

Another knock sounded, and he gritted his teeth before answering. "What is it now!"

He scowled as the door opened and Mr. Quartermane stepped into the room, hat in hand. "Good morning, my lord."

"Mr. Quartermane." He'd been avoiding the man all morning and was not happy to see him.

"I was sent to fetch you for our outing," he stated, looking about the room curiously.

"I told your maid that I was busy right now," he told the man, wishing Quartermane would hurry up and go.

Unfortunately, Quartermane was a man of many words when it was a subject he liked. "We could wait a few moments, or I'm sure Mr. Thompson wouldn't mind returning later."

"Yes, of course," Thompson agreed, standing.

Everett didn't care for that. If he was going to wriggle free of the parson's noose, he'd better escalate his belligerence. He gestured Thompson down again as he stood and rounded the desk to face the interloper. "This matter will take most of the day to sort out."

"Is something wrong?"

"Nothing is wrong. I merely have much work to do."

"Perhaps I could be of help," Quartermane offered, smiling with an enthusiasm Everett did not share. "I know a fair bit about the trading of cattle and such."

He regarded his future father-in-law with growing annoyance. Everett had been managing Warstone for a decade, and before that, his father had included him in every major decision for the estate. He wasn't a young man wet behind the ears. He didn't need or want Quartermane's advice on how to make his herd more profitable. He wanted Thompson to learn from him. "As do I," he insisted. "Have an enjoyable outing with your family, sir."

"We're to visit Twilit Hill," Quartermane murmured, finally appearing annoyed with him.

"Give my best to the family." Everett smiled tightly, determined not to give any ground on the matter. Quartermane had approved of him, and to be free before the wedding day, the man would have to disapprove of him.

Quartermane finally took his leave, casting a disgruntled glare over his shoulder. Everett walked to the door after he'd gone and locked it decisively to keep out any further interrupters.

He turned back to Thompson to find his friend grinning. "Not one for calls this week?"

Everett shook his head. "The first rule in working for me is for you to ignore every one of Quartermane's suggestions," he told Thompson.

"Good," he agreed. Thompson's grin widened. "I don't envy you your future with *him* in the family. He's a bit of a braggart, isn't he?"

"Indeed, and much too free with his advice for my taste. For the record, should the subject ever be raised to you, I would never countenance a large-scale logging on the estate. That is something Quartermane has yet to accept."

"Right you are," Thompson agreed. "I suppose you hardly need the blunt anyway now," Thompson teased with just the faintest hint of envy.

Thompson knew little of the costs associated with maintaining an estate yet, but he soon would if Everett had his way. "My coffers are not endless, man. Economy and good management are essential for any estate to thrive."

Thompson shifted nervously. "My father throws money

around and makes everyone else worry about the details."

Thompson's father was rumored to leave his eldest son a nightmare of debt when he passed. "I am not like that, and I am also not in debt like your father, or ever plan to be," he promised. "I'll teach you how to avoid it, too."

Thompson sat up straighter. "Trees, cows. Careful spending. What else?"

"Tenants," he said, and then summarized his suspicions for future repairs needed. "An inspection is required before winter."

Thompson nodded enthusiastically. "I can start on that today as I introduce myself as your man here, and make notes of their concerns as I go."

"That is a very good place to start." It was a relief to have someone to talk to again. Someone who had no personal agenda where the estate was concerned. Thompson was a personable fellow. The men he'd employed for the cottage repairs had seemed to like and respect him. That too was essential for the efficient running of an estate.

When they were done, Everett took Thompson with him to explain the changes to his butler and housekeeper. And then escorted him to his new lodgings, the cottage he'd worked tirelessly on for weeks.

Chapter Twenty

---◆---

The sounds of a carriage arriving reached Whitney's ears, but she refused to go and look out to the drive. It would probably be Miss Quartermane and her parents calling again, casting pitying eyes on her because she was a spinster and firmly on the shelf. She needed a moment to prepare for that conversation again.

Whitney had *chosen* not to marry in the pursuit of her dream, because if she married, she feared she'd never be able to travel. A husband could prevent her leaving and using her own money. A husband would want a family. A son.

If Whitney ever married, had a child and gave up her dream, she feared she would grow to resent her husband and child because she felt unfulfilled.

Whitney refused to martyr herself.

If she married at all, then it would be after her dreams had come true first. Few understood. Miss Quartermane always dismissed her desire to improve herself as inconsequential.

"So this is where you are hiding," a stern voice complained suddenly.

Whitney spun about at the hail. "Exeter! What the devil are you doing so far from London?"

"Tagging along with my nephew's family." The Duke of Exeter strolled into the room. He seemed a bit crumpled but grinned nonetheless. Dear Lord, he was an appealing devil to look at. Tall, slender, and handsome, but he was also very easy to talk to, despite his lofty title.

"Miss Crewe," he said formally.

Whitney curtsied. "Your Grace."

They both laughed.

Whitney was glad of the distraction. Exeter was fun. He had never taken her teasing seriously. She narrowed her eyes. "Are you running away from your horde of admirers, or is it that you couldn't bear to let the twins out of your sight again?"

"You know me too well." He chuckled. "Twins are always a handful. How are you, Trouble?"

"Quite well," she promised him.

Exeter drew close and peered into her eyes, then shook his head. "Say that again and mean it this time."

Whitney laughed awkwardly and dropped her gaze. "You know me too well, too. But I don't want to talk about it, if you don't mind."

For a moment, she thought he might argue, try to get to the bottom of her troubled thoughts. He was a frightfully observant man, and very kind, despite or because of his exalted rank and vast wealth. Thankfully, he let the matter drop with his next words. "Come and show me about this gigantic pile of rubble. It's been a while since I've visited Twilit Hill."

Whitney finished tidying up, removed her paint smock and led Exeter back the way he must have come, into the heart of the house. "Tell me the news of London."

"Oh, much the same." He talked of mutual acquaintances as they moved toward the study. Whitney led him to the whiskey and poured him a glass herself without calling for a servant to do it. They would be busy elsewhere in the house, settling the new guests most likely.

"To ease the ache travel brings," she murmured as she slid a full glass toward him.

"Are you suggesting I'm getting old and infirm?" he protested, but took up the glass anyway.

"You *are* old," the Marquess of Ettington announced as he joined them. He rubbed his hands together. "I thought I heard whiskey calling my name. May I?"

"Of course." Whitney poured another glass for Lord Ettington and handed it over. She knew these men well. They were just like her cousin, too. They were good to be around, safe and easy to tease. "It's good to see you, too."

"It is nice to see you, Trouble," Ettington promised. "How is the work of making Taverham appear regal going?"

She laughed. "Very well, indeed. I'm surprised to see you here."

The marquess sipped his drink. "Didn't Taverham tell you to expect us?"

"Not at all. He mentioned the Carringtons the day before they arrived, but had not named anyone else."

"Perhaps he wanted to surprise you with the arrival of your great admirer," Ettington chuckled.

Whitney blinked. "My admirer?"

Ettington glanced between herself and Exeter, one brow raised.

"Nephew," Exeter growled. "That's enough nonsense."

"Is it? You only agreed to accompany us after you learned Miss Crewe was here."

"He's following the twins," Whitney joked, but she felt just a tiny bit uncomfortable. She liked Exeter, but not romantically. "And he knows I have no interest in matrimony, as everyone should by now."

The duke nodded, eyes alight. "Which makes Miss Crewe the safest female acquaintance to have at a country house party. Plus, there's never a dull moment with Trouble around."

"Now that is high praise, coming from you." Ettington shook his head and stepped back.

The duke took a mock swing at his nephew and the marquess backed all the way out of the room with his hands raised in surrender. "I'll leave you to it."

When he was gone, an uncomfortable silence settled between her and Exeter.

After a moment, the duke cleared his throat. "I regret I ever listened to my sister and encouraged that boy to talk."

Whitney grinned. "Duly noted."

"He's wrong, you know." Exeter sighed. "I just enjoy being myself with you."

"So do I," she assured the duke. After a moment, she decided it wasn't too early to take a drink herself. Just one before the ladies returned downstairs. She was about to pour a glass when Exeter took the decanter of sherry from beneath her fingers and did the honors.

"So, tell me," he murmured. "Who is he?"

"Who?"

"Ettington would say he's my competition."

"Ettington would be mistaken," Whitney advised as she took her first sip.

"I've seen that expression on your face far too often these past months. Who is the man who claimed your heart but makes you sad when you think of him?"

She shook her head, staring into her glass. "It's not like that."

"Well, it damn well should be if there is any justice in the world," he complained loudly.

"Exeter! What's gotten into you?"

He scowled fiercely. "I tell you now if you have a chance to claim the one you love, do not hesitate. Do whatever it takes, break every rule to be happy."

"I *am* happy," she promised. She looked up into the duke's face and frowned. "Did you lose someone you loved once?"

"No. I don't know. Perhaps?" He shook his head. "And that, my dear, the unknown, is the worst of it at my age. I might have been in love once, but now I'm not sure it isn't just my advanced years convincing me I might have missed something important in my life."

"I'm sorry," she whispered.

He snorted. "Don't pity me. I've had a damn fine life. And make sure you never pity yourself, either," he exclaimed. "You deserve to be loved for exactly who you are. You are remarkable."

"Exeter!" She fluttered her lashes at the compliment. "Such ardent adoration will give me unreasonable expectations."

"Only if I was twenty years younger, perhaps," he warned. "I'm much too old for someone of your tender years."

Whitney laughed heartily. "You don't seem that old to me."

He studied her a moment, but thankfully let the subject of love drop in favor of talk of mutual acquaintances and the latest scandals making the rounds of the *ton* until the ladies joined them.

After that, Taverham's guests—Exeter, Lord and Lady

Ettington, the Carringtons and a few other couples—settled into a cozy chat until dinner was announced.

But through it all, Whitney couldn't forget what the duke had suggested to her about chasing love. She'd not truly tried to win a man she admired for herself. She'd given way where Lord Acton was concerned, allowed him to go ahead with his ridiculous plan to choose another to marry.

But that spark of desire still burned hot between them, and she wondered about it more and more. She saw yearning in Acton's eyes, eagerness swiftly followed by regret. Was there more between them than desire? Could there be? Did she dare find out before it was too late?

She was leaving the country, and she'd warned him she might never return. What might happen if she gave in to the pull toward him and actually chased a man?

Would Acton run away? Continue the engagement with Miss Quartermane, a woman he'd claimed to have never kissed? And if Whitney were brave enough to take a chance on loving him, would he grant her every wish she'd ever had and consider joining her on her adventures?

She had no answers, but time was certainly running out to decide if she should find out.

Chapter Twenty-One

Everett dismounted on the drive of Twilit Hill and handed his horse off to a waiting groom. The sun was at its highest in the sky, only a soft breeze blew against his face, so it seemed like a good day for a party.

He had been surprised by the tone of Taverham's invitation to luncheon. The marquess had been quite insistent that he must come today, and that was not like him.

So here he was…but uneasy about the summons.

He did not know what sort of reception he'd face, and hoped he wasn't about to be lambasted over Emily in front of everyone.

He dawdled toward his carriage and was not in time to help anyone out on purpose. Mr. Quartermane took his wife and daughter on each arm anyway, so all that was left for Everett to do was lead the way around the house toward the sounds of laughter with Thompson at his side.

Making it clear his interest had waned in the Quartermane's daughter was a frustrating process. He'd deliberately missed sharing the breakfast room with her father this morning again, cursed within Mrs. Quartermane's hearing, and been less than attentive to Miss Quartermane.

Instead of listening to the woman drone on about her season, he'd sat about with a silly grin on his face, remembering the pleasant hour he'd stolen with Whitney Crewe the other day.

His decision to ride to the Taverham estate today had been an unpopular choice with the Quartermanes, but he'd claimed a problem to fix first and sent them off ahead of him with Thompson. He'd caught up with them halfway along the Twilit Hill drive.

He strode ahead of them now without looking back, and immediately saw the scene had irrevocably changed since his last visit.

The rose garden Emily had loved and tended for the past decade was gone as if it had never existed. Even the paths and garden borders had been torn up. Soon, Emily would be no more, and all that would remain was her legacy of pain that he hoped would fade in time, too.

Beyond the barren patch of earth, a collection of tables and chairs had been assembled and a party atmosphere prevailed. The Carrington children ran about between tables and people, squealing their heads off. And there seemed to be a number of additions he'd not known were coming.

The Marquess of Ettington and his wife were standing together under the sun.

"Oh dear! Oh my," Miss Quartermane exclaimed, primping her hair suddenly when she spotted the newcomers. "Exeter has come."

Everett saw the duke across the lawn and nodded politely to him. He did not know Exeter well, but the duke had been much around Whitney this past month. "So it seems."

He glanced behind him, noted mother and daughter had turned to each other and were each inspecting the other's gown for flaws. "That will have to do, my dear. You look lovely," Mrs. Quartermane whispered to her daughter.

Three children raced past, waving at Everett.

"I hope it will be quieter when the children are sent inside for the luncheon," Mrs. Quartermane whispered again as she clung to her daughter's arm and boldly strode to the fore.

He noted the smaller tables and chairs from the nursery had been unearthed and were set behind the larger table, and places had been set for everyone on them. "I think they might be staying out here with us for luncheon," he warned, searching for one face in the crowd. His new friend seemed to be absent, and keen disappointment caught him by surprise.

He scanned the group again, catching a flash of familiar red hair lower down. He moved toward Whitney Crewe, discovering her seated with a very young child bouncing on her knee. Dressed in pink as usual, she appeared breathtakingly fresh and lively.

She looked up into his eyes and his worries fell away. He smiled. "Miss Crewe."

"Ah, you're here at last, my lord."

Their eyes held a long moment, but then Whitney turned her attention on Miss Quartermane, who had suddenly appeared at his side and claimed Everett's arm.

"It is so good to see you again, Miss Crewe," Alice exclaimed, as if they'd not seen each other every day for the last week.

"Miss Quartermane," Whitney murmured, her smile slipping as she bounced the dark-haired child on her knee. "You must come and hold Ettington's son. This adorable young fellow is Garret. His twin, Georgiana, is delightful, too, but I think she's been taken off somewhere else."

Miss Quartermane approached, seating herself primly on the edge of a chair next to Whitney. The contrast between the two women was remarkable. They were as night and day.

"He looks a sturdy lad," he said to Whitney.

Whitney tickled the child again, who bent his face to Whitney's fingers as if he wanted them in his mouth. The boy persisted, and Everett shuddered that young Garret appeared to be drooling. "Is that normal," he asked, knowing very little of children except that one day he'd need a son of his own.

"Of course," Whitney promised. "I suspect he's growing his teeth."

"Ah, well. You must know more than I do."

Miss Quartermane leaned closer to the child, suddenly vying for Garret's attention, but the boy cuddled up to Whitney's creamy white shoulder and hid from her.

Whitney's smile widened as the boy appeared to put his obviously wet lips and chin on her bare skin. "He's adorable. Would you like to hold him?"

Miss Quartermane stared at the damp spot on Whitney's skin, and lifted her hands to her own neck protectively. "Perhaps later. My lord, do you…"

Everett tuned her out, directing his attention over her head.

"Where is Taverham today?"

"Not far," Whitney murmured, a half smile lifting her lips as she resettled the child to face everyone else.

Damn, she had a pretty smile.

The appeal of the child was soon forgotten by Miss Quartermane in favor of gossiping about the Ettington's and Exeter's unexpected arrival. "I had no idea they were coming," Whitney promised Alice. "But I am glad they have."

"I am too," Alice whispered quickly as the Duke of Exeter approached the pair. Whitney immediately passed the boy to his great uncle and the trio were soon laughing together, all attention on the child and his attempts to draw the duke's fingers into his mouth.

A firm hand settled on his shoulder. "You caught me by surprise the other day," Taverham murmured.

"I apologized."

Everett moved back a step to keep Taverham at a safer distance.

"You shouldn't have needed to. No matter what she did, she's still family."

"My family," he clarified, and glanced around, feeling decidedly uncomfortable in this garden. He would normally have greeted everyone, joining in where he could and laughing with them. However, no matter what Whitney claimed, he believed himself a risk to others.

He looked for her quickly but she was already gone. He craned his neck and spotted Whitney, the duke and Alice walking toward the house together. Mrs. Quartermane soon scurried after them, too.

Most women coveted Exeter's attention, no matter their age. Exeter's title and wealth were a definite lure, but the man had steadfastly resisted matrimony. Some said Exeter had developed an interest in Whitney but Everett could not credit it.

He tracked Whitney as far as the doorway to her studio, and then they all disappeared inside together. "I did not expect to see so many of your friends today."

Taverham moved to stand beside him. "It's quite a change, isn't it? Having so many people around? A year ago, the only noise around here was the tap of mother's cane upon the marble floors."

And Emily singing. He glanced away swiftly as pain flared in his chest. "Did the dowager come?"

"No, not even Exeter's arrival stirred her from the dower house. It's not often he travels but she refuses to eat out of doors still. She did promise to make an appearance later."

He snorted. "So generous."

"None the less, I'm pleased with events. Without her stern looks, the children will not need to be shushed so much," Taverham promised.

Everett laughed. "The dowager was the same way when you were young. Do you remember? Noise of any sort wasn't ever tolerated, except for Emily's music."

"Christopher gets away with doing what he wants, though. He's somehow managed to wrap the old duck around his finger."

"I'm glad for his sake."

"So am I. I want him to feel safe here. I want him to feel at home and know everyone here wishes him well." Taverham sighed. "You look tired. How is she?"

"Fevered again last night. They sent for me at nine."

"Does that happen often?"

"More often than I care for."

Taverham fell silent, and so did Everett. He was weary to the bone but glad that he'd come. He disliked being at odds with Taverham, his oldest friend. When Emily was gone, he'd have no one else to discuss the past with.

Taverham's son and another child ran up to the marquess, and Everett moved back a discreet step to give the children room to pester him.

Christopher dragged his father away, laughing.

Everett felt a tug on his coat and glanced down in surprise. The little girl had lingered, Mabel, he thought her name was, and stared up at him with a wide smile. "Can I sit on your shoulders?"

He shook his head and stepped back.

"She doesn't bite," Whitney murmured as she stepped between them and took the child's hand in hers. "Now Mabel. What did we talk about earlier?"

She bent over to put her face at the height of the girls, presenting Everett with the most awkward and arousing glimpse of her backside he'd ever had.

"You said not to bother Lord Acton today," Mabel said quietly.

"That's right. He works hard at his estate and he's often very tired. There will be races later, and the gentlemen need to gather their strength if you want them to carry you around."

"There are races?" he cut in.

"His Grace suggested it," Whitney told him as she straightened, adjusting her gloves. However, she bent back down to Mabel a moment later. "You should ask the duke to be your pony. Garrett is too little to join in this year, and I don't think anyone has asked him to carry them yet."

"All right." Mabel grinned then skipped off looking for the duke.

"I can't wait to see how he likes her request." Whitney's dark chuckle warmed him all over. "Ah, there he is."

Mabel approached the duke, and the man surprised Everett by kneeling down to talk to the girl. Whitney sighed like a woman in love, and his heart twisted painfully in his chest at the idea he'd misread her interest in the duke. He looked down at his feet. "Will he do it?"

"I would say not. Exeter isn't the running-around type of duke, but he's very good at organizing others to take his place. See, he's conscripted a footman to be her pony already." She threw a smile his way. "You, however, *are* the running-around sort, under normal circumstances."

He spluttered. "Thank you, I think."

"You're very fit," she said before throwing him a sultry smile that warmed his blood. It was hard to miss her meaning when she looked at him that way again. She knew what he looked like beneath his clothes. She had touched him intimately.

"You are more muscular than I thought you'd be too," he whispered.

"I knew you'd peeked at me when I was changing in the smithy," she said in whispered shock, but then lifted her gloved hand to her lips to hide a wicked laugh. "Thank you for being so improper, my lord."

He glanced around quickly, as she licked her lips. He would like to kiss Whitney. He'd had a hard time thinking of anything else since they'd parted company two days ago. "Anytime."

She cleared her throat suddenly. "The races will be held after luncheon, so that will give you time to think up a reason to leave early if you think you should not stay," she told him.

His mood soured at the thought of slinking away. "I would stay if it wasn't for…"

"I know," she added, and then laughed softly. "You would have been such fun to ride, too."

He glanced at Whitney quickly and saw her eyes sparking with devilry. It was the very same glance she'd leveled at him the night they'd met. He felt warm all over, and dug a finger under his cravat for some air.

Whitney chuckled again.

"You are asking for trouble," he warned.

"Oh, no. I *am* Trouble. I am sure I explained that during our very first conversation."

"You probably did, but I confess I might not have been paying attention," he told her. "You had me rather wound up that night."

She hummed. "I had you in hand."

His cock perked up at the memory, and he shifted on his feet and tried to think of something unpleasant to diminish it.

He closed his eyes briefly, realizing this was an attraction he couldn't dismiss as inconsequential. Talking about the past only made him want Whitney more. She was begging to be chased, tossed onto her back and made love to until dawn, and at any other time he might have considered obliging her. But he was still committed to marry a beautiful young woman and had a sister dying of consumption. It was the worst possible time to chase any woman, but he couldn't help thinking that having Whitney in his arms again would do him the world of good. If he caught her…

What might have happened if Whitney had not possessed more morals than him that night? Would he have even bothered to call on Miss Quartermane the next day if he'd kissed Whitney on the night they'd met and learned who she really was?

"Everett," she whispered softly.

He opened his eyes slowly as the answer formed. No, he wouldn't have. He had absolutely pursued and won the wrong woman's hand in marriage if he felt like this still.

They both knew it, too. She'd told him he'd chosen wrong that night.

He met Whitney's stare without bothering to hide the desire that stirred in him. He couldn't have her. Not anymore. He would only bring her disgrace. Yet yearning filled her eyes, too, when she held his gaze. Her hand settled on his arm and squeezed. "What can I do?"

"You cannot help me. Let me go," he whispered, and when her hand slid off his arm, he turned toward his future bride with grim determination to continue his sabotage of their engagement so that he might be free to have Whitney one day in the future.

He joined Alice's conversation easily, hands shoved in his pockets, aware he'd rather be anywhere else. As it happened, the talk he interrupted was of their impending marriage.

Exeter smiled warmly, a child of Ettington's held securely in his arms. "What time is the happy event?"

"Eleven," Alice told the duke.

"Eight," Everett countered, thinking on his feet.

Alice took the correction without batting an eye, but her mother's quick-darted glance promised daggers.

"Oh, so it is," Alice agreed with an awkward little laugh. "How silly am I, to get the time of my own wedding wrong?"

"I'm sure it will be a perfect day," Ettington soothed.

"It will not be perfect without Miss Crewe, but we must make do without her, I'm told," Alice complained.

"Oh," the duke said with a heavy frown. "Where will Miss Crewe be?"

"Oh, haven't you heard?" Miss Quartermane stepped closer to the duke. "Miss Crewe is to travel. Alone, of all things. Perhaps you can persuade her to forget her foolishness, Your Grace."

His bride went into great detail to the duke, outlining Whitney's plans in a way he'd never heard described before. She made Whitney's adventure sound frivolous, and even scandalous.

"She will have paid companions," Everett reminded everyone, rising to defend Whitney. "A married couple familiar with the journey."

"But still, anything could happen to her alone on a ship like that," Mrs. Quartermane warned.

"She is traveling on one of the Fremont ships," Everett

remarked. "They are well known and a well-run operation."

"Indeed, they are," Exeter promised. "I own a stake in that line, so you can rest assured her journey will be uneventful and quite safe. I can guarantee her an uneventful journey."

Everett did hope so, too.

"Do you have many interests in shipping?" Alice asked him as lunch was announced.

"A few," the duke murmured before he wandered off to hand the child he held to a waiting servant.

Alice followed the duke a few steps and Everett turned away from her, pleased her attention was directed elsewhere. His eyes immediately fell on Whitney. She was helping seat the children, who all seemed to want to sit at the larger table instead of the shorter one. Although he longed to join her, assist her, he found himself a chair far from his bride and heaped his plate high. Missing breakfast had made him very hungry.

As all the seats filled, he discovered only one remained beside his.

And Whitney seemed the only one without a chair, by the end.

She joined him with a wry smile. "You saved a spot for me. Thank you."

He looked at the table as a footman placed a jug directly before him, but deposited no others along the table. Curious as to why, he peered inside quickly. It looked like...water?

Water sloshed over the edge as he righted the jug.

Whitney laughed softly. "Careful, my lord, or you'll get wet again," she warned.

"You be careful too, Miss Crewe, or you might become so too."

He could almost swear Whitney moaned softly at that prospect.

Chapter Twenty-Two

Whitney clutched her sides, attempting to stifle her laughter so as not to wake the children resting in the next room. It had been an extremely enjoyable day. The luncheon was long over but not the merriment. Lady Ettington, slightly tipsy, was revealing a whole other side of her husband that most never knew could exist.

"Well, how was I to know he liked me when we argued all the time?" Lady Ettington admonished, as she rocked her daughter gently in her arms. Little Georgiana was slowly falling asleep, despite the hysterical confession her mother had just made about her near-disastrous first season and courtship by the Marquess of Ettington. "He acted with such highhandedness, and I never liked him once he started to act so top lofty. He was quite unbearable to me once."

"I trust he's mended his ways now?" Lady Taverham asked, laughing too.

"Oh, gracious no. He still tells everyone what to do. My husband will never change," the marchioness promised as she handed her daughter over to a maid to take back to the nursery, brushing her fingers over the girl's blonde curls. "But I wouldn't give him up for the world, or our darlings, even if sometimes they try my patience. If not for Sinclair stealing them away so often, I'd never get a moment's peace."

"Sinclair?" Miss Quartermane asked, her face twisting into a frown at the unfamiliar name.

"I meant Exeter," Lady Ettington said gently. "I'm sorry. The duke is quite insistent on informality with me. It may have something to do with casting up my accounts on him last year," she confessed with a look of chagrin.

Another round of laughter swept through the room, but Alice gaped. "You threw up on the Duke of Exeter?"

"Well, I did try not to. He would not listen when I warned him to stay back. I was quite ill for a time when I carried the twins, and he was much too concerned for my welfare. He had no one to blame but himself for putting himself in harm's way. He knows full well that I'm prone to disasters."

That earned more laughter from the ladies and Whitney chuckled softly along with them. Exeter was very obviously a family man, and very forgiving. "There are not many unmarried gentlemen who would put up with that, I suspect," Whitney mused.

"No, there aren't," Lady Ettington agreed. "We are really very lucky. He is simply wonderful with the children. He says my daughter constantly reminds him of his late twin, my husband's mother."

"He should have married," Miranda murmured.

"Perhaps there's still time for him to get around to it," Lady Ettington stated before casting a quick glance about the room. Her gaze lingered on Whitney a moment too long for Whitney's comfort.

Whitney stared back, giving the tiniest shake of her head.

The marchioness tilted her head, a question in her eyes. "I would like to see him settled with someone he likes very much. My husband would, too."

The message couldn't be clearer. If Whitney did like Exeter enough to consider an offer of marriage from the duke, should he ever make one, she'd get no opposition from the Ettingtons.

Unfortunately, Whitney did not consider Exeter in a romantic light, and never had. He merely reminded her of the family, the uncles, she no longer had. He was a comforting presence, and a man she felt safe around. That other people had noted their ease around each other could become awkward if she were to remain in England for much longer, she suspected.

Whitney shook her head a little more firmly again and Lady Ettington sighed. Whitney did not want anyone, least of all the Ettingtons, to assume she was eager to marry.

Lady Ettington slipped from the room. She was gone several minutes, and they sat in silence until she returned with a triumphant smile. "Done."

"Now the babies have gone to sleep, might we please escape outside," Lady Carrington asked with a hopeful expression.

"The older children have gone to the stables with the marquess," Whitney reminded everyone. "Perhaps we could walk in the direction of the dower house instead."

"Yes, let's call on the dowager," Lady Ettington exclaimed. "I have a question I must ask her for a dear friend."

They made their way downstairs and out into the late afternoon sunshine.

Lady Carrington and Mrs. Quartermane led the way, strolling easily together and discussing the manner of raising children. Whitney was glad to be spared that conversation. Mrs. Quartermane always seemed to end her statements about motherhood by looking directly at her. It was unnerving how the woman had singled her out as if she had the right to tell her what to do. Whitney did not disapprove of marriages that were made for the right reasons, or of children. But saying so out loud would bring unwanted attention and her feelings about Miss Quartermane's impending marriage might become exposed, when she'd always done her best to hide her disapproval from her friend.

Miss Quartermane attached herself to Lady Ettington's side, coaxing her into discussing the delights of her new country home and married life. "Have you known the duke long?" Alice asked of Lady Ettington.

"Since I was a girl," the marchioness said with a smile, and began to extol his virtues in great detail.

That was another discussion Whitney was pleased not to be involved in. Married life, being beholden to a man, was not in her future. Learning more of Exeter wasn't a good idea at this juncture, either.

Miranda seemed slower on her feet today, and not inclined to participate in either discussion, so Whitney happily remained at her side. They wandered along in pleasant silence for a while, glancing about them at the beautiful Twilit Hill grounds.

Miranda smiled her way. "She's rather obvious, isn't she?"

"Who? Lady Ettington?"

"No. I was speaking of Miss Quartermane. She's very easily impressed by titles." Miranda gestured to the pair laughing ahead of them. Whitney heard Exeter's name, and frowned that they were still talking of him.

"For all that she is engaged, I fear her interest might easily become diverted if given sufficient encouragement," Miranda asked.

Whitney gaped. "Diverted from Acton? When? How?"

"Don't you see it?"

She stared ahead at Miss Quartermane and saw nothing unusual. Alice behaved much the same in Town as she did now. Happily chatting to anyone she met. Always eager to join a conversation, graciously accepting any man who asked her to stand up with him for a dance. Since the engagement had been announced, Alice had been positively overwhelmed with her increased popularity.

Miranda patted her hand. "You're a good friend, Whitney, and easy to talk to, but I fear Miss Quartermane is not quite the friend you imagine. She's thrived in your company."

"We are friends," Whitney protested.

"New friends only this season, despite the seven years difference in your ages. While other young ladies gather together, she chases after you." Miranda grimaced. "Miss Quartermane's increased popularity is due to you not her engagement to Acton. She had made good use of your connections these past months and sought friendships with many years above her in age. Because of that she has been invited to every event you attend."

Whitney gaped. "So have many women."

"This is deliberate, Whitney." Miranda stopped altogether and faced her. "She copies you and envy's your ease with gentlemen."

"She has Acton."

"She has her eye on more distinguished game," Miranda warned. "Have you really never noticed how Miss Quartermane lights up when Exeter enters the room?"

Whitney laughed, her relief instant. "Many women do that around him. I tease him about his universal appeal constantly."

"And *he* rarely notices anyone but you." Miranda's brow rose, daring her to deny it. "Are you willing to let another woman steal his attention from you."

Whitney frowned. "I don't think of him that way. He knows I don't."

"He does?"

Whitney nodded quickly. "He is only my friend, and he understands that is all we can ever be."

"Speaking of friendships," Miranda murmured as she took Whitney's arm. "You seem to have become Lord Acton's friend somewhat quickly. I thought you disliked him."

"It's not sudden," she protested. "I can see now that he is being kind to you, and that pleases me."

Miranda drew Whitney after the others. "Is that all it is?"

"Of course!" Her eyes widened in alarm. "Why?"

"Because I know another lady who lights up when a certain gentleman arrives at my door, and looks glum when he doesn't show his face for several days." Miranda slowed her steps. "I saw you with him the other day, too. Outside the kitchen garden where the children were playing."

Whitney gulped. "I dumped a pail of water over his head that day. He had quite a lot to say about my impertinence."

"But he wasn't cross." Miranda laughed softly, eyes alight with amusement.

"Well, he was at first, but he proved he has a sense of fun by the end of our conversation." Whitney glanced ahead quickly, her face flaming. "We should catch up with the other ladies."

Miranda stopped her, her expression troubled. "Just remember that no matter what you might think could happen, he's an engaged man. I don't want you to be hurt by setting your cap for the wrong man. Your cousin would never forgive me if I didn't do all I could to protect you."

"There is absolutely nothing to protect me from," Whitney insisted. Acton was engaged, but he might be attracted to her still because of the nature of their history. "Acton is marrying, and I am leaving the country. Most likely we will never meet again after this week. You worry for nothing."

"It is in my nature to worry. I was married for my dowry and thought for a long time that I would never be happy," Miranda murmured. "You know how well that turned out for me."

"But Taverham loved you then, and loves you still. Very obviously, too."

"Does Acton love her?" Miranda shrugged and jerked her chin toward Miss Quartermane. "I wonder sometimes if he has made a mistake there. They are so painfully formal with each other."

Whitney gritted her teeth. "I don't wonder. But as you once said, it is none of our business what he does."

"True." Miranda hugged her quickly, and when they reached the dower house garden gate, she winced. "Forgive me for bringing that up. Taverham says I'm imagining his indifference."

She wasn't. Only time would tell if Acton and Alice could turn their arranged marriage into more than the cold alliance it seemed now. She hoped so, for his sake. "Perhaps he has something besides Alice on his mind?"

"What else could be more important than his own marriage?"

Whitney suspected he was often thinking of his sister, worrying quietly how she fared so far away. In that, she couldn't fault his preoccupation, but she couldn't speak of it either to explain. "I'm sure I don't know."

The dowager peeked out the window and Whitney waved. "Shall we join everyone?"

"Into the dragon's den," Miranda murmured, as she waved, too. "Let's hope she's in a better mood today than the last time I visited."

"She will be," Whitney said out the side of her mouth. "I sent her the sketch of Christopher she so admired yesterday—in your name, of course."

Miranda shook her head. "Now who's meddling?"

"Me!" Whitney winked. "Invite her to dinner tonight, too, and seat her beside Exeter. She'll enjoy his company more than anyone's, I suspect."

"I'll try."

The dowager welcomed Miranda with more warmth than Whitney had ever witnessed. She hid a smile as the dowager insisted Miranda accept a glass of cool water and a fan for her hot face. Whitney wanted to cheer. The dowagers stern fussing was quite sweet in its own way. Perhaps all was not lost between the pair. It was most considerate, and for once the pair seemed finally at ease with each other.

Miranda smiled at her mother-in-law after thanking her. "We've missed you at the main house these past few days. Will you do us the honor of joining us for dinner tonight?"

Given everyone's attention was on the Dowager Marchioness of Taverham's answer, the older lady had no choice but to graciously accept the invitation.

Chapter Twenty-Three

---◆---

Everett strode toward his home from the stables, full of grim determination. After the rigors of today's outdoor luncheon, and an exhausting visit with his sister, he didn't have the fortitude to keep up the charade of happiness any longer. All he wanted was to sit down and forget about illness and marriage, not that the two situations had much in common. One led to an ending, one to a beginning, unless he did something to stop the only one he could control.

Unfortunately, he'd not the patience to care whose feeling he would hurt by the confessions he planned to make tonight.

He could not live a lie anymore. Didn't he deserve passion and love, and to give those in return one day?

He hurried through his gardens, past windows flung open to enjoy the cool evening breeze after a hot day, and heard his name mentioned. He paused, head cocked toward an open doorway as he discovered Miss Quartermane was talking of him inside.

"Lord Acton isn't like that," Alice promised. "He would never keep secrets from me."

"Nonsense, my girl. He is a man," her mother argued. "It is hardly a secret that all men appreciate a fine-looking woman. Where does he go at night, I ask you?"

"I don't know what you are talking about," Alice protested. "He is always here."

"Are you sure he's not got some woman tucked away on the estate? My maid tells me he's always riding off alone somewhere."

"He wouldn't do that to me, would he?"

"He shouldn't, but you know the nature of titled gentlemen. Their heads are turned by every pretty face to cross their paths," Mrs. Quartermane said soothingly. "Now, don't trouble yourself about the future, but it is best to go into this marriage with your eyes wide open. Your father, bless his heart, has never strayed into another woman's arms, but he was not a man born to wealth and privilege as Lord Acton is. The lords and ladies of higher society are used to that sort of thing, and you must become accustomed to it, too."

There was silence within. Everett held his breath, waiting, expecting Miss Quartermane to defend his character from such ridiculous slander. He had never imagined taking a wife and a mistress. He had expected, anticipated, desiring his own wife from the very beginning. He wanted what Taverham and Miranda had, a marriage of equals, more than anything.

That he didn't love Alice was the issue. He'd convinced himself that love could be acquired, given enough time and intent. The future he'd ruthlessly pursued was a myth. He wanted more. A lifetime of love or nothing.

"As long as he never embarrasses me, I will overlook it," Miss Quartermane concluded. "I will do my duty as you suggest and not expect more."

He shuddered. Should his love not be worth fighting to claim and keep?

When he thought of love, he imagined laughter.

Long pleasant walks, holding hands, making love in a starlit field on a warm summer's night.

Togetherness.

He smiled at the memory of Whitney Crewe walking beside him through the woods of his estate, fingers entwined with his, smiling and laughing together. If they were married, they could sink to the earth and pledge their hearts and bodies to each other again and again.

Alice's intentions to merely do her duty to their marriage demolished any chance they could have a contented life together. He did not anticipate contentment with her now. He could not get his imagination past her ever being only his houseguest.

That was why he was about to drive an immovable wedge between them and prove he was not worthy of her. She should marry a man who could love her, even if she didn't understand that yet.

Everett made himself known to his guests by stomping into the room. Caught unawares of his approach to the house, both Mrs. Quartermane and Alice appeared startled to see him, and very guilty as they glanced at each other.

"My lord," Alice exclaimed.

He glanced between them and did not smile. "I hadn't considered I'd ever want a wife and mistress both. I had hoped they would be one and the same to me."

Miss Quartermane gulped but quickly recovered. "I apologize if you overheard what should have been a private conversation."

"You are in the drawing room of my home. Many servants of the house pass through this chamber, too. They are not above gossiping." He nodded. "Anything you wanted to know about me, you should have asked me directly."

He moved farther into the room, poured himself a drink, and then took a chair by the open doorway, basking in the swirling breeze and the sounds of the woods just beyond.

"Anything?"

"Anything," he agreed. It was time to clear the air between them once and for all.

Alice bit her lip, and there was clearly something she wanted to ask. After a moment of consideration, she squared her shoulders. "There is a rumor I heard in London. It is said that you caused trouble for Lord and Lady Taverham. That you may have tried to prevent her return to her marriage."

"That is a little stretched, but I certainly distrusted Miranda upon her return. I could not imagine why she would treat my friend so poorly as to abandon her marriage for so long."

"And the boy?"

"Well, of course I distrusted her word that the boy was Taverham's heir. He appeared out of nowhere, fully grown almost."

Her mother latched on to that. "Do you still disbelieve his claim? Was Miranda unfaithful to her husband?"

"Of course not," he protested. "I have the facts now, which Taverham rightly did not share with me in the beginning. I understand Miranda better now, too, and wish her every happiness in her marriage. We are on the way toward being friends, I hope."

"I am glad."

He raised a brow. "Those were questions about other people, though. What do you want to know about *me*? There must be something."

The skin of her face pinked brightly as she wet her lips. "Was it you who lost those breeches at the Fairmont Ball?"

"Yes," he admitted defiantly. "A tryst gone awry."

"A tryst?" Her mouth fell open as she stared at him. "That was the night before we met!"

He shrugged, disguising any shame he might still feel about his state of mind that night with indifference. "I went to the ball, met a lady who captivated me, and the rest you can probably guess."

"A lady?"

"Most definitely a *lady*—of very high principals, too. It was not her intention to embarrass me, I assure you. When she discovered my plans to marry, she rightly scolded me and ran off—accidentally taking my clothing with her."

Mrs. Quartermane covered her daughter's ears. "Have you no shame, discussing such a scandalous subject with an innocent young woman?"

Everett turned his attention to the older woman, noting Miss Quartermane was attempting to escape her mother's censorship. "She asked, and I answered. Do you find honesty offensive, madam?"

"I find your confession most disagreeable indeed," she promised, as Miss Quartermane set herself free at last. "A gentleman should not behave in such a fashion."

"I will not wring my hands and beg forgiveness from a young woman I'd not even met at that time in my life," he exclaimed. "And I would rather get these truths out in the open today, so perhaps you could be quiet and let your daughter speak for herself for once."

He turned his attention back to Miss Quartermane. She had

paled a little at his tirade. "Do you have more questions?"

That earned him a half smile of gratitude. "You said she scolded you. Why?"

"She claimed I was unromantic and something of a scoundrel." And he had been, too.

"For flirting with her when you were to marry?"

"For attending a bachelors ball while knowing I would pursue you for marriage the next day," he corrected.

"Did she know me?" Alice seemed so appalled at that possibility that, from this point on, Everett decided a little discretion was called for. It would save Whitney a world of distress later, should Alice prove to have loose lips.

"No, but I described you. That was enough for her to brand me as a thoroughly unromantic man."

Miss Quartermane sank into a chair. "How exactly did you describe me to the stranger?"

"Well-bred, innocent, and blessed with a generous dowry. Remember, we had not met, and I had only your father's correspondence for my information about you at that time."

She raised her hand to her face, caressing her cheek with the tips of her glove. Her lips lifted in a smile. "How would you describe me now?"

"Well-bred, innocent, and still blessed with a generous dowry. All of that remains true."

Her eyes lifted to his—disappointed. "But?"

He frowned at the woman he'd given his word to make his wife. "But what?"

"You don't love me, do you?"

"Not in the slightest," he informed her. It may be cruel now to be so honest, but he'd rather not be married for his title alone, or chosen based on false assumptions about the state of his heart. "By that token, you don't love me either, I suspect. I asked you once why you agreed to marry me, and your answer was anything but romantic."

Her brow wrinkled, and then she reached for her mother's hand to hold. "I don't love you."

"And we have never so much as shared a kiss, have we?"

"Is that important to you now?" she asked, frowning.

"Not so much now, but it is very telling that I never have. I suspect you have kept your parents close so you did not have to be alone with me."

"That is not true!"

"But that is exactly what has happened. Even this private conversation has been shared with one of your parents. Do you think we might have both made a mistake?"

"You, my lord, have an agreement to marry my daughter," Mrs. Quartermane boomed in a voice too loud and forthright to be ignored.

"I never intended not to keep my word," he said, as he stared at Alice. "I am a gentleman. No matter what I feel, or cannot, I will honor my promise to marry you, Miss Quartermane."

Lack of love on his part was no reason to terminate a contract to marry, and they all knew it. He had no power in this situation unless he wished to suffer Lord Carrington's fate. Being snubbed by society would be uncomfortable, but he'd survive it somehow. Whether or not Miss Quartermane felt that lack of feeling on his part was enough to end their engagement, remained to be seen.

He cleared his throat. "Many couples marry without love and do very well—coming together to make children but living vastly separate lives."

She stared at him.

"You've made it clear over the past weeks that you prefer Town to the country, while I feel the opposite. So, after the wedding, after my heir has been conceived, there is no reason why you cannot live in London as much as you like."

"You don't want me living here?"

"There is a situation I've not felt comfortable discussing with many people as yet, but it cannot wait another day." He glanced at Mrs. Quartermane with an apologetic smile and saw her fanning herself as if she was about to faint. "It concerns my sister."

The older woman breathed a sigh of relief. "Oh yes, Lady Brighthurst. Such a well-regarded lady ought to be here by now. She would never condone your behavior or this scandalous discussion."

Emily was hardly in a position to criticize him after what she'd done.

"You hardly speak of Lady Brighthurst," Miss Quartermane

accused. "When is she due to arrive for the wedding?"

He shook his head firmly. "Unfortunately, my sister has for some time been unwell, and cannot attend."

"I am so sorry to hear that," Alice murmured. "Please convey my hope for a speedy recovery in your next letter to her."

He shook his head again. "Writing is not necessary when Emily lives on the estate, not far from here. I visit her every night, and most days, too, to sit by her bedside and entertain her. She has no notion of current events in my life."

"Every day you sit at her bedside? Why have you never said a word about it?" Alice's eyes widened in shock, and then she stared at him in horror. "What is wrong with Lady Brighthurst that you could not tell us before today?"

He would not discuss Emily's obsessive love for Taverham and the distressing things she threatened to do if ever released from Rose Cottage. He would keep the shame of her madness private forevermore. Only the loyal servants tending her had any idea of her confused state of mind, and of course, Whitney Crewe, had discovered it on her own.

"Emily has consumption."

Miss Quartermane shot to her feet, jerking Mrs. Quartermane up, too. "Consumption?" The pair huddled together. "But...that cannot be right. You said she was eager to meet me."

"I am afraid I did lie to you on that score."

Both Mrs. Quartermane and daughter gaped at him. Only Alice found her voice. "She doesn't know we are to marry, does she?"

"No. Her physician suggested that any sort of emotional upheaval might prove too unsettling and speed her decline." He glanced between his guests, wondering if they were really as afraid as they seemed. "The only way you could ever meet to speak with her is at her sickbed, and even then, I would ask that you not say anything about our marriage."

When he had told Miss Crewe of his sister's situation, he had sensed shock and a brief moment of fear that had quickly faded. Miss Quartermane's reaction was quite different. She looked at him now through narrowed eyes. Accusing eyes. "Are you ashamed to marry me?"

Now that was a ridiculous suggestion. "Of course not. I gave my word and cannot go back on it." He stood and took a step toward the pair, hands outstretched. "Emily suffers in seclusion, and I was told she would not have very long. However, she tenaciously clings to life. I always considered her headstrong, but I do not know how long she has left. I wish to remain at her side until the end comes, and perhaps it would be prudent to delay the wedding until she has passed."

"Weeks of illness?"

"Perhaps longer. I am unsure of when she first began her decline."

"All the time we have been here?" Mrs. Quartermane whispered, blanching and clutching her daughter's hand to her chest as he nodded. "And you have slipped away to visit her every night without ever a warning hint to anyone."

"My staff and tenants nearest the cottage know the situation well enough to keep a distance. Sometimes I have been recalled to her side more than once a day, especially lately, as her fevers grow more frequent. When her temperature rises too high, she becomes confused and needs me to calm her."

Miss Quartermane pulled her mother back one step, and then another, until many yards separated them. "I am very sorry to hear of her situation, my lord, but I cannot..." Her eyes filled with tears, and he saw a decision about their marriage had been made, and made very decisively, even if she would not say so. "My mother is not well, and we simply cannot remain another moment longer."

"Of course," he agreed. Everything about her demeanor reeked of fear. "By all means, retire to consider what the future holds for us. Let your father know I intend to remain in the countryside until the inevitable comes to pass, but I was warned she could be ill for many months more to come. I am afraid we won't have a very jolly start to our marriage, so a delay is probably for the best."

And in that time, he hoped Alice Quartermane would find someone to love. He smiled apologetically, forcing away his anxiety about Emily's uncertain future to deal with Alice. "I will look forward to speaking to you again at dinner."

"Yes, at dinner," Alice agreed, all the while backing her mother from the room as if he were the one suffering from consumption instead of Emily.

He let them go without another word, knowing he had been somewhat heartless to let them think he cared so little about their welfare and that they might have been callously exposed. It was a possibility, but he was confident he'd been careful enough around his guests, and he had not kissed Miss Quartermane at all.

If he had become infected, the only person in the slightest bit of danger was Whitney Crewe. She was the only woman he'd almost kissed recently, and that was after she'd already learned about Emily's situation.

Left to his own devices for the afternoon, he poured himself another drink and sat in Emily's favorite chair by the open window, listening to the birds in the woods and considering the difficult future immediately ahead of him. There would be talk of the delay in their marriage, and unfortunately there was nothing he could do to prevent some of the blame attaching to Alice Quartermane if she eventually released him from their engagement.

It wasn't her fault he couldn't love her.

He was already in love.

The muffled rush of feet upon the upper floorboards proved something of a distraction for the next hour. When the note came, delivered by the Quartermanes' stammering maid, he read it, hopeful of what it might say of his future.

He sighed as he folded the note, and immediately sent word to cook that the formal dinner the Quartermanes had always enjoyed so much could be canceled for tonight. Dinner could be served on a tray for the Quartermanes that night instead.

There was no mention of the marriage, or agreement for the delay he'd asked for.

He was still unfortunately engaged.

Chapter Twenty-Four

Whitney held out her hands to the little girl and spun them around and around until they were both horribly dizzy. Little Mabel laughed and laughed when released.

"Again. Again," she begged as she rushed at Whitney.

"Oh no," Whitney said as she steadied herself against a low wall. "I think that is enough spinning for this morning. I need to sit down a moment."

Mabel hugged her legs tightly. "I want to stay with you."

"Let's find a good spot in the shade, shall we." Whitney smoothed the girl's hair back from her hot face, collected her sketchbook, and looked around the garden. The Taverhams' guests were spread everywhere in the formal gardens. Small groups of people had gathered together, taking advantage of the warm day, fine food, and comfortable chairs strewn about to talk or relax in the perfect weather.

The children ran between them, playing their own games, grasping at crumbs of conversation thrown their way by the adults. But most of the children were more interested in each other than the adults. That was usually the way with children; however, today young Mabel had attached herself to Whitney and refused to be drawn away.

Whitney did not mind the company, but choosing a place slightly away from the other guests was essential. Mabel was something of a chatterbox and was quite often warned to be quieter. Whitney liked her chatter, though. The girl was inquisitive about everything girls usually took no notice of. She had a fine mind that needed stimulation. The child reminded Whitney of herself at that age. Orphaned and eager.

Whitney could draw well enough while the girl prattled on, and preferred privacy anyway to complete her sketches, of which Mabel was one subject.

Tomorrow was the day she would leave her friends behind, and the thought of it made her momentarily sad, a feeling she quickly shook off. It was impossible to achieve her objectives if she allowed timidity or apprehension to slow her down.

They found an empty square of blanket and sank to the ground under the shade of a tree. As soon as they'd chosen their place, a servant hurried over, tray of food, pitcher and two glasses in hand, and offered to bring anything else they required. Whitney requested two pillows—one for her back, and the other for Mabel to rest her head upon should she lie down.

When the man returned, Whitney and Mabel settled in to a generous feast, washed down with Twilit Hill's excellent mulberry wine and water for Mabel.

Mabel all but sat in her lap after they'd eaten in her eagerness to be friendly. "Do you have a daughter?"

Whitney smiled at the question and shifted the girl a bit farther away from her elbow. She set her sketchbook against her knees. "I don't."

"Do you want one? She could be your friend too and you would never be lonely."

Whitney stroked the girl's cheek with the back of her fingers. "I'm not lonely, my dear, but perhaps when I'm older I will want a child."

The girls face fell.

Whitney hugged the girl to her side quickly. Mabel was a pretty little thing with a heart easily disappointed. "I have good reasons. I am not married, for one, and two, I don't have a home."

Mabel gasped. "Are you an orphan?"

"I suppose I am still," she confessed. "My parents died when I was a little older than you. I only have one older cousin, and although he would prefer that I lived with him, I wish to travel."

"Where is your cousin?"

"He is at home with his wife and daughter, I imagine."

"Did they leave you behind because you were bad?"

"No, she is very good indeed," Exeter answered before she could.

Whitney looked up at the Duke of Exeter, who had wandered in their direction. He was grinning down on them, obviously very amused with himself today, judging by that smile.

"We parted ways in London when I came to visit Lady Taverham. After this visit is over, I'm off to see the world."

Exeter surprised her by sitting on the other side of the blanket, stretching out in front of them. "She's very brave," he told Mabel before winking. "Most ladies are not as adventurous as our Miss Crewe."

"Thank you," she murmured, feeling slightly uncomfortable with the compliment. She thought she was brave sometimes, too, but it was the "our Miss Crewe" that made her nervous. She was her own person. She answered to no man, or woman for that matter. She made her own way, paid her own bills now, and would decide the course of her life without interference.

Mabel, eager to act as hostess, offered the duke the platter. There were only a few little bits left to tempt him. "Are you hungry?"

"I could be persuaded to eat." He selected a piece of cheese and ham and thanked the girl.

Whitney turned the page and made a few small adjustments to a sketch she'd started of the duke earlier in the week. She had not quite captured the warmth in his expression well enough in her opinion.

Mabel returned to her side. "I think Whitney should get married," she exclaimed.

The duke chuckled. "Do you now?"

"Yes, and then she could have a daughter. She could look after you, too."

The duke appeared to be highly amused, given the way he pressed his lips together and his eyes sparkled with mirth. Whitney hurriedly tried to capture his emotions on the page. She almost had his image perfect when he spoke again.

"What do you say, Miss Crewe? Is she right? Should I marry?"

Whitney had only been listening with half an ear, and frowned at him. "Hmm, you could if that is what you wish for. Just make sure to ask the right woman."

Mabel pushed the tray under his nose. "I would look after you. I'd be the best daughter ever."

Whitney's breath caught at the plea in the little girl's voice, and she set her sketch aside. "Darling, of course you would, but you are a daughter already. Lord and Lady Carrington love you very much, and I don't think they could part with you for any reason."

The girl's eyes filled with tears, and then she crumpled against Whitney's side. "They don't want me anymore," she whispered.

"Why do you say that?"

"They're always talking about having too many children underfoot."

Whitney hugged the girl. "They do not mean it that way. But you must remember it takes a lot of work to support a large family. Everyone must help each other," she reminded her.

"And we must be quiet," Mabel whispered.

Clearly the girl had heard that request a lot lately and taken it to heart. Whitney remembered what the fear of being discarded had felt like too well. Her aunt Ester had abhorred noise of any sort, and Whitney had not been a quiet child, either. "Quiet, but not utterly silent."

"Mabel," Lady Carrington called. "Come over here for cake, sweetheart."

"See, you are wanted. She made sure you would not miss out," Whitney pointed out.

"I'll be back," Mabel promised without a backward glance, and then sped across the grounds to join the line of waiting children.

"Goodness, she's fast on her feet," Whitney exclaimed.

She smiled as the child was moved into her place in the line— by age, if Whitney was not mistaken—and waved back at her.

Whitney returned her attention to her sketches, checking each one off. The portrait for Lady Ettington was done and could be given away tonight, as could the one she'd just completed of the duke. She turned the page and found herself looking into Lord Acton's eyes.

She was slightly ashamed of having drawn him again after promising that she never would. She couldn't seem to help herself; no matter the time of day or night, the dratted man was always in her thoughts. Even when he was with Miss Quartermane, she could not forget the weight of his hand covering hers, or wrapped around her waist as they rode together. It was not right and it was not fair. If only she could have liked someone else, she might not be in such an uncomfortable position.

Whitney covered Lord Acton's face with another page.

Exeter sat up suddenly, glancing around, and so did Whitney. Many of the guests appeared to be rushing away, most returning indoors with the children. She glanced up at the sky, noting there were still enough hours left to enjoy the countryside before darkness fell.

As far as she knew, there were no entertainments planned for that evening, so she could not understand why everyone was leaving.

"I wonder where everyone is going in such a hurry," she mused, unwilling to follow them.

"I've no idea, but I am glad." Exeter cleared his throat. "Do you really think it's not too late for me to marry at my age?"

"You're not old, Exeter, you are merely well seasoned."

"Seasoned? That isn't complimentary."

She smiled, turning her pages. Yes, her work was complete on all but the family portrait for Lady Taverham. "On the contrary. Older timber burns hotter than greenwood."

He laughed. "Then I will take that as a compliment after all."

"You should. You are very handsome."

"Do you think so?"

"Everyone says so."

"I meant you."

She looked at him more closely. "Your face is very pleasing to look at. Beyond that I will say no more, because I am sure you've heard it all before from your slavish admirers."

"Slavish?" He frowned. "You make it sound as if they are mindless imbeciles."

"Some of the more eloquent ones are. Make sure when you choose a wife that she is able to discuss more than the cut of your coat or the curve of your lips as you smile. Otherwise, you might find married life a touch, well…boring."

"I will keep that in mind. What else should I look for in a wife?"

Whitney laughed and climbed to her feet unaided. She had to complete her work this afternoon. To delay, even for conversation with the duke, wasn't in her best interests. "I really don't know. I rarely play matchmaker."

"But you have an idea?"

"Everyone has an idea of who would suit and who does not. Compatibility surely is more than a meeting of position, connections and pocketbooks."

"I think so, too. I've little interest in marrying a woman whose only recommendation is her appreciation for my position in society."

"I quite agree. A man or a woman's standing in society can change so swiftly through no effort on their own. Take me. My father was a gentleman of modest income, his brothers were in trade. I am only wealthy now because they died and left me their fortunes. Thanks to my connection to Lord Louth, I am invited everywhere and my eccentricities are overlooked. Mostly," she amended.

"But that is not all to recommend you," Exeter murmured. "You make me laugh."

"Anyone could make you laugh if they tried hard enough. Did I see that even Miss Quartermane managed it the other day?"

He conceded her point with a nod. "She surprised me by not being boring."

"I'm glad," Whitney murmured. "She likes you very much, I suspect."

Whitney kicked herself for uttering that observation out loud. Alice was about to marry Lord Acton, and that was that.

She turned away, but Exeter stayed her with a light touch on her arm.

"I prefer your laugh to hers," he confessed.

"I like yours, too," Whitney promised. "When you exert yourself to make the attempt. But come tomorrow, you're going to have to find someone new to amuse you."

"So you are determined on going?" he asked.

"Of course," she exclaimed with a frown. Had he suddenly become dense?

"And nothing could change your mind?" he pressed.

Her thoughts skipped back to Lord Acton, and for a moment she was almost temped to say yes. If, and it was an impossible if, Lord Acton somehow did not wed Miss Quartermane, she might have reason to stay for his sake. She knew the agonizing torture that came when someone you loved was dying very slowly before your eyes. Whitney did not care for Emily, but she did care a great deal for the earl. She wished there was a way to stay and be his friend through the hard weeks or months to come.

But he would have Alice to comfort him. To be his wife. Whitney was not needed here.

"I highly doubt it," she warned. "It would take more than a few pretty words to convince me."

"Perhaps this will change your mind." Exeter leaned close, attention locked on her lips.

She was sure she uttered "stop" but before she knew it, she was in the duke's arms, and the recipient of a passionate and lengthy kiss.

Chapter Twenty-Five

◆

Everett ran up the lower garden steps when he heard Whitney cry out *stop*.

He rushed toward the sound of her distress, rounded a garden pond featuring a statue of Athena, and found her struggling in the Duke of Exeter's arms.

The duke was kissing her, but Whitney was beating at his shoulders as if she wished he wouldn't.

Blood boiling, Everett wrenched them apart, putting Whitney firmly behind him for safety. "I believe the lady said stop."

The duke blinked at him, and then drew back, fury in his eyes. "This has nothing to do with you, Acton. Kindly take yourself somewhere else."

He flexed his hands at his side. He wasn't a man prone to violence—unless Whitney Crewe was being ravished against her will, it seemed. He steadied his temper. One did not attack a duke without personal provocation. "I don't think so. I could hardly consider myself Miss Crewe's friend if I abandoned her to a man who did not listen. She said stop. Very clearly, Your Grace."

Whitney clutched Everett's arm, her actions supporting his decision to protect her as she used him as a shield. "Don't fight," she whispered.

"Very well. Miss Crewe, we will talk about this later."

Whitney trembled. "There is nothing to discuss. You misunderstood everything I said, Your Grace."

"You're a damn tease, then."

The duke was asking for a good drubbing.

"I said there were others that admired you. I never said it was me!"

He glanced at Whitney over his shoulder. "Is the person who likes Exeter an acquaintance of yours?"

Whitney nodded quickly. "I just can't say who it is right now."

Puzzled but taking Whitney at her word, he faced the duke. "You owe the lady an apology. For not listening, for the kiss, and the insult. Now."

Whitney flexed her fingers around his arm, and he covered her hand with his.

"I apologize, Miss Crewe," Exeter said stiffly at last. "For not listening, for the kiss, and the insult. I misunderstood your interest."

"Granted," she whispered. "I would prefer that we never speak of this again," she begged.

"That I can do, since you're leaving anyway," the duke said, before he spun on his heel and stalked off.

Whitney sagged against Everett's back, burying her face in his coat collar. "Damn. Damn. Damn."

Everett warmed all over. Not from her cursing but the feel of her against his body. "He thought you liked him?"

"He did," she whispered. "But I don't. Not the way he wanted me to."

A silly smile burst over his face, which he tried to force away.

Whitney thumped his back. "You don't have the right to look so pleased about it."

But he *was* pleased. He was utterly delighted that the distinguished Duke of Exeter stood no chance with Whitney Crewe. But if she didn't like the duke, and clung to Everett with such fervor now, did that mean it was not too late for him. For them? "Are you all right?"

"Mortally embarrassed, but I'll survive." She laid her cheek against his shoulder with a beleaguered sigh. "I thought he understood that we could only ever be friends."

"You do tend to make an impression," he suggested.

"Obviously the wrong sort, in his case," she said, and then released him. "How am I ever to talk to him again? I will have to guard every word I say to make certain there are no further misunderstandings."

He sighed. "It will be all right. You are leaving tomorrow."

"I must. Even more so now." She raised her fingers to her lips, eyes wide like saucers. "Oh, hell, this is the worst mistake I have ever made."

He tried not to smile again. Almost making love to him could have been the worst if she had not liked the experience so much. He was buoyed with hope, a rare feeling these days. Thinking to help her in any way he could, he offered his aid instantly. "Then perhaps you would allow me to shield you."

"Shield me?"

He rocked back on his heels. "I am at a loose end today. Unless Emily succumbs to another fever, I had hoped to spend the rest of your last day here. With you."

"I see." She glanced toward the house, frowning. "Does that mean Miss Quartermane is inside?"

"No, she is not inside," he promised, not bothering to explain where Alice was for now. The words to say he was no longer engaged had stuck fast in his throat, too.

Alice and her parents had left his home already, a note left behind to explain that the engagement had ended. "I walked across from Warstone on foot. I've no notion of when you might see Miss Quartermane again."

All of that was true. The Quartermanes' carriage had left his estate early that morning while he'd been with Emily. He had wondered if the family might have called here and taken their leave of everyone. Perhaps they had not after all. Perhaps the end of his engagement might remain a secret for a few days more. The awkwardness could come later, after Whitney was gone. He rather hoped it might, because he did not want to discuss why he wasn't upset about Miss Quartermane with everyone.

"Might I keep you company on your last day?" he asked.

Whitney's answering smile was unusually shy. "I would like that."

Everett held out his arm to Whitney and, when she wrapped hers about his, he silently vowed to make this the best day of their entire association.

Rather than return and be confronted by the Duke of Exeter in a temper again, he took Whitney to the stables and introduced her to Lion. His horse draped himself all over Whitney, who laughed and fed him a treat from his pocket.

"Oh you are a lovely old fellow, aren't you," Whitney told his horse as she patted him.

Everett stood aside to watch her with his horse. She seemed very confident. "Do you ride often?"

"Indeed, I usually do in the countryside, but haven't spent much time on horseback this last season in London. I dislike the congestion on the roads. I prefer a good long gallop."

He smiled. "I host a hunt each year."

She nodded quickly. "I knew that. The last hunt I attended was two years ago now, but great fun. I plan to acquire my own horse on the continent. I do regret the days when I cannot ride about."

He sighed with pleasure at her confession. "I feel exactly the same way."

Next, they returned to the kitchen garden where they'd almost shared a kiss. Behind the privacy of those high walls, he captured her hand and held it. "I would like to return tomorrow to see you off on your journey, too."

For a moment, he saw sadness in her eyes. "I asked for the carriage to be ready for eight o'clock. Is that too early?"

"I will be here no matter the time."

He released her hand when they left the privacy of the kitchen garden and strolled toward the open drawing room doors, where everyone appeared to have gathered. The sound of happy chatter drifted out to greet them as the sun set, and Whitney clutched his arm again when she saw the Duke of Exeter was in the room.

He patted her hand soothingly. "You can do this, Whitney. We can do this together."

He led her inside and responded to hails of welcome, but he kept himself near Whitney all evening. The duke watched her in brooding silence and then left the room. Everyone suggested he would likely end up in the nursery, doting on his great niece and nephew yet again. It appeared no one but them knew about the kiss, and he was relieved beyond words that she was spared any awkwardness.

Everett threw a smile at Whitney, which she returned. After that, the woman he loved relaxed and enjoyed her last night at Twilit Hill in the company of good friends. He did not question his feelings for her anymore. Now that he no longer had the prospect of marriage looming over his head, he could see his feelings for this woman had always been just beneath the surface.

He had gravitated to her smile, like a drunk takes to drink perhaps. They might disagree on certain topics—marriage and decorum, to name just two—but they had always spoken together about them. Impassioned and eager to hear the other's words. Nevermore would he feel she dismissed him as just another titled gentleman who thought too much of himself and his position.

After an excellent dinner attended by every guest, the ladies left to take tea and the gentlemen consumed port and cigars. Everett kept a distance from the duke, but kept an eye on him.

Not that he considered Exeter stood a chance of changing Whitney's mind now.

Few probably could.

The Marchioness of Taverham approached him as soon as the gentlemen rejoined the ladies. "Were you not going to share the news with everyone that the Quartermanes left your estate today?"

He glanced at her quickly, and then around to see who was listening. No one else was paying them any attention, and Whitney was surrounded by other women and laughing once more. "It hadn't been my intention, no."

Her expression softened to regret. "I am so sorry."

Judging by the sadness in her eyes, she wasn't just speaking of the Quartermanes' abrupt leave-taking. Somehow she had already learned that his engagement had ended, too. "How did you know?"

"A feeling. Your smile when you look at Whitney has changed today. It is the same eagerness Taverham often reveals when we've been apart." Miranda sighed. She nodded toward her guests. "Does she know yet that you are free?"

He quickly shook his head. "There is no need to spoil her evening with talk of my situation. It would be entirely selfish to darken the evening. She would want to talk about what happened. Let her be happy tonight. She is due to depart so early in the morning."

"Did you never think she might return your regard and not

wish to leave after all?"

"She wishes to leave no matter what I say." Whitney might feel something for him, but at this late stage in her visit, he couldn't countenance upsetting her. They were good friends, with lust as a silent counterpart to every discussion they'd ever had. But further complications were unwise at this juncture. He would not hold Whitney back. She deserved to travel, to grow beyond society's expectations without letting a little love and his sudden availability cloud the air.

He loved her too damn much to deny her the life she wanted.

He would keep this one secret from Whitney, and hope that perhaps one day she might return to him.

He glanced at Lady Taverham, and saw her eyes had misted with tears. "I wanted so much for you both to be happy," she whispered.

"Please, say nothing further." Happiness would have to wait in his case anyway. There would never be a better time to lay what remained of his secrets bare to his friend's wife. So he squared his shoulders, ready to begin the most damning confession of his life. "Lady Taverham, there is something else I must share with you."

"Miranda," she murmured, before linking her arm through his and drawing him to an open window.

"Thank you, but..." he started, and further words stuck in his throat as a warm breeze battered his face. It was a perfect night, and he very much regretted that he would upset a lady he'd come to admire.

Miranda sighed. "If you are about to confess to Emily's whereabouts, rest assured I've known all along exactly where she is...and her unfortunate diagnosis."

He stared at her in horror, expecting a similar reaction to her husband's. "You know?"

"Everything." Miranda nodded. "We shared the same physician for a time, but he begged to be excused from attending me in future. I do wish you'd not told my husband about her living nearby though. He's turned into a bear and is hovering worse than ever. It is not good for him, or for my heart, when he worries incessantly."

"I'm sorry that you have been worried." He studied Miranda, who, at the moment, did not seem at all angry, as she had every right to be. "I have no choice but to leave her there indefinitely now."

"I know her situation grows worse every day," Miranda murmured. "Whitney was kind enough to explain the progression of her parents' illness. They died of consumption too, you know."

He groaned. "She never told me that."

"It was a long time ago," Miranda murmured. "She was nine when they died, within a few days of each other. After that, she was shunted all over the countryside to every loving relative she had, before she landed on Lord Louth's doorstep with her last uncle in tow. She has endured a lifetime of loss in her short years. That was why I'd hoped she somehow might find a home finally, as your wife. She likes it here very much, and you are good together."

"Lady Taverham, I—"

"How many times must I insist you call me by my first name?"

He raked his hand through his hair as he stared at Whitney. "I never meant to cause trouble for anyone."

"Then don't. I know we've not known each other very long, and you might feel this is none of my business, but you simply must tell her how you feel about her." Although he gaped, Miranda's attention switched to Whitney Crewe. "She's not as open to expressing her feelings as you might expect from someone so opinionated about everything else."

He remembered how she'd clung to him after the Duke of Exeter's kiss. She had needed his support and had expressed her need without words. "I will do nothing to halt her adventure, but neither can I join her because of Emily."

"Are you sure letting her go is wise?"

He looked at Whitney again, felt that longed-for happiness well up inside him. The feeling threatened to wreak havoc on his good intentions, but he could not be selfish. "I care about her too much to let what I feel stand in her way. She leaves tomorrow, and I will remain to care for Emily in her last days."

Miranda was silent after that for many minutes, and when Whitney slipped from the room, he decided he would follow her discreetly in a few moments.

Miranda's breath caught. "You love her."

"Yes, Miranda. I have loved her since the night we first met." He bowed. "She has always been the sun upon which my world turns. Excuse me."

Chapter Twenty-Six

Painting had always been her refuge. Whitney bent over the last canvas, the one depicting the Taverhams in this room, and added small details to what had become her best work. She was done with it, and she could leave first thing in the morning.

A deep sadness filled her. She had packed and repacked her trunks several times, deciding that she had to get rid of more than a few possessions before she traveled.

She straightened and groaned as her back protested. "There."

The door lock turning made her shiver, as did the question asked in a voice she'd never hear again after tomorrow. "Are you finally done, Whitney?"

A shock of longing filled her at the sound of Lord Acton whispering her given name. They had not spoken very much more than a few words together since their return indoors, although he'd followed behind her silently all night and, true to his word, had kept the duke from approaching her again.

But what she felt for Acton was impossible to act upon. She had not expected that he would remain so late. He had guests at home he should be entertaining. "Yes, I believe so."

She took her paintbrush and wiped it clean on the silk breaches that she'd once taken from him by mistake and, without looking around, began to pack up her painting case in readiness for tomorrow's journey.

He came closer, boots striking the boards softly. "May I view the masterpiece?"

She nodded. "It's time to show it off now anyway."

There was silence behind her for a long time and eventually she turned. Everett had raised both gloved hands to his lips and stared at her work. "This is…"

He stretched out his hand but thankfully did not touch the canvas where some parts would still be wet.

"This is incredible," he said, and then turned to Whitney wearing a huge smile. "I had heard you had talent, but this is more than I dreamed possible. I understand better why you wish to seek out others of similar persuasion."

A blush crept up her cheeks at his praise and she looked away. "I can do better. That is why I am going away, to improve myself."

She was also going away so she could forget him.

Acton came closer as he spoke. "You don't need to improve, change, you just need to be yourself. You shame the angels with your gift."

"Hardly an angel," she whispered, glancing at him swiftly as her heart began to clatter in her breast.

"You are to me, Whitney Crewe," he promised with a soft smile. "You make me a better man."

"Everett," she warned. "Don't talk that way."

"If not now, when? Oh, Whitney, I'm so tired of being alone."

"You're not alone," Whitney promised him. "You have Alice."

He shook his head. "I never kissed her."

Her eyes widened. "Because of your sister?"

"No. It is not that." He winced. "It seems I am like you. I'm not romantic. Not with her."

Whitney trembled with shock. "But you're to be married."

He lifted his chin. "We were never left alone long enough for anything to occur. She sought me out only once, but only because you suggested she should."

Whitney trembled. "She wanted to know if you loved her."

"I don't." He cleared his throat. "In fact, I thought she seemed more interested in *your* suitor than with me."

"Exeter was never my suitor, and it cannot be true that she prefers his company over yours. The duke is very charming and funny, and you've been so very grim of late." She closed her box. "Alice was raised to be a very proper young woman. If anything is to happen before you become man and wife, then I think you will have to pursue her."

"It has not been easy," he confessed as he picked up his breeches and folded them neatly. He held them out to her to pack away. "And that might be a problem. I just…"

Whitney added his breeches to her belongings, feeling better for keeping them. "What?"

"I wanted my relationship with Alice to be as easy and as uncomplicated as it is with you."

Her heart beat wildly against her ribs. "Perhaps it only seems easy since I'm not the one you'll marry. I'm hardly ever proper."

"You're proudly eccentric," he whispered, as he captured the cuff of her sleeve to admire the fine details she'd painted there when she'd first come in.

"I am," she agreed, but wished it were not so. If she'd been different, would Everett have considered her as more than a friend by now? "We've had our ups and downs."

"Yes," he said softly. "It's why I like you. I never know what to expect. You never let me get ahead of myself, and for that I am grateful."

Whitney turned away. "Nonsense!"

His hands skimmed her arms, and she shivered with the impulse to turn around. "It's true. You changed me. I'm glad you never met my sister properly. I think Emily would have hated everything about you. She would have convinced others not to like you, too, and I am ashamed to say I might have gone along with her once upon a time." He leaned toward her and inhaled. "But I don't dislike you at all. I think…no. I *know* I fell in love with you long ago."

Her breath caught as he fitted himself to her back and wrapped his arms about her waist. She didn't resist him. She couldn't catch her breath easily. The warmth of his body seeped through her gown and she started to turn around to face him.

"Don't move," he warned. He tightened his grip and drew her into him as they were. "I just want to hold you for a moment before we part ways. I need this."

"Everett?"

"Nothing has changed since the night we first met, has it?"

"No." There was comfort and pain in being in his arms again. She'd never thought she'd fall in love, and yet she was certain she loved him, too. "I still want you as much then as now," she confessed.

Whitney let out a shaky breath as he splayed his fingers over her stomach. He was wearing gloves as usual but it made not the slightest difference to what she felt. His touch set her body on fire, and she longed for some way to end the torture.

She tipped her head back to rest upon his shoulder, gazing up at the intricate ceiling and wishing it was an open sky filled with stars instead. Everett nuzzled her hair with a tortured groan as his fingers rose to capture her breast and squeeze until she moaned, too.

Whitney loved the way she felt with Everett surrounding her. Her body began to tingle everywhere, even if she knew he would leave her unsatisfied. This man had caused her so many sleepless nights.

But she loved him, and that meant making sacrifices and taking chances.

She glanced toward the door, remembering he'd locked it. She couldn't be with him once he'd married Alice. Opportunities like this would cease tomorrow.

Whitney closed her eyes, lost in a fierce battle with her conscience and her desires as he began to arouse her in earnest. She was betraying Alice, a woman she'd considered a friend for a very long time.

But *she* had met Everett first—and he was the one for her.

"Make love to me," she whispered.

"I can't," he gasped as he caught hold of her hips. "But I swear I would love to do nothing more than that tonight, and all the nights of my life."

Whitney let out a frustrated groan that had Everett chuckling against her hair.

"I love that you want me this much," he whispered. "It makes the torture bearable knowing it is shared."

"There is a way for us to be together without risk," she said and caught his hand, inspired by a wicked idea. "Come with me."

She led Everett across the room to an open window and drew

him outside, into the night.

She ran with him to a secluded corner of the garden she'd discovered, where two stone benches had been placed opposite each other.

They were set far enough apart to surely be considered a safe distance by him.

His brow creased in the moonlight. "What are we doing?"

She pushed him down onto one and spun around to sit on the other.

"We are going to make love together, but separately." She inched her gown up her legs a little, and then undid the top button on her gown.

His eyes widened. "Almost like the first night we met?"

"The beginning," she promised. She smiled as she undid another button on her bodice. "I won't run away with your breeches this time."

"I can't promise not to take a souvenir of my own," he warned with a wide smile before tossing off his coat. He unbuttoned his waistcoat, loosened his cravat and caught the first button of his breeches. "I could steal your whole gown."

Whitney licked her lips. "That would mean others might see me naked."

"No, I do not want that. I want you all to myself. I'll have the chemise your wearing instead." He smiled warmly. "Have you done this before?"

She should tell him now about her past so that the last of his shocks were over for him. If he did not like what he discovered, then he was not the man for her. "I'm not innocent, if that's what you're asking."

He smiled. "I'd already gathered that, and I don't care either way."

"I'm not promiscuous," she promised. She licked her lips as he removed his shirt and exposed half his beautiful body to her eager eyes. The man was sinfully attractive. "But…"

His lips quirked. "You have trouble staying away from men you consider handsome?"

She held up three fingers, and his eyes narrowed.

"Is that three before me?"

"Including you." She shrugged. "I know we stopped, but you

were so memorable, I concluded we may as well have shared a bed together."

"There wasn't a bed anywhere in sight," he said darkly. "I was planning to have you up against the wall."

Whitney's breath caught, and she quickly finished unbuttoning her gown. She left it on but parted to tease him.

"Be naked with me," he whispered. "I would like to see you tonight. All of you."

She rose to her feet as she slipped her gown off her shoulders so it fell to pool at her feet. Clad in only a sheer chemise now, she glanced at her lover.

Everett moaned. He had opened the fall of his trousers and now idly stroked himself with the edge of his thumb.

Her smile grew as he became bolder about it. "Remind me of what you have there," she asked, hands shaking with the need to grasp him again.

He shuffled to bring his breeches to his knees. Whitney had of course seen Everett naked before, and her imagination often brought him to her bed, but the visual added to her arousal to such a degree that her palms became damp.

He brought his hand to his cock and began to stroke. "Is this what you need?"

She nodded, breath coming even faster. She lifted her chemise a little higher, so he would glimpse her quim. She ran her fingers through her red curls and he moaned again.

"I'm wet," she told him. "Again."

He laughed once. "I'm in hell," he complained. "Again."

Whitney leaned back on one arm and began to play in earnest, sliding her fingers through her slick folds, dipping the tip of one finger deeper into where he could be if he wasn't so concerned for her health and her future.

"Take it all off," he growled.

Despite the frustration of not being able to touch him, she loved him all the more for his demand.

"Everything?"

"Leave your slippers and stockings on," he decided with a nod. "The stones might hurt your feet."

She tugged her chemise over her head and then returned her hand to her quim. She had never pleasured herself before another but found it wildly exciting with him looking on. They fell silent, each watching the other, each touching themselves with unabashed need.

His hand stilled and his chest heaved.

Dressed in nothing but stockings and shoes, she felt free, she felt beautiful as she stared at him.

"Lovelier than I could have imagined." He shook out his cravat. "Don't move from that pose."

Whitney closed her eyes, but she slowed the movement of her fingers. She was very aroused. Very ready for him to touch her sensitive skin if only he would.

She opened her eyes suddenly, realizing he'd moved to stand over her, his nose and mouth covered by his folded cravat.

She met his hot gaze, heart hammering painfully against her ribs. She needed him. Her attention dropped down his body, lingered on his stiff cock. He held himself tightly, gripping the base without moving.

"Widen your legs farther for me," he demanded, his voice hot and dark and so eager, she shivered.

Whitney parted her folds, reveling in Everett's loud groan in response.

She longed to touch him as a lover would. Give herself over to his pleasure and an uncertain future. Yet she was too emotional to speak.

The moment was perfect. Raw with emotion, and yet she had to tell him what was in her heart. "I love you," she whispered.

Everett dropped the cravat and fell to his knees beside her bench, close but too far away to touch. "Show me your passion, Whitney," he begged. "Make yourself come for me."

So Whitney groaned desperately and, while he watched, gave her body and soul to him completely.

Chapter Twenty-Seven

———◆———

Mornings had always been Everett's favorite time of day, but not this particular morning. This was it. Goodbye. The day he'd once longed for but now dreaded. The sun was just rising over the Twilit Hill estate and Whitney Crewe would be out of his life at any moment.

He should be pleased that she would be happy, and yet his soul was being ripped in two.

He stood on the sidelines as she bid farewell to the friends she'd made here and tried to smile. Although it was very early, all of Taverham's guests had dragged themselves from the warmth of their beds to share a few more words with her.

Even Exeter had put in an appearance, despite Whitney's rejection of him.

Everett yearned to speak to her privately again but, despite what had happened between them last night in the garden, he couldn't think of a single positive thing to say just now.

"Don't forget to write us. We want to hear all about your adventure." Lady Ettington grinned. "And when you come back home, I have another idea for a painting to surprise my husband with."

Whitney leaned close to the marchioness' ear, and what she said caused Lady Ettington to burst out laughing.

"He recovered from the shock of the last one very quickly, I promise," she explained with an arched glance for her husband.

Lord Ettington acted as if he understood nothing of their conversation, but a telling blush was creeping up his neck and over his cheeks.

Now what had Whitney done? He shook his head, amused rather than alarmed. He did not need to know everything she'd done. But typical of Whitney. She must turn everyone's head as well as his own.

Whitney was beaming with mirth as she looked up at the Duke of Exeter. Everett saw the challenge in her gaze as she dared the duke with one look to remain angry with her. "Farewell, Your Grace," she said happily.

The duke appeared a little awkward as he bowed to her. Everett hoped the misunderstanding in the garden had not irrevocably caused a rift between them. Even though Whitney was leaving the country, the loss of the duke's good opinion would influence others in society to think meanly of her.

Whitney seemed to be making a valiant attempt to put the whole mistaken kiss business behind her firmly, but the duke wasn't as sanguine.

"Miss Crewe, I wish you all the best for a safe journey and swift return." He spoke very formally, more formally than he usually did with her.

Whitney's smile slipped a little. "Thank you," she murmured, before moving on to Lady Carrington.

Everett watched the duke a moment longer and then returned his attention to Whitney's farewells.

"The children should have been here," Lady Carrington was telling her.

"Oh, goodness. Don't wake them at this hour. Besides, I've left them a message and gifts for each one of them upstairs with the maid, and there is something for you, too."

"That was very kind of you."

"I am sure they will be thrilled," Lord Carrington agreed as he took Whitney's hand. "Until we meet again, dear girl."

He lost the rest of the conversation as Miranda leaned close. "What do you think she gave them, Everett?"

"I'm sure I have no idea." But he did think she might have had time to sketch each child during her visit. She was kind like that. Although she had promised never to sketch him again, or that she would want to, he'd noticed a very good likeness of him in her studio last night. He'd made no mention of it at the time, but his heart had lightened at the sight.

The friendship that had grown between them had begun poorly, but he was certain of her now. And after last night's tryst, he would always dream of her. He might feel some trepidation over what could happen to her when she left England behind, but he trusted that Whitney knew what she was doing. He could not follow her and abandon his sister, and he regretted that very much still.

He chose to believe that she could take care of herself in any situation until he could be with her again.

"Surely another week will not make much of a difference," Miranda complained as Whitney stopped before them.

Whitney laughed and hugged Miranda tightly. "It will mean the world of difference to me," she promised, looking at Everett over Miranda's shoulder before turning her attention back to the marchioness. "I have friends expecting me to visit them, too."

"You have friends here. What of the Quartermanes? Did you even say goodbye to them?"

Everett's breath caught at Miranda's query. She should not say anything about the Quartermanes that might lead her to change her plans. Not now.

Whitney squeezed the marchioness' hand. "I have said all I need to say to them."

He let out the breath he held. Whitney still believed he was an engaged man, and now, at the very last minute, was not the time to confess Miss Quartermane had run away from the danger Emily presented.

Whitney wanted independence, not a proposal that would tie her to him, to this county, because of the family they might eventually have together. Those were the things he alone wanted.

He had to let her go, but it was not easy to pretend indifference after last night's passion.

Whitney stepped back from Miranda, eyes twinkling with her customary good humor. "Take care of yourself, and that handsome husband of yours."

"I will," Miranda promised. She leaned forward and kissed both of Whitney's cheeks. "Write to me soon, and tell me of your trip and where to find you. I expect you to visit me the moment you return to England."

"I will." Whitney laughed softly then turned toward Everett. Her expression gave nothing of her feelings away. It was as if their intimate tryst last night hadn't happened. He wished he were assured his own face was as inscrutable, but he stepped toward her, feeling coldness clutching at his heart.

His palms grew damp in his gloves, and he said nothing at first as he looked down upon her happy face.

He drank in the face that had grown most dear to him. Lips made to speak mischief, eyes that often spoke uncomfortable truths, wild red hair that always made her look as if she'd only just stumbled out of bed. He had never expected this to happen, but he loved Whitney more than words could say. She was everything he'd never known he needed in his life...and he had lost her before he'd ever truly had a chance to keep her.

A smile trembled on her lips. "Will you shake my hand, Lord Acton?"

"Yes, of course. But before I forget, I have something for you." He dug in his pocket for the paper he carried. "I have a small property in Dover. Inherited some years ago and never used. If you find your accommodations while you wait for your ship untenable, please do not hesitate to present yourself at this address. I've sent a letter ahead to my staff to expect you, and render you any assistance you might require."

She clutched the paper, read the address, and then folded it neatly. She added it to her paint box. "Thank you. That is very kind."

"Well, goodbye, Miss Crewe. Pleasant journey." He shook her hand firmly, yearning for the soft smoothness of hers against his bare palm. It felt a lifetime since he'd touched her skin, and he regretted he might never do so again.

She squeezed his hand tightly, and then slipped from his grip once and for all.

Lost to him forever but taking a piece of his soul with him, he was sure.

What had begun as a pleasurable distraction one scandalous night had turned into the most important affair of his life. He would always think well of Whitney, hope for nothing but happiness for her—but he would also fear for the next poor fellow she managed to bedevil.

He couldn't ask her to write, to inform him of her safe arrival in Florence. He would have to rely on hearing secondhand from Lady Taverham, and hope that Miranda would allow him to eagerly devour every word of her letters.

Whitney curtsied, and when she rose, her eyes caught his briefly. Pain flashed through them before she hid the emotion behind her excitement and departed the room in a rush for her waiting carriage.

The silence left in her wake made his unsteady breathing uncommonly loud. He followed everyone else out to the front drive to wave her off, feeling utterly desolate, now that she was really going.

His throat tightened as the door shut and when the carriage lurched forward, he had a brief moment of insanity as he considered chasing after her. But reason soon return. Even though it hurt, he was doing what was right for Whitney.

He watched the carriage go, searched for her face at the window until the carriage disappeared from view.

"Goodness, but waking at this hour has made me famished," Lady Ettington murmured as she faced the Taverhams. "I think I could devour everything set before me today without complaint."

"I feel the same. Everything was to be laid out as soon as Miss Crewe's carriage departed," Miranda told everyone. "Please go inside and help yourselves."

Everett held back. He did not think he could eat anything today. He spared one last glance for the empty drive then faced the steps and the other guests.

The Duke of Exeter was watching him. The older man crossed the distance to Everett and thrust his hand out. "Now I understand why she's been unhappy, and why she would not ever speak of the reason. You lost a treasure today, too," he said quietly, so his words did not carry far. "Look me up when you find yourself in London again. I suspect you and I could become great friends one day."

Everett reluctantly shook hands, astonished by the duke's words. Had he and Whitney been seen together in the gardens, or had their parting been too obviously bittersweet to be mistaken? He suspected the latter.

Knowing he must say something, he nodded. "I would like that."

Taverham and Miranda and the dowager joined them, and the duke made a hasty escape inside.

Taverham clapped him on the shoulder. "Dinner tonight?"

"I don't think so." He noted the couple held hands yet again. "I'll be with Emily."

The dowager scowled, and Taverham looked instantly stricken as he darted a guilty glance at his wife.

Everett frowned at them all. Had they not discussed Emily together yet? He was too tired to worry that he'd upset the applecart. They each knew what he did for his sister, and they had each claimed they understood.

"I understand why you might not wish to return for a while," Miranda murmured as she set her hand to his chest briefly. "But do come back and see us soon, and if you ever need anything, don't hesitate to send word day or night."

The dowager was nodding right along with Miranda, which made a nice change. The dowager had been much too fond of Emily and dismissive of Miranda from the very start.

"Thank you, Miranda." He nodded to Taverham. "Have an enjoyable day."

Miranda slipped her arm through her husband's, who was gaping like a fish at their conversation.

Miranda sighed. "Don't even think of making a fuss right now."

"I can explain," Taverham promised. Everett turned away, catching the last of their conversation.

"There is no need to explain anything," Miranda promised her husband. "Everett is family. Lady Taverham, will you join us for breakfast?"

"Yes, I think I am hungry enough to eat at this hour, too," the older woman decided, and shuffled slowly into the manor. Taverham offered his arm at the stairs and, together, they all headed inside.

Everett sighed with relief that his friend's family was slowly growing closer. Managing a family could be very complicated. He did not envy Taverham the stress of bringing those pair, his wife and mother, into harmony.

He turned away, walking the fields he, Taverham and Emily had ridden across together as children. Before he reached his own lands, he was in tears over those faraway memories. He wiped them away irritably, and soon found himself facing another summons before he'd even walked through his front door.

Without the need for secrecy now, he mounted his horse on the front drive and rode hard and fast for Rose Cottage to spend another day sitting at his sister's bedside. It could be her last, but he fervently wished it wasn't.

Chapter Twenty-Eight

Whitney handed her card to the butler of the neat redbrick building overlooking the channel, heart in her throat. She hoped she was doing the right thing by imposing upon a connection, because the alternative was too horrible to bear. "I believe Lord Acton told you to expect me."

The doorway widened to admit her immediately, and an old man without a scrap of hair on his head smiled widely. "He certainly wrote that it was a possibility you would come. Welcome, Miss Crewe."

She spared her companions a quick glance of relief then entered. Whitney stepped into a pleasant front hall and sighed at the peaceful atmosphere surrounding her.

"Ah, what a charming home." The past few days and nights had not been ideal for her. Everett's generous offer of his unoccupied property, save for a pair of servants, not far from the port, was perfect for her needs. It was close enough to her ship and a relieving distance from the unsavory characters who had appeared suddenly at the inn she'd settled into. Staying, despite the changed mood of the place, had been essential until her companions had arrived to join her. She was very glad to have an alternative so readily available to her party.

"May I introduce my companion, Mrs. Roberts? Her husband, Thomas, will be along shortly with our luggage."

"Pleased to make your acquaintance. Lord Acton was very keen to be of assistance, should you require his help." The man rang a bell to his left. "There's just the two of us, myself and the housekeeper, who will come along at any moment to settle you in. Let me first help with your luggage."

A rail-thin older woman appeared and ushered Whitney into a nearby parlor. "Would you care for tea, my lady?"

"It is *Miss* Crewe," Whitney stressed. "And tea would be lovely indeed."

She fretted until her luggage was carried inside, but directed the servants to store almost all of her belongings in the dining room. She would need very little luggage for the one evening she planned to stay in Everett's home.

The butler shut the front door and rejoined her. "There now," he said with a satisfied smile. "His lordship will be very glad to know you have come. He was quite concerned for your welfare in his letters."

"Letters?"

"Yes, indeed. There have been several about you."

Mrs. Roberts nudged her. "He *is* still thinking of you."

Whitney sighed, realizing she had blubbered on Mrs. Roberts' shoulder far too much since meeting the woman. She couldn't seem to help herself, and laughed nervously, hoping to make light of the matter before Everett's man. "He's very kind."

"He must have truly been in love with you," Roberts whispered. "Men only fuss this way if they care about a woman very deeply."

Whitney swallowed, fighting another bout of tears, resolutely squaring her shoulders and trying to put what might have been firmly behind her. "When you have the opportunity, please convey to his lordship my appreciation of his generosity in allowing me to stay," she choked out.

"Tell him he may very well have saved her virtue, too," Mrs. Roberts added.

The butler's eyes widened in alarm. "What has happened?"

"Nothing. Nothing at all," Whitney promised the fellow before he was too shocked, casting a sour look at her new companion. The woman was as blunt as a well-used axe. Whitney usually liked that trait in her friends, but not so much today.

Nothing had happened, thanks to the stout wood and locks on her door and the timely arrival of her traveling companions. Discovering she wasn't invulnerable at the inn had been a very nasty shock. "The inn was much too crowded for me to remain another day."

"Noisy?"

"Ooh yes, until all hours."

"That ain't even the half of it," Mrs. Roberts said in a loud, clear voice. "The tavern weren't fit for a lady. I told my Thomas we should have come earlier than we promised."

Thomas Roberts, a great hulking fellow with the sweetest disposition toward his wife, lumbered into view, holding the Roberts' pitifully small trunk. "Should have listened to you. I know."

Mrs. Roberts beamed at her husband and he went on his way.

"Oh, dear," the butler grumbled. "You were staying at a tavern? I could have told you it was the worst possible place for a lady if you had come here first."

"Well, we are all here now." Whitney felt her optimism in the good of mankind returning but rubbed her brow. "I've hardly slept a wink with all the strangers pounding on my door by mistake," she admitted. "Half the patrons at the inn seemed incapable of finding their own rooms without directions."

Instead of laughing, the poor butler appeared even more stricken. "Then we are glad you have come. His lordship said we were to look after you as if you were part of the family. You can be assured of our protection and discretion and privacy."

"I don't require protection, now that I have Mr. and Mrs. Roberts at my side, but I do thank you for your concern." Whitney forced a smile. "All I require is a bath, a meal, a peaceful evening, and a bed to sleep in later. I expect a caller very early tomorrow morning. Captain Williams will come and provide instructions for our voyage."

"Of course," he murmured. "Let me show you around and to your room. His lordship suggested that the master bedchamber be prepared. It is the best room in the house."

Whitney pushed away her despair. She would have enjoyed the room more if Everett could have joined her there. But today was the day of his wedding, and it was past time to stop thinking of him.

She followed the butler upstairs, encountering the housekeeper on the way down, and stepped into a warm room. Dark wood, rich fabrics, and wide-open windows surrounded her. There were no drapes in this room and the sun warmed the space perfectly.

"How lovely," she murmured as she ran the tip of her finger along the damask comforter, thinking of the man she loved sharing this bed with his wife. She curled her fingers into her palm. She could no longer think of Alice as her friend. She could no longer consider herself Alice's.

Was Everett nervous?

She lifted her gaze along the bed and encountered a letter resting on the pillow. "What is that?"

"It is a message for you," the butler advised, taking one last look around the chamber and nodding. "Lord Acton sent it with hope that you might come and read it before your departure."

Her hands trembled but she did not rush to snatch it up. "I will read it later," she promised, turning toward Mrs. Roberts. Her companion appeared intrigued, but then she sighed. "I could use a nap, too, after this morning."

"Your room is this way, Mrs. Roberts. I directed your husband there before you came upstairs."

Mrs. Roberts left the room and the butler promised Whitney tea and biscuits soon. They left Whitney, and she busied herself by unpacking the few things she would need for the night. Anything to stop herself from snatching up that letter.

When the housekeeper arrived bearing a tea tray, Whitney was as calm as she could be. The housekeeper backed out with a quick glance at the unopened letter. Whitney let out a sigh and collected it before returning to sit in the window seat overlooking the street. She ran her fingers over her name, deciding Everett had handsome handwriting, and broke the seal.

She covered her lips as she read the first lines.

My dearest Whitney,

I cannot thank you again for the pleasure of your company and friendship. The hours we spent alone together have been the best of my life, and I am bereft that you have gone away, my darling girl.

Nothing has changed here since I saw you last. Emily's health remains in decline, and she is as ever utterly unrepentant of her past misdeeds. I know you wish me to be angry with her, furious, but I cannot in my heart turn aside the years of affection that existed between us. Her doctors have stopped suggesting I have hope now.

The Taverham house party has finally ended, and immediately after your carriage left, I was invited by Exeter to call upon him when I visit London next. I thought he seemed genuinely cast down by how things ended between you. I know he considered you a great friend, and I also suspect he knows how I feel about you. Do let me know if you wish me to pursue a friendship with him for your sake? I've no doubt you could again enjoy his company upon your eventual return.

Will it surprise you to learn that Lady Taverham, Miranda, knew of Emily's location all along? Miranda and I have spoken of Emily's health on several occasions, and she has been more of a comfort than I deserve. I remain astonished that she accepts what I've done for Emily's care, though I know she remains a little anxious about it all. She also admonished me for informing Taverham about Emily. She says Taverham has become unbearably concerned and worrisome. Taverham's open devotion to Miranda reminds me every day that I should never have let you slip through my fingers. I have never been happier than when I am with you.

Since you are reading this letter, you must be in my house, in my bedchamber hopefully, enjoying the view of the sea through the front windows. How I wish I could be with you. My servants will look after you well enough in my stead, and I truly hope you can be comfortable and happy there.

Now I must beg a boon from you. I know you will tease me for suggesting it, but I beg of you to write to me no matter where you go in your grand adventure in the years to come. I could not rest easy without having a letter from you tucked beneath my pillow at night, and will cherish each and every one you send. If I cannot see you, I must hear from you, as often as you can bear to write me, and I promise I will write to you very faithfully each week.

You will find me at Warstone Manor until the worst comes to pass. After Emily is gone, I have decided I will spend the mourning period traveling, hopefully abroad. I should like to call on you one day, if you agree to see me again after all that has happened between us. I very much look forward to having you show me the places you've written about. If my health continues to be strong after six months has passed after Emily, we could deepen our friendship if you still like the idea. For that to happen, please write with your new directions as soon as you are settled abroad, and tell me of your journey.

Yours most faithfully,

E

Whitney wiped at her streaming eyes hurriedly. Damn him. Now she would look for him coming every single morning. The last days had been hard enough without the torture of hope.

She read the letter again, memorizing every loving word. She missed him. She missed him so much that it hurt. As she scanned the last lines of the letter for the third time, she frowned. He spoke only of his own future, and said not one word of Alice, or his marriage.

...we could deepen our friendship if you still like the idea.

Whitney's breath came fast and shallow all of a sudden. Everett spoke only of remaining at Warstone for Emily's sake. He said nothing of traveling with his new wife. What wasn't he telling her? Had something gone wrong with his engagement to Alice?

Concerned and hopeful all at once, Whitney covered her face with both hands and muffled a soft scream of frustration. Alice and her parents had been suspiciously absent that last day, when they had previously been always calling upon the marchioness daily. She should have asked Everett what had kept the Quartermanes away the day she'd left Twilit Hill.

Had the engagement been broken before she'd even left Twilit Hill?

For a moment, Whitney considered swooning.

There was no other reason for that sweetly worded letter than to express hope of a future together. That beautiful, secretive, idiotic, darling man might not be married, and could have been hers to claim.

He should have told her he was free. She would have delayed her journey to wait for him.

Whitney sprang to her feet, searched every room in the house until she found a writing table and paper, and then penned an expansive letter to Everett, telling him everything of her last few days, assuring him that she, too, could not wait to see him, and then asked after the new Lady Acton.

She did not think he would lie to her in a letter.

Once that was sent and on its way, she ate, bathed and then, exhausted, slid between the sheets of her lover's bed. She fell asleep to dream that the man she loved had not married, and that he was racing along dark roads to join her. Their reunion had been so happy that she woke in tears as the sun rose and, for the first time in her life, considered giving up her voyage to return to him.

Chapter Twenty-Nine

A firm hand settled over Everett's shoulder. "She is at peace now," Taverham murmured, as the last of the townsfolk drifted away from the burial ground high on a hill overlooking Warstone.

Everett continued to stare into the grave as it was slowly filled with earth. "She loved you till the end, you know."

Taverham sighed. "I'm sorry."

"So am I," he whispered. "I wish she'd fallen in love with someone else. Maybe she could have been happy if she'd just let you go."

Taverham's grip on his shoulder tightened. "Come away. Miranda and Christopher are waiting in the carriage to take you home."

He was concerned the boy had come. There had been no need for him to learn that Emily had lived so close to him for so long.

The dowager was here, too, a grim figure in black mourning at the edge of the crowd. She bowed her head to him and returned to her carriage without a word. That was for the best. He still did not know what to say to her. The dowager had cared deeply about Emily once and been utterly betrayed.

"I can't leave with you," he whispered to his friend. "I cannot be in a carriage with them, or anyone. I was holding Emily's hand as the end came," he admitted.

He would not willingly put Taverham's family in any danger.

"Oh," Taverham, said and then fell silent. "I didn't realize."

"Where else would I have been when the last of my family slipped away? Emily did not die without a struggle," he confessed, heart growing heavy again.

It had been a ghastly night, knowing the end would come sooner than he was ready for. He'd expected months more, not a mere week. But they had talked every day. Discussing the past, and the future she wouldn't live to share. He never told Emily about Alice, but he'd told Emily *everything* about Whitney Crewe. How they had met, how she challenged him on every level. Her eccentricities were already known to Emily from gossip, and while Whitney's character had concerned Emily in the beginning, she had come around by the end of her life.

She had made him promise to pursue her. Sadly, it may have had more to do with Emily's keen interest in the size of Whitney's fortune than the woman herself. Emily had happily listed a number of improvements he could make at Warstone with the additional funds when he wed Whitney.

However, any marriage would be for Whitney to decide in the end. It was her future, her life he wanted to bind with his. If he lived after this.

Emily had coughed her final breaths in his arms, struggling for air.

He took a step away from Taverham before he faced him. "Until I am certain I am safe, allowing enough time to pass to be sure, I must keep a distance from everyone."

Taverham nodded slowly, his expression grim. "How long?"

"I've been thinking about that. I think at least six months must pass before I can relax my guard and be at ease around others again."

Taverham frowned. "What about the wedding?"

Everett glanced at the carriage where Lady Taverham and her son looked on, clutching the window frames tightly. It was good of Miranda to come when she had never been a friend to Emily, and Emily had despised everything about Miranda.

Miranda climbed out, urged the boy to remain behind in the carriage with his grandmother, and moved to join them.

He smiled her way quickly and then faced his friend. "The day I told Miss Quartermane about my sister's illness was the day she fled my estate and our engagement ended."

Taverham gawked. "Why didn't you say something to us?"

He winced a little. "I said nothing because I was not unhappy about it. I did not need pity."

Taverham brushed his hand over his mouth, likely holding back a question.

He shrugged. "I only have myself to blame in the end for making a match that was not based on love. Seeing you and Miranda together again has reminded me of what was missing in my life. Miss Quartermane and I did not suit, and I am grateful that she released me before it was too late. There is nothing I want to do to change the situation. I hope you will remember that when you meet her again in London."

"Of course we will be kind to Miss Quartermane," Miranda promised. "You can depend on us to make sure any gossip we hear is turned so it is favorable to both of you."

Taverham squinted at him. "What did you *do* to make her give you up?"

"Give up being my countess, you mean?" At Taverham's reluctant nod, he shrugged. "I confirmed it was me who lost my breeches at the Fairmont Bachelors Ball. That scandalized her mother quite a bit."

Taverham's eyes widened. "That was you?"

He nodded quickly. "But when I finally told her about Emily's poor health, it was too much, apparently. I discovered Miss Quartermane and her mother have a mortal fear of illness. As soon as I told them of Emily, her current situation and prognosis for life, she practically ran from the room. It took her one night to decide to end the engagement and pack her bags. They left early the next morning while I was visiting Emily."

"That must have been a terrible shock to discover they were so rude as to leave without saying goodbye," Taverham said

"Actually, it was a relief not to have to pretend I was happy to be with them anymore."

"It was for the best." Miranda held out her hand. He glanced at it, reassured himself she was gloved too, and took her fingers lightly in his. "You know we worry for you," she said.

He shivered as a chill swept him, and for the first time in his life he felt oppressed by the close growth of the woods. He wanted to get away. He needed to be somewhere else soon. "Thank you both for coming."

"Of course we would come to support you at this terrible time," Miranda murmured.

"If you ever need anything, you know where we are," Taverham began.

"I will write," he promised, earning a startled glance from Taverham. "I'm going away, you see. I would prefer it if you could keep news of my travels to yourself for a while."

"Leaving? No. Stay." Taverham grasped his shoulders, appearing stricken. "If you become ill, I swear we will always look after you."

Everett broke free of Taverham's grasp easily. "I'd never ask you to, but should that be my future, I want to see something of the world now. While I am well, I'm going to spend the mourning period traveling abroad," he told Taverham. "Like we always talked of doing with Emily."

"Will you call upon Whitney?" Miranda asked, her eyes alight with speculation.

"That woman does bear watching," Taverham warned, seemingly without a clue that Everett's interest in Whitney was slightly more romantic in nature than protective.

"I will, but I will keep a distance for her sake," he promised Miranda. "It is not my intention to curtail her time there."

Miranda smiled. "I am glad you are doing what is needed. You both wore such long faces the day you parted ways, but I understand why you could not stop her going, even if you should have told her the truth."

He frowned. "I will not risk her health, but I harbor a small hope that she will agree to accept my companionship for a while," he murmured.

"If I have learned anything about Miss Crewe, it is that she will hardly care for the proprieties." Miranda turned away. "Come, husband. Let us not delay Everett a moment longer. He has a long journey ahead and a heart to recapture."

Taverham fought his wife's managing. "What the devil are you talking about? What heart?"

Miranda succeeded in steering him away a second time. "My dear husband, always so slow to grasp the obvious. Let me explain. Your best friend has fallen head over heels in love with the most eccentric woman we know."

"With Whitney Crewe?" he exclaimed a little too loudly as he turned back.

Miranda dragged him on, whispering now, but clearly enough that Everett heard. "What better woman should he pursue than the one who already loves him?"

Miranda all but forced her husband into the carriage, and they moved off and turned down their drive within minutes.

He idly wondered how the rest of that conversation would go. Would Miranda admit to everything she'd pieced together? Everett suddenly didn't care.

He had a plan. The carriage was already packed for his trip and waiting beneath the shade beyond the cemetery.

He had today and tomorrow to reach Dover, and the docks to book passage on a fast ship. Whitney was a full week ahead of him, but an easy crossing could make the interval much longer.

He hoped he would not have to wait long for a ship that would deliver him straight to Whitney's side. He had memorized her plans, but there was always the danger she might change them, too. He wanted to tell her face to face that he wasn't a married man as soon as possible. He caressed the letter from her in his pocket.

Whitney had promised she was eager to see him, and would always look for him. He was glad to know she'd taken up his offer of accommodation.

He smiled, thinking of her enquiry about Lady Acton's happiness. He worried that his letter had given him away, and that Whitney suspected he'd been untruthful.

He bid one last farewell to his sister and turned for the carriage. He set his cap upon his head, and looked up to find only the Blakes and Garrett Thompson had lingered after everyone else had gone away. The Blakes were holding hands, and he suddenly wanted the chance of love returned that he'd given up when Whitney had gone.

He wanted her so badly he ached.

He forced a smile for their sake to hide his distress. "Thank you all for coming."

"It's no trouble. Are you all right, my lord?" Nancy peered into his face. "You're very pale today, if you don't mind me saying so."

"Merely tired," he promised, restlessness gripping him a little tighter. He had spent his nights wondering if telling Whitney he wasn't getting married would have made any difference to her plans. When morning broke through the trees and bathed his bedchamber in light, he had wanted to run after Whitney immediately and tell her before it was too late. The agony of waiting for her reply to his letter had only been appeased by hope when he received it. But there had been Emily to consider, to care for until now. Now she was gone, and he was truly free to do and say what he felt in his heart. "A little time will do me the world of good. Is there anything you need?"

"No, nothing." As Everett shuffled his feet, anxious to be on his way, Blake's smile grew. "You're going to chase after the redhead now, aren't you?"

"Yes," he promised. "It may be some time before I see you all again."

"A merry dance she'll lead you." Blake laughed softly. "Knew you should have chosen her the day she stood in my workshop and you kept blushing."

"Now Blake, don't tease him." Nancy linked her arm though her husbands and smiled up at him in delight. "She's just what he needs, and everyone who met her agrees with me. Redhead always make the best wives," she said proudly, quoting Whitney back at him.

He believed it, too. When he'd spoken to the vicar, and after he'd explained that there would not be a wedding involving Miss Quartermane, the man's first response was to enquire about whether he had considered asking for Whitney Crewe's hand, instead.

It seems Whitney had been more sociable than he'd realized, and there was a greater disappointment that she had gone away than expressed for the Quartermanes' hasty departure.

"Thank you. I don't expect to return soon, so if you need anything, just call at the estate and Thompson here will take care of you both."

"Well, I won't need any new dresses for many years," Nancy said with a laugh.

They had reached his carriage, but he turned back. "Why is

that?"

Nancy beamed. "Miss Crewe gave me an armload of gowns and frilly things she said she couldn't possibly take with her. Some of it were too fine for me, but she said I could do what I liked with everything I didn't want. Miss Jones has a pretty new gown for her wedding day, Mrs. Jennings a fine shawl for church, and Miss Lambert has a sturdy pair of boots and thick stockings for the coming winter. It's almost as if she's already your lady and taking care of us."

"That was very generous of her, and of you to share," he said, and he was more than pleased. Whitney would make an exceptional countess one day. "I hope upon my return to bring her home with me."

He did not say how long that might take. He'd no notion how long Whitney's travels and adventure would take, but he wanted to be at her side for all of it. If she would have him. He would wait until he was sure he was well and healthy before even mentioning the possibility of fulfilling his dreams, of marriage and a family, with her.

Chapter Thirty

"**I** do apologize for the inconvenience," Captain Williams told her, fidgeting and looking uncomfortable amid the delicate chairs of Everett's parlor for the third time this week. "I'm under orders to wait until the weather improves."

"Well, you can hardly be blamed for poor sailing weather." Whitney nodded, peeking outside at the fine day. How the wind could be so brisk here and absent from the port where the ship remained at anchor confounded her. "How soon do you think we might be able to get underway?"

"That is in the hands of the weather gods. Sunrise tomorrow, or it could be as long as three days hence."

Whitney had already been delayed days, and now there seemed no choice but to be patient a little longer. "I see. Well, thank you for coming all this way, Captain Williams. I shall extend my stay here and remain in readiness for your eventual summons."

He touched his cap politely, and Mr. Roberts showed him out. Once she was alone again, she flopped back in her chair and groaned. "This is so unfair!"

"Did you say something, Miss Crewe?"

She turned, discovering her companion hovering at the door. She'd become very comfortable around the kind woman, since making her acquaintance. She considered her as much a friend as a paid companion already. "Only complaining of the lack of wind."

"Would you like a cup of tea?"

She considered a moment but then nodded. Why not? She had nothing else to do and no desire to paint. "May as well. Thank you."

"I'll be back in a moment. Oh, and now that you're not leaving today, could Mr. Roberts slip down to the market for me?"

"Of course," she said.

"He won't be back for at least half an hour. I hope that suits you."

"I'm not expecting any other callers today." She smoothed out her skirts as if she'd not a care in the world.

But once Mrs. Roberts had gone, she put her head in her hand and cursed softly under her breath, dispirited by the delay that would keep her stranded in the port town. It was not fair. She was ready, more than ready to leave everything behind and start again.

She heard a door open and close somewhere in the house. Mr. Roberts, undoubtedly running off on his errand.

"Am I doomed never to leave England," she whispered.

"If you are doomed to stay, I shall be the happiest of men, Miss Crewe," Everett replied as he stepped into the room.

Whitney sat up so fast her head spun. "Everett?"

His lips twitched with a smile. "Hello, Trouble. What the devil are you still doing here?"

Whitney squinted at him again. Yes, Everett was truly here, one brow raised, and looking more handsome than was possible. Her heart beat wildly at the sight of his pretty face as she stood. She drank in the joy of seeing him again. He looked very good in his dark coat, and although she should be ashamed, she rushed across the room and threw herself into his arms.

He caught her and held her tightly against his warm, hard body.

"What are you doing here?" she exclaimed.

He released her slowly and then stepped back. Whitney drank in his appearance again—and then noticed he wore a dark band about his upper left arm.

"Oh, Everett. I'm so very sorry for your loss."

She hugged him tightly again, but he seemed eager to escape

her embrace.

"Be careful," he warned.

Unfortunately for him, she happened to like holding him. "This is careful enough."

He cupped the back of her head gently, holding her firmly at arm's length. "I missed you."

"It's been a week," she reminded him. Far to many horrible lonely hours where she was denied his company.

He brushed his gloved fingers across her cheek softly. "And in that time so much has changed that I could not wait to speak with you again."

That reminded Whitney that he was supposed to be a husband. Or had the wedding been put off because he was in mourning now. "Where is Alice?"

"In London."

Relief was instant and overwhelming. Alice loved London, and Whitney loved Everett. "What brings you to Dover?"

"You," he said.

"When did your sister pass away?"

"A few days ago." He closed his eyes briefly. "It was quite simply the worst night of my life."

She took his hand in hers. "I am so sorry."

"She is at peace now, buried the day before yesterday."

Whitney led him to a chair and pressed him into it. "You came all this way to tell me?"

"Yes. No." He sighed deeply. "I came, not expecting you to still be here."

Was fate yet again tipping its hat in her direction and giving her one last chance to be with the man she loved? Unfortunately, she was at a loss for words at that moment. She simply stared at him, trying not to smile because he was in mourning now.

"I want to tell you something important that I hope will please you." He smiled quickly. "It seems you were right."

"That would be a first," she quipped. "But what about?"

"I could have met you as a married man today."

"Could have?"

He nodded slowly. "If Miss Quartermane hadn't cast me off, I would have been married to a woman I could never love. You were right that I should never have offered for her."

Whitney forced her mouth to close so she could swallow. "When did she end the engagement?"

"The day I told her about Emily's poor health. She was quite upset and fearful. They left my estate the next morning while I was away, in something of a panic I'm told."

"What day was that exactly?"

He bit his lip, and then winked. "The day before you left Twilit Hill."

"So they were gone before we made love in the garden? That would mean I was not the worst friend in the world for wanting you."

His grin returned. "I was not engaged to Miss Quartermane then, and you are the best friend anyone could ever want."

She shook her head, eyes filling with tears at his deception. "Why didn't you tell me you were free?"

He leaned forward, hands clenched together between his knees. "I couldn't risk that you might stay. Because of what happened between us, I was afraid you might think I expected you to change your plans for me. I learned about your parents from Miranda, how they died, and I could not risk it. I could not abandon Emily, and with my houseguests gone, I spent every moment with her until her last breath."

"You were a good brother."

"I'm not so sure." He shook his head, and Whitney lowered herself to kneel at his feet.

She clasped his hand and laid her chin upon it as she looked up at him. "I suspect I know why you feel that way. I really do. When my parents were ill, at the very end of their suffering, I just wanted it to be over. For an end to their pain, and mine."

He tightened his grip on her hand. "How well you know me. I didn't want to lose her, but I wanted her to go so she would not suffer again."

Whitney nodded, feeling the sting of tears in her eyes. "It isn't fair that anyone should suffer."

He brushed his thumb across her cheek. "No, it wasn't fair."

Whitney rubbed his thighs briskly, shaking off her sadness. "Now what for you? Are you returning home soon?"

He shook his head. "I made a promise to call on you. Do you still care for me, Whitney?"

She narrowed her eyes. "Such a foolish question. I am kneeling and touching you while we talk, aren't I?"

A ghost of a smile crossed his face. "So you are."

"I would be sitting in your lap and kissing you if I thought you would allow it," she admitted with a soft laugh, hoping to divert him from his grief.

His eyes sparkled with warmth and her heart melted. "When do you leave?" he asked.

"I await the wind and tide, unfortunately. One of which seems to have vanished completely. All of Fremont's ships are becalmed in the harbor for the present, or so Captain Williams keeps telling me."

"What rotten luck for you," Everett said with a slow grin as he pulled her to her feet to stand with him. He brushed his thumbs over her rings. "But how fortunate for me that I arrived before you could sail. Do you have plans for today?"

"I am entirely aimless," Whitney confessed.

"Let me spend what time you have left ashore with you. There is so much I want to say to you, now that I can."

"I'd be very grateful for your company." Whitney grinned widely. "Where shall we go? What shall we do?"

"I think our first step is to find me somewhere else to stay," he said with a wink. "The proprieties must be observed."

"You could stay. This is your home, and Mr. and Mrs. Roberts make wonderful chaperones."

He glanced around. "So you truly did hire someone?"

"I would be foolish to travel alone, wouldn't I? There are any number of scoundrels who could seduce me," she teased.

"I'm one of them," he confessed. He seemed to consider the matter a few long minutes but then nodded. "We must always take care of your reputation."

"And yours, too," Whitney agreed, and saw him smile again. She walked her fingers up his chest. "I'm glad you have come, and I know what you're thinking, my dear man."

He cast a quick glance around the room. "I am calculating how many hours it will be until we can undress ourselves," he whispered.

"Exactly." Whitney grinned. "Mr. and Mrs. Roberts retire early every night. You'll like them, I think, and they will like you, too."

He laughed softly. "Now, about that conversation we must have. I am now free to say—"

The man was simply too adorable. Whitney flung herself into his arms again and held him tightly. "I feared I'd never see you again."

"I did too." He kissed the top of her head. "I am free to speak from my heart at last. I love you so much, Whitney. I think I must have fallen the moment you beckoned me close."

"And I love you, too, but it will do us no good. I am to leave any day now."

"I don't want you to stay," he promised her.

Whitney drew back, staring at him in astonishment. "You love me but don't want me?"

He caught her fingers and tugged her into his lap. "You crave adventure, and I love you for it. I will not forge bonds between us that destroy your dreams. I had responsibilities until my sister's passing. I would never want you to give up what you hold dear. So you will travel the world, discover new sights and paint them, but I hope that from time to time you will think of me fondly, and write on occasion, so that I may know that you are well and happy and safe."

"I always think of you. It is most distracting." Whitney tugged on the ring encircling her thumb. She couldn't bear to let him think her indifferent. "This belonged to my father. I want you to wear it always."

She held the beloved relic before Everett's hand and found a finger the piece fitted. He stared at it. "Do I dare imagine this means we are engaged?"

"You can. I will not be away forever, even if I cannot say when I will return. Can you bear to wait for me?"

"Only if you wear this." He tugged his signet ring off and placed it on her bare thumb. "Wear this and know I will always be yours," he whispered.

Whitney admired the ring, deciding it looked perfect on her hand among her others. "We are engaged."

"We are indeed." Everett pressed his head to hers. "I will wait for you, for however long it takes."

Whitney's eyes filled with tears, and she lifted her face to his, yearning to feel his lips slide across hers just once. They stared at each other, but Everett merely pulled her into his arms and held her close. "I don't want to hurt you."

"You couldn't ever," she promised. Holding each other close had to be enough. For now. "I see your face whenever I close my eyes," she whispered.

"That must be distracting," he said with a chuckle.

"It is wonderful. You know I find you very pretty," she murmured.

"Ah, about that. You know that I love your unconventional ways, from your enjoyment of wetting me to your fondness for wearing pink, but do you think you might describe me as…well…a little less feminine in future? We are engaged, after all, and the other sounds almost insulting."

She laughed loudly. "My dear Lord Acton, if I should speak the truth of how well I admire your body, we would both be cast out of good society for at least two dozen years."

"Two dozen? Well, I'll risk it to hear the truth from your lips just this once."

"You are the man of my fantasies, a most arousing package of masculinity that makes my knees weak and my breath catch every time you are near. I am in love and lust, my dearest lord, and I fear I am quite mad for you."

"Mad for me is better than being mad *at* me," he whispered. "I confess I experience similar desperation that soon you will be so far away. So I have a compromise to offer: take me with you, Whitney Crewe. I'll carry your bags. I am, as I have forever been, all yours."

"So wonderfully romantic of you." Whitney grabbed his head and drew him close to deliver the kiss she'd waited her whole life to offer the person who'd claimed her heart.

Epilogue

Six months later...

Whitney twitched in her mourning gown, staring out at the changing colors of the sea one last time from the terrace of her temporary home with a feeling of great trepidation. She was leaving today; beginning the journey to England after the sudden death of a man she'd come to admire so much. She once would have given everything she owned not to have to go back home but accepted she must.

But she couldn't be selfish. She had achieved her dream, studied and painted every day, learning so much about the life of a painter, too. Enough to know that her art would always be important to her, but it wasn't enough to satisfy her now.

Whitney was about to set off on a new journey that would consume the rest of her life.

She rested her hand over her churning stomach and sighed. Everything was about to change. Her whole world was about to alter, settle into place—if she were fortunate.

"I think we have everything ready to go," Everett promised as he strode across her terrace, his strong voice evidence of his good health and vitality. Coming to Florence to mourn his sister had done wonders for his outlook on life. He no longer frowned so much. He even ran about a bit after the local boys when they tried to play tricks on him.

She could have turned to face him, admire his tanned features, yet she knew them by heart. She could never get enough of looking at him, and, if she had her way, she never would have to. "Did you have Roberts check under the bed?"

"At my villa and at yours."

His hands closed over her shoulders and he drew her against him, pushing her grief aside. She had been mentored by a little-known painter she'd met one night at dinner, who had charmed her and Everett both. Roland had become her staunchest supporter, and the hardest taskmaster she'd ever had. Under his watchful eye, she'd stretched herself as a painter. Under his discerning gaze, she'd come to understand where her greatest strengths were as a person, too. "I saw his wife this afternoon. She wished us a safe journey."

"I spoke to her, too, just a few minutes ago." He squeezed her shoulders. "She will be all right without him. She has her children and grandchildren to support her. She is surrounded by family and her friends here."

"I'm glad she has them." She fell silent, enjoying Everett holding her. Whitney wasn't sure what she would have done if she'd lost him, as he'd feared she might. They had lived largely separate lives for the sake of propriety, but she was more in love with him than she'd thought possible.

Whitney had found keeping a proper distance from him, one he'd claimed was required for her health, incredibly frustrating. He merely winked whenever the topic of forbidden pleasures came up and soon changed the subject, most often to her latest work or someone else's they'd recently seen. They had maintained an independence from each other and slept alone every night too, but, now they were going home to England, Whitney wanted the separation to end. "When are we going to talk about it?"

"Today." He let her go.

Whitney turned around, aware that the future was something they'd always avoided talking about. He'd only recently put aside his mourning clothes, and was colorfully turned out at last. She wet her lips before she spoke. "You're not afflicted with consumption."

"So it seems," he said, then laughed softly. "No lingering

death for me."

She breathed out, allowing the tension in her to fade to nothing. "I am so glad. The world would be a lonely place without you in it."

"I hoped you might feel that way." He lifted his hand to her face and gently moved her red hair back from her cheek. He still wore gloves around her, and if the danger had passed there was no reason now that couldn't stop. They could touch, kiss and become proper lovers.

She looked him up and down, longing for him. It had been a month since Everett had last posed for her. Nude, of course. "Remove your clothes, my good man."

He grinned widely and tugged off his gloves. "In a moment."

He took her hand in his very tenderly. It had been a long time since they'd kissed, or touched skin to skin, and the torture had been acute for Whitney.

He slid his palm over hers and then laced their fingers together tightly. "I want to do this right this time."

Whitney was returning to a life of dull and proper behavior soon, to balls and dinners and morning calls and everything she'd ever resisted. Conforming to society's expectations had never appealed before, but it was what Everett would want, and because she loved him, she intended to try to fit in. "We've done nothing else right, have we?"

He grinned. "These past months have been the best of my life, and I have only you to thank for that. I have discovered so many things about myself, and about you most of all."

"Such as?"

"That you only have to look in my direction to make me happy. I never imagined this life, but I am grateful to you for showing me another way to live. I think I would have been very miserable if not for you."

"I feel the same." She leaned close. "And I feel I must confess that you only have to walk into a room to excite me unbearably."

His grin widened. "Imagine making love where we actually touch?"

Her breath quickened. "I always do."

They pleasured themselves in each other's company only infrequently, and when they couldn't, they would whisper about it in the most inappropriate locations. Whitney had never felt so beautiful as when Everett told her his desires.

"Tonight," he promised. "Tonight, I will be with you."

Tonight was hours away.

"Now," she countered. "There is nothing to hold us back anymore. To hell with my reputation. I have waited long enough."

His grip on her hand tightened. "Whitney, I need you."

"I need you, too." She leaned forward to claim a kiss but he drew back.

"Life is very relaxed here, but we cannot continue this way once we are back in England," he warned her.

"Because people always gossip," she agreed. Everett particularly did not like when the talk involved him or Whitney. He was rather funny when his feathers were ruffled by rumors and innuendo.

"People always do. I want to be with you so much that when we get home, I think we need to marry immediately." He drew her hands upward and pressed soft kisses to her knuckles. He met her gaze, and Whitney's knees almost buckled under the love she glimpsed in his eyes. "I know your dreams are not over, and that you will paint and sometimes scandalize the high sticklers, but I don't care. I want to be with you, at your side forever. I hope there might be room for me in your dreams, too."

"You are in them." She slipped his grip and touched his dear face, sliding her fingers into the lengths of his hair. She adored this man because he had never asked her to change. "My dreams are filled with you and the life we can have together. I would be honored to be your wife."

His expression changed to delight as he pulled her closer against his chest. He rested his hands on her hips and squeezed. "What do you dream for us?"

"Many things." The feel of him against her at long last made her pulse speed up. She toyed with his cravat, trying to put into words the future they could share. "We're going home to be married, to meet our mutual friends together as man and wife, and we are going to start the family you have always wanted. I have always known I would have children. I want yours soon."

"What else will we do?"

"We will most likely spend part of the season in London, but most of the time we will be home at Warstone, moving your cattle from field to field, keeping your horses long after they are fit to ride. Making love under the stars or in the woods. Calling on your friends in the village and making sure they are well and happy, especially the Blakes."

He grinned widely and spun them both in a tight circle. "I have loved you since the night we met."

Whitney laughed. "Are you attempting to rewrite our history, my love?"

"Of course not." He laughed with her, something she'd not thought him capable of the second time they'd met. "But upon reflection, I cannot believe I didn't understand why seeing you always angered me. Why you laughing with other men annoyed me so much. I think I was plagued with the most horrid jealousy when you smiled at other men I unconsciously deemed unworthy and my rival for your regard."

"You wanted to be the one I flirted with instead?"

"Of course," he promised. "Not that I ever understood my feelings for you until it was almost too late."

"Will you feel any better should I tell you that I fell for you the night we first met, and it was only out of friendship and loyalty that I had no choice but to detest you?"

He looked surprised at that. "You detested me?"

Whitney nodded. "I hated that you didn't try to win me, because you know I *do* possess a fortune, so you could have married me instead of proposing to Miss Quartermane."

"I know that now," he agreed with another laugh. "Fortunately for you, I've never been interested in marrying for monetary gain. You have won my regard by your own merits."

"So why the rush to marry at all?" She grinned, knowing her question was foolish. They were in love, and love was the most troublesome of all emotions to contain.

"Because I cannot get you out of my mind and heart...and I don't want to. I demand the right to tell everyone that you hold my heart."

Everett lowered himself to one knee and produced a shiny bauble from his pocket. It was not an overly large ring, but Whitney loved it on sight. Rubies and diamond were her favorite stones. "I collected this last month from a silversmith. I had it made especially for you. I wanted you to finally have a ring of your own to pass down to our children, along with those of your aunts and uncles. No one else has ever worn this before."

Whitney felt her eyes prickle with the warning of tears as he slipped it onto her finger and stood again. "Oh, Everett, that is so sweet of you to have this made, but I already have your ring."

She fisted her fingers and waved his signet ring under his nose.

"One to claim you, one to keep you," he whispered. "I made such a mistake trying to do everything that society expected of me, and I even asked the wrong woman to marry me, thinking I could learn to love her," he confessed quietly. "I'm so sorry."

"You don't have to apologize," she promised.

"But I need to explain. I grew up with the right example right before my eyes, and lost sight of that somehow." He met her gaze. "My parents' marriage was arranged, but they were a love match from the very start. My mother and father were never very obvious about it, but it was in everything they did and said, and sometimes what they didn't say. They lived for each other, in later years they finished each other's sentences too. They were never apart for longer than two days at a time. Wherever Father went, Mother was at his side, and vice versa. I want that for us."

"So do I," she whispered, cupping his cheek. "I need you in my life so very much."

A smile lingered on his lips. "Mother believed in waiting for the right moment, and this is it. She told me the love of my life would light a bright flame inside me and when I found her, that yearning would never go out. That flame is the love I feel for you."

Whitney stared at her hand a moment, at his rings surrounded by those of her long-dead family, and her eyes filled with tears. "Oh Everett. That is just the most beautiful thing you've ever said to me. I'd love nothing more than to spend the rest of my life having you at my side, having you finishing my sentences. That could be very interesting…and wicked too."

She threw her arms about him and clung to the love she'd been waiting for all her life.

Everett nuzzled her neck. "Are you ready for me, Whitney?"

"Indeed. Ready, waiting, quite impatiently."

Everett swept her into his arms, carried her inside, and upstairs to her bedchamber.

He deposited her beside her bed and cupped her face. Slowly, painstakingly it seemed, his lips met hers. Their second kiss excited her more than she thought possible, and when his tongue swept past her lips and tangled with hers, she swooned against him.

Everett's arms tightened around her as he plundered her mouth. She clung to him, kissed him back for all she was worth and more. She felt the tugs at the buttons on her gown and then the sweep of his hands across her bare upper back.

His touch was firm, possessive, and she could not get close enough. She began to undress him, removing his cravat and unbuttoning his waistcoat before sliding her arms about his narrow waist.

She relaxed her grip as he struggled out of his coat, let his waistcoat fall to the ground, and then he yanked his shirt over his head.

Whitney moaned as she laid her cheek against his bare chest. "I've missed touching you."

"I've missed it more," he told her with a laugh as he removed her gown and stays. Her chemise disappeared quickly, and then they were kissing and naked together, nearly fused from hips to lips.

They broke apart to remove his trousers.

Whitney fell backward onto the bed and lifted her legs high. Everett grasped her ankles briefly, then divested her of her shoes, garters and stockings. He crawled on top of her and pressed his whole body against hers. "I can't believe I'm finally in bed with you."

"Believe it, lover," she whispered, winding her arms about his neck and pulling him down for a long, steamy kiss. Whitney widened her legs, her body already humming with lust. "You'll stay until dawn," she told him.

Everett cantered her hips and positioned himself where she needed him most. "Will that be long enough to sate us?"

Whitney squirmed, attempting to bring him into her. She admired his restraint, even if she didn't need it. "I don't think so.

Come into me."

"We have more nights ahead than this one, darling," Everett whispered softly against her ear. "We have the rest of our lives. My God, I love you, Trouble."

Whitney set her hands to the smooth curve of his bottom and tugged. "Start now," she demanded, as she pulled him all the way into her and made them both moan.

Second Epilogue

⸺ ◆ ⸺

At the Fairmont Midsummer Ball
London, 1815

Once upon a time, making merry hadn't come easily for the Earl of Acton. Everett had once lived a proper life of propriety and duty. Thankfully those dull, dreary days were long gone.

He sipped champagne slowly, casting an admiring glance over the lovely ladies who glided past his spot—certain he was where he was meant to be.

Those who'd come to enjoy the midsummer ball on the grounds of the Fairmont estate were having a marvelous time yet again.

Within the manor behind him had been the usual gathering of mystics and fortune-tellers, selling hopes and dreams, determined to predict anyone's future in exchange for coin. He'd pressed through their number without partaking or being taken for a fool. He did not need a fortune-teller to determine what his future path would bring into his life. His happiness was already assured.

Everett had come to this unholy revel in pursuit of his eccentric bride-to-be, but had not yet captured her. She was a wily one, for all the softness of her heart.

He would take a bride with a fortune tomorrow and live happily ever after.

But not quietly, he suspected.

His intended bride, Miss Whitney Crewe, was somewhere about the place, basking in one last night of spinsterish freedom, she'd teased, while in the next breath inviting him to come and be wicked *with* her.

He could barely hide his excitement, for this was the place they had first met, where he'd lost his heart to a beautiful and maddening creature who had lightened his soul with her nonsense and love.

A flash of long bright red hair caught his eye at the edge of the darkness, and he wasted no time in setting off in pursuit. Whitney liked him to chase her about, but was always willing to be captured if he delivered kisses when he did.

Whitney wore gypsy garb again—with silk caressing the curves he adored and gems glittering on every finger under the torchlights as she spun about. Even her thumbs sparkled with gold bands, treasures of the family she had once, long ago. But among them now were two additional rings—one that had belonged to his family for generations, and another that was new from him alone.

She lifted her skirts a little as she danced with careless abandon, revealing slender calves and bare feet gliding upon the neatly trimmed lawns.

He drew closer, beguiled by the way she moved with unhindered sensuality and confidence.

He wasn't the only man who noticed her, either, and he was very glad he'd already staked his claim. She always drew a crowd of admirers, handsome gentlemen, and even ladies flocked to her. People stared, smiled at her transparent energy, and made a game of trying to copy her movements with varying degrees of success.

Everett was as entranced as he'd always been, and found a spot to watch as she grabbed a lady by the hand, swinging her into her dance. They laughed in giddy joy, and soon the entire crowd was swaying along with her.

That was Whitney's gift. She made everyone fall in love, but none more than him.

Whitney suddenly held out her hand to him, as she'd done that first night, fingers wriggling in invitation. The gems winked and he swayed forward, helplessly spellbound still.

Redheads were his weakness, but only this particular one had brought him to his knees.

He took her bare fingers in his and raised them to his lips to kiss them all. "Enjoying yourself, darling?"

"I am now," she promised, sliding into his arms as she always did.

Her body was soft and warm under his palms, and he didn't ever want to let her go. "Are you thirsty yet?"

She nodded, and led the way inside by taking his hand. He admired her hips gently swaying under her gown, and then requested punch for both of them.

She drained her glass quickly. "Why did you not join me in dancing?"

He requested another beverage for his lady. "I had something on my mind."

Her smile widened and her eyes glowed with delight. "You are too adorable, my lord. Did you not read your invitation? Guests were supposed to leave their cares at the door."

"Life cannot be all fun and games." He grinned. "Sometimes we must be serious."

"You did enough of that before," she insisted as she set her glass aside. "A little fun never hurt you."

He pulled her close. "Do you think so?"

"I know so. Come, I want to show you something." Whitney caught his hand and pulled him across the room and into a familiar long gallery. Holding his hand firmly, she ignored the paintings of their hosts' ancestors this time and marched him toward an adjoining room they were both quite familiar with.

The door closed with a resounding snap that sent a shiver over his skin. "I think you've lured unwary gentlemen to this room before."

"Perhaps I have. Only once, though, and I'm sorry to say I left him in an unforgivable condition last time." She threw aside her shawl. "I stole the poor fellow's breeches, too."

"He has forgiven you for that. A long time ago," he promised. Everett grunted as Whitney pressed against him.

"Do I have to I remind you this is a bachelors ball and indiscretions are expected? You're a bachelor, and I'm a willing and amorous spinster."

"But I am an engaged man, about to marry an eccentric heiress," he warned her.

"A devoted heiress," Whitney corrected him, as she unbuttoned the fall of his breeches. "Now where did I stop the last time I had you here?"

He looked down at himself. "I had less clothing on, I believe."

"Hmm, I think that can be arranged." Whitney made short work of stripping him off until their appearances matched the very night they met, and the precise moment they parted company. "What would have happened next?"

"You had me in hand," he whispered, and moaned as she reenacted the events of that night in exquisite detail. "I wanted to kiss you but you refused me."

"Not tonight," she whispered, lifting her eyes from the cock she stroked. "Tonight I am feeling very romantic toward you."

Her eyes twinkled with mirth as she squeezed him a little harder.

"Such a relief," he whispered as he lowered his lips to claim hers. They had of course kissed many times since he'd proposed. There was no reason not to, since his intentions were honorable and hers always urgent. The journey home to England had been very pleasant and very satisfying for both of them.

He turned Whitney against the nearby wall and hitched her skirts above her knees, even as he pressed his hips against hers.

Whitney smoothed her hands over his shoulders and then stared at his face. "Has anyone every told you that you are a very pretty fellow?"

"Yes, you," he said, feeling his cheeks heat with embarrassment. "Every time we make love. Every morning I woke up in your bunk aboard ship to find you drawing me again."

"I never get tired of sketching you." Her lips curved into a broad smile, and she brushed her fingers across his cheek. She held his face, studying him. "I am so glad we found each other."

He crushed her lips under his.

When they parted, he was panting.

"Can I have you?" she asked, rather than demand, as she'd done the night they'd first met. "Here. Now."

He was no longer surprised by her forthright desire. What could it hurt this one last time to taste temptation before he became a properly devoted husband, anyway? "For tonight and then forever?"

She nodded quickly, and he positioned himself to claim her. He had become adept at reading Whitney's moods. She was often impatient to be with him, and tonight seemed no different. As he slid inside her tight little body, she let out an alarmingly loud moan that suggested she was very far gone in lust already. He drew back and returned to her, burying himself to the hilt.

"Oh, that feels so good," she promised. "I missed you."

They had made love a few days ago, in the carriage as they traveled directly to London after leaving the ship. He had gone to see about a special license as soon as he had deposited her at her cousin's home. "Wait for me, my love."

"For you?" She met his stare through eyes gone hazy with lust as she writhed against him and tangled her fingers in his hair. "If I can, but I may disappoint you."

He pinned her hands to the wall and let go of any hesitation. Whitney took everything he gave and more, but soon she began to thrash and cry out his name. She tightened around him provocatively until he was in serious danger of losing control entirely.

"Darling, you never have disappointed me, and never could. That's why I'm yours forever," he managed to say, just as he gave up the fight.

Loving Whitney was all he wanted, all he needed, for the rest of his life.

Married by Moonlight

The marriage mart is murder!

Chapter One

London,
May, 1815

Gilbert Bowen, Earl of Sorenson, burst through the swirling fog into the torch-lit rear courtyard of Lady Berry's home in a violent temper a little before six o'clock in the morning. Mr. Albert Meriwether deserved to be horsewhipped, and so did the Runners for going along with this arrest.

A tall, narrow fellow, probably one of them, too, peeled himself off a wall by the servants' entrance and moved to block Gilbert's path.

Gilbert wasted no time on pleasantries. "Where is he?"

The man looked him up and down, taking in his fine clothing and superior size. "Who are you?"

"A man not to be trifled with." He passed over his card and letter of introduction from a mutual acquaintance, hoping the man knew how to read.

Apparently, he did, for the Runner's eyes widened and he swallowed hard.

The man handed them back, hand shaking a little. "We were not told to expect you, my lord."

Gilbert scowled. "My presence should not have been needed if reason had prevailed. Take me to Mr. Meriwether, now."

"Of course, my lord. He's still interrogating the suspect inside." The man smiled quickly. "The name is Davis."

Gilbert recognized the name but made no further comment. Bow Street Runners were generally good men, thorough and effective at their jobs on most occasions.

Except this one. They had little reason to rub shoulders with members of the *ton* or they would not have detained the man inside at all. He hated to think what had happened overnight inside Lady Berry's home.

Davis may be one of the best. But Albert Meriwether, the investigator wrongly holding a suspect inside for interrogation, was definitely not of that quality, from all he'd heard tonight. Gilbert was here to put a stop to his interrogation before any lasting harm was done.

Davis led him swiftly down halls overflowing with chairs, folded tables and piles of soiled linen ready to be taken into the country for laundering. Gilbert should have attended the ball held here last night. Unfortunately, fate had not been on his side.

He stepped into a disordered drawing room and took stock of the situation.

Lady Berry was sobbing on a fainting couch by the far window, a maid hovering ineffectually at her elbow wearing an expression full of fear.

Gilbert swung his gaze to the man tied to a chair in the center of the room like a criminal. His temper did not improve to see fresh blood spotting his friend's shirt front. His cream knee breeches were soiled by old blood too, likely the victim's.

"Meriwether!"

The investigator looked up slowly, his expression annoyed. "Sorenson? What the devil are you doing back in London?"

Gilbert raked his gaze over Meriwether, noting his bloodied knuckles and the sheen of sweat glistening on his face. "I'm here to rectify the grievous mistake you've made tonight before it is too late."

"There is no mistake," Meriwether insisted, circling his innocent captive.

"There most certainly is," Gilbert insisted, withdrawing his orders from Bow Street and holding them out. "Read this."

The investigator snatched them up and read every line—twice, he suspected. Gilbert moved to check that Lord Carmichael still breathed. He turned his friend's face up to the light, appalled by what he saw. "Dear God. What has been done to you?"

Carmichael shuddered. His left eye was swelling shut and his lip had been split from a beating and was dripping blood down his chin. Meriwether had not been gentle or within his rights to do this. The magistrate would not be pleased.

"No. This case is mine," Meriwether complained. "He's all but confessed to the murder. He's covered in her blood."

"Old blood, judging by the state of his knees." Gilbert grimaced, reaching into another pocket for a week-old letter. "You should read this, as well, before you say another word to implicate him further."

Meriwether read the letter Gilbert had recently received from Lord Carmichael and Miss Berry, announcing their impending wedding, and their request that Gilbert come to London for the announcement last night. Rain had prevented Gilbert from reaching London in time.

"Lord Carmichael was in love with Angela Berry, and she with him. He would not kill her when he was about to announce their marriage, of that I am certain."

"This gives him motive if she refused him," Meriwether crowed. "Look at him."

"Did you not read her own words in the letter?"

"Anyone could have written it."

"Show her mother and have her disprove it is her handwriting."

Meriwether rushed to Lady Berry and thrust the letter at her face. "Is this your daughter's writing?"

Lady Berry sat in shadows, but the maid rushed to bring a candelabra to her so she could read. After a long wait, she began to nod. "That is her penmanship. I would recognize it anywhere."

Meriwether swung around, scowling at the maid.

Gilbert shook his head. "It is known he was found with the body and was nearly incoherent when questioned. He would have attempted to revive her, which is why his clothing is soiled with her blood, you fool."

"She was cold when I found her," Carmichael mumbled, clearly in pain, judging by the slurred nature of his speech. "Never even had a chance to announce we would wed…"

Carmichael sobbed and turned his face away from everyone.

Meriwether sneered. "Isn't that a convenient tale?"

"Actually, he's never been a good liar. *I'm* the reason he had delayed announcing they would marry last night. He wanted me here—which the magistrate believes too," Gilbert told the fellow. "Now, I have Bow Street's approval to release him, and you may go and track down a *real* criminal in any other case you have on your hands. You are done here. Leave the Runners behind. They are under my command now."

"Damn nonsense! You titled bastards always protect your own," Meriwether complained as he began to straighten his clothes. He pulled on his wrinkled coat in a furious rush, scowling like thunder. Clearly the man was unhappy but that was just too bad. "I'll speak to the magistrate about this immediately."

"Good. He's expecting you," Gilbert told him, glad to have the investigator gone.

Gilbert gently untied Carmichael's bonds, noticing red stripes had formed around each tightly bound wrist. Meriwether would have a hard time explaining to the magistrate why he'd treated a peer with such contempt. "Carmichael?"

Carmichael turned his head, squinting at him through his long hair. "What kept you?"

Gilbert brushed his hair back, continuing to assess the damage Meriwether's fists had caused to his face. Nothing so far suggested Carmichael would bear any scars. "The roads from Kent were muddy," he apologized. "I had only just arrived in London when a Runner I know well came with the news you were being held as a suspect in Miss Berry's death."

Carmichael carefully dabbed at his split lip with his shirtsleeve. "I'm innocent, Sorenson."

"I believe you, but Meriwether does not know you like I do. He will be reprimanded for this, I swear."

He put his arm around Carmichael and hauled him up onto his feet. Carmichael was unsteady and Gilbert held him tightly. "Let's get you out of here, all right? My carriage is waiting in the mews to take you away."

"I want to help catch Angela's killer," Carmichael protested.

"You're in no condition to do anything but what I say, my friend. When you're rested, we'll talk again. Bow Street has given me complete autonomy in the matter. I'd like to keep this quiet for now, to protect your reputation and Bow Street's. I am sending you to my home, where my man will tend to your injuries in privacy. As soon as I finish up here and sort through this mess, I'll return home to take your real statement and discuss what will happen next."

Carmichael nodded but then turned. He looked across the room to where Lady Berry watched their slow progress through puffy eyes. She still had the letter from Carmichael and her daughter clutched in her hand. Her expression was decidedly ashamed.

"Thank you for believing in me," Carmichael whispered to Gilbert.

"Don't thank me yet," he warned. London policing was an imprecise business at best. "Meriwether is fond of beating confessions out of his suspects, whether they be true or not. He could still cause trouble for you."

Reputations were made or lost because of harmful gossip, and Carmichael's standing in society was in jeopardy now.

Lady Berry drew herself up and thrust out the letter to Gilbert. "He said it had to be him," she whispered. "He said there could be no one else."

"I loved her," Carmichael protested. "We were going to marry next week by special license and go home to Edenmere. Angela had already chosen the bedchamber that would become yours. I swear to you, I could never harm her," Carmichael promised the older woman. "I'll find out who took Angela from us if it's the last thing I do."

The older woman seemed to crumple back onto the fainting couch, covering her face as she began to cry again. Gilbert tried to hurry Carmichael away but the man was barely able to move.

"Be gentle with her," Carmichael begged of him once they were a distance from Lady Berry. "As prickly as she's always been with me, she adored Angela. Meriwether is a convincing bastard. I almost believed his arguments myself."

"No, you didn't," Gilbert disagreed. But he would need to ask some hard questions of her and everyone in the household again. There was no telling what sort of nonsense Meriwether had coerced the household staff to say to implicate Carmichael. Getting to the truth might take a while.

He pulled Carmichael through the rear door and paused to catch his breath.

"Can I help you, my lord?" Davis asked, rushing forward.

"Indeed you can," he said as Davis took on Carmichael's extra weight. "Carmichael has attended too many lavish dinners this season."

"So I could be with Angela," Carmichael added with a groan. "Any excuse."

Tears flowed from Carmichael's eyes now and mingled with the blood smeared on his face.

Although he should say something to comfort his friend in his grief, he couldn't delay out of sympathy or concern for his well-being. There was a crime scene to inspect before anyone else disturbed the remaining evidence.

He loaded Carmichael into the carriage with Davis' help

and sent him on his way through the subdued foggy streets of London's early morning traffic.

Gilbert looked around and then up. The fog was thinning but the clouds overhead suggested the bad weather had followed him from Kent. It would rain soon if he was not mistaken. "I'll need you with me at all times, so there can be no question that my loyalty is to the truth," he told Davis as he turned toward the house again.

"Very good, my lord," Davis said as he hurried to catch up. "I was itching to get inside from the get go, but Meriwether kept us all away."

He looked at Davis in surprise. "Every single Runner was kept out?"

"Yes, my lord. Meriwether preferred to work alone on the interrogations, as he always does."

Gilbert cursed under his breath. Beating a man to a false confession of guilt was abhorrent to him, and very easy to do without witnesses. Thank God he'd arrived in time to rescue Carmichael from Meriwether's ham-fisted tactics. "That is not how it should be done. You will witness every interview from now on so the evidence brought before the magistrate is without reproach. Form your own opinions and we'll discuss our conclusions in private afterward. Agreed?"

"Sounds fair." Davis frowned though. "I am sorry about Lord Carmichael, my lord. It didn't sit right with me the way he was held like that, but Mr. Meriwether wouldn't hear reason."

"He wanted the conviction, not the truth." Gilbert handed over Carmichael's last letter to Davis. The Runner would have all the information Gilbert uncovered, and help spread the word that Carmichael was wrongly accused and an abused mourner, should any gossip arise.

"Well, I'll be damned." Davis nodded and handed the letter back. "That's clear enough for me. The poor woman is this way."

Gilbert stepped into the conservatory, noting the room was

well lit and quite crowded. There were cushioned settees, little side tables, and a few books scattered about the room.

He dropped his gaze to the floor. As Carmichael had alluded to in his many letters about the woman, Angela Berry had been pretty.

Dark auburn hair curled wildly around a pale, lifeless face. She'd been stabbed in the chest, a blow that most likely pierced her heart. Death would have been inevitable, if not instant from a wound like that.

"Hello, Angela," he murmured. "I'm sorry we never had a chance to meet."

Davis drew close. "What was that, my lord?"

"I was just introducing myself to the victim. I never had occasion to meet the deceased while she lived. She used to add a few lines to Carmichael's letters occasionally, but that was the extent of our association. I should have come to London more often this past year."

Davis made a noncommittal sound.

Gilbert drew in a breath and then got to work, noting the arrangement of her limbs, the location of the wound, and the blood smeared around her on the Indian tiles. "Did you read the initial reports?"

"I did. Maid found them together on the floor, Lord Carmichael holding her in his arms. She thought she'd stumbled on a tryst until she noticed the blood."

"What brought her to this part of the house at that precise moment?"

"A cry for help."

"From whom?"

"The report did not say."

"We'll need to question the maid again and ask about the cry." He turned to look around. Angela Berry had fallen not far from the doorway. She might have been waiting here for Carmichael, or someone else perhaps.

Gilbert moved away from the door and the body and investigated the perimeter of the room. There was a narrow path behind the potted palms lining the walls. It was possible to walk completely around the room behind them, he discovered. Along the way, he tested every window and doorway latch. The last glass panel gave way with a gentle push, revealing a hidden exit.

"Well, I'll be!" Davis said as he joined Gilbert. He slipped outside and looked left and right. "Access to the street, and to the mews at the back."

"I take it Meriwether did not discover this?"

"He looked nowhere but to Lord Carmichael once he arrived." Davis scratched his head. "There are other suspects in my opinion, my lord…if you'd *like* my opinion."

"I would, but first things first. After the maid, tell me who else Meriwether might have spoken to. We need to re-interview everyone about Miss Berry's movements from the moment she was found to the last time she was seen alive, to be sure they have not been influenced."

"At least a dozen. There is a footman who is missing though."

"We need to find him as soon as possible," Gilbert said, making notes for himself in his pocketbook. "Tell me what else you know."

"Miss Berry was last seen alive around eleven last night during the height of the festivities of her mother's ball. There were thirty-three members of the *ton* invited, most present, and a dozen extra staff hired for the event."

A hoard of suspects but the wrong one detained. "I'll need Lady Berry's guest list as soon as possible. Bring me the maid, and then the housekeeper and the butler, separately."

"Right you are." Davis stood straighter. "It's good to have a proper investigator back in London, my lord."

"Thank you, but I'm not happy about this at all." He shook his head and looked down upon the deceased again. "I came for a wedding, not a funeral."

More Regency Romance
from Heather Boyd...

Saints and Sinners Series

Book 1: The Duke and I
Book 2: A Gentleman's Vow
Book 3: An Earl of Her Own

Rebel Hearts Series

Book 1: The Wedding Affair
Book 2: An Affair of Honor
Book 3: The Christmas Affair
Book 4: An Affair so Right

The Wild Randalls Series

Book 1: Engaging the Enemy
Book 2: Forsaking the Prize
Book 3: Guarding the Spoils
Book 4: Hunting the Hero

Miss Mayhem Series

Book 1: Miss Watson's First Scandal
Book 2: Miss George's Second Chance
Book 3: Miss Radley's Third Dare
Book 4: Miss Merton's Last Hope

And many more...

About Heather Boyd

Determined to escape the Aussie sun on a scorching camping holiday, Heather picked up a pen and notebook from a corner store and started writing her very first novel—Chills. Years later, she is the author of over thirty sexy regency historical romances. Addicted to all things tech (never again will Heather write a novel longhand) and fascinated by English society of the early 1800's, Heather spends her days getting her characters in and out of trouble and into bed together (if they make it that far). She lives on the edge of beautiful Lake Macquarie, Australia with her trio of mischievous rogues (husband and two sons) along with one rescued cat whose only interest in her career is that it provides him with food on demand and a new puppy that is proving a big distraction.

You can find details of her work and writing at
www.Heather-Boyd.com

www.ingramcontent.com/pod-product-compliance
Lightning Source LLC
Chambersburg PA
CBHW032128180726
48284CB00002B/704